The Last Orphan Train

Books by F.M. Parker

Coldiron *series*
Coldiron
Shadow of the Wolf
The Shanghaiers
Thunder of Cannon
Spoils of War (a.k.a. The Thieves)

Novels
Skinner
Nighthawk
The Searcher
The Highbinders
The Far Battleground
The Shadow Man
The Slavers
The Assassins
The Predators
Winter Woman
The Seekers
The Highwayman
The Last Orphan Train (a.k.a. Girl in Falling Snow)
Wife Stealer
The Harvester
Soldiers of Conquest
Dream Hitcher

The Last Orphan Train

F.M. Parker

SPEAKING VOLUMES, LLC
NAPLES, FLORIDA
2022

The Last Orphan Train
a.k.a. Girl in Falling Snow

Cover design by Hannah Linder

ISBN 978-1-64540-688-4

For Louise

Foreword

From 1854 to 1929 an estimated 150,000 homeless children, orphans and abandoned children, were shipped by train from New York City to farms in mid-west America to be "taken in" by a family. There are an estimated 1,000,000 descendants, most of them alive today, who trace their roots to the boys and girls that rode the orphan trains.

In 1979 Bruce (Utah) Phillips, an offspring of one of the Orphan Train girls, wrote a song about the Orphan Train.

Orphan Train

Once I had a darling mother, though I can't recall her name
I had a baby brother who I'll never see again
For the Children's Home is sending us out on the Orphan Train
To try to find someone to take us in

Chorus -   Take us in, we have rode the Orphan Train
Take us in, we need a home, we need a home.
Take us in, oh won't you be our kin
We are looking for someone to take us in

I have stolen from the poorbox, I've begged the city streets
I've swabbed the bars and poolrooms for a little bite to eat
In my daddy's old green jacket and these rags upon my feet
I've been looking for someone to take me in

The Children's Home they gathered us, me and all the rest
They taught us to sit quietly until the food is blest
Then they put us on the Orphan Train and sent us way out west

To try to find someone to take us in.

The farmers and their families they came from miles around
We lined up on the platform of the station in each town
And one by one we parted like some living lost-and-found
And one by one we all were taken in.

Now there's many a fine doctor or a teacher in your school
There's many a good preacher who can teach the Golden Rule
Who started out an orphan sleeping in the freezing rain
Whose life began out on the Orphan Train

Chapter One

Street of Waifs

The old section of New York City, December - 1929

Alice stole silently through the shadows of late evening lying dense on the weed choked yard of the ancient and abandoned two story frame house. The windows were broken, the porch roof sagged. The door hung open on one hinge.

Alice was twelve years old, slender, face finely chiseled, big eyes, and a mouth of a generous size. She was scruffy; reddish brown hair tangled, face smudged and a large purple bruise marred her left cheek.

She wore a rumpled gray coat with a rip in the sleeve over a dark blue dress, and a badly worn pair of leather shoes. Everything needed soap and hot water. She was tired, cold and hungry, with the half eaten sandwich in her coat pocket begging to be devoured.

A stiff gust of cold wind struck the decaying old house and it groaned.

Alice jerked to a halt, poised to turn and run. She stared intently ahead as she dug a knife from a coat pocket and pried the blade open with a thumbnail.

She listened closely and letting seconds pass. With no more sounds, she continued her slow sneak upon the house. She stepped upon the porch and halted and listened for sounds from inside. All was silent and she warily entered through the sagging doorway.

Alice moved warily and silently through the dimly lit bottom floors littered with trash left behind by others, homeless like her, and dust and leaves blown in by the wind. She halted at the stairway to the floor above and stared upward just as a stiff blast of wind gave a keening whistle as it was cut by a broken window glass. Alice flinched, but held her tight focus up the stairway.

She strained to catch any sound that might signal someone was present above. Seconds passed and no sound came to her other than those of the wind and the groaning and creaking of the decaying house.

She adjusted the blanket roll on her shoulders, and holding the knife out ahead, crept up the rickety stairs. The rotten wood of a step squeaked under her foot and she halted and cocked her ears. Only silence from above and she climbed upward and cautiously lifted her head above the attic floor.

In the weak light coming from the single small window in the end of the attic, she saw the room was long and narrow. The ceiling was peaked and consisted of the underside of the roof. Cobwebs that had been spun by summertime spiders hung in tattered strands from the dusty wooden rafters. In the end of the room most distant from her, dark shadows masked what could be lurking there. She climbed into the attic and stared into its far recess. A form wrapped in a red blanket and barely visible lay on the floor. Someone had beaten her to the possible refuge.

Alice started to back away. Then she stopped. The form did not appear to be that of an adult, perhaps someone like herself searching for a place to find shelter during the coming night. If that was correct, then there was less danger threatening her. Further there was more than ample room for her to spread her blanket without crowding the lone occupant.

"Hello," Alice called, hoping the person would allow her to remain until the night ended and daylight lit the world.

No response came from the blanket wrapped figure.

"Hello. May I share the attic with you until tomorrow?" Alice questioned.

Still there was no reply or movement from the blanketed form on the floor.

"Are you all right?" she called in a louder voice.

Again there was no reply. Alice slowly crept closer and looked down at the still form. She knelt and touched what she judged to be the shoulder. The figure within the blanket was hard and rigid. Alice jerked her hand away.

She stared down at the blanket wrapped figure for several seconds. She had to know the condition of the person. Was he or she dead or alive? Slowly, hesitantly, she reached out and began to pull the thin blanket away from the figure.

The last fold of the blanket fell away and Alice saw a boy of seven or eight hugging a doll-like girl half his size in his arms. Their gaunt bodies were dressed in grimy, raggedy clothing. Both had fair skin and light brown hair. The girl's eyes were closed. The boy's blue eyes were open and staring down unblinkingly at the girl. Alice thought his expression was one of worry and love. She wanted to believe they were brother and sister, that the brother, unable to feed and protect his little sister and unwilling to leave her, had lain down and died with her. Alice knew the tykes were dead.

The girl's eyes flashed opened, and swiftly widened to round circles of surprise when they fell upon Alice. "Help me," she cried out.

Alice flinched back at the dead girl suddenly coming alive. "Oh, my God," she exclaimed.

"Big Brother has been holding me tight for a long, long time and won't let me loose," cried the girl. "And I've got to pee.

"Yes. Yes." said Alice with sudden understanding of the girl's predicament. The boy had died and his body had become rigid in death and from the cold temperature. The girl had become imprisoned within his arms.

"Yes. Yes. Let me help you get loose from him."

3

She took hold of the boy's stiff arms and pried them a few inches apart. The girl wiggled free and Alice hastily released her hold on the boy's arms.

The tiny girl looked angrily at the boy. "Big Brother never was mean to me like that before."

"I'm sure Big Brother never meant to hurt you," Alice said.

"He wouldn't talk to me even when I yelled at him and I don't like it when he won't talk."

"Your brother is dead and his spirit has gone to heaven."

"Big Brother dead!" The girl began to cry. "Our mom died and went to heaven," she said through her tears.

She scooped the little girl into her arms. "Don't cry for you'll make me cry," she said.

"All right," the girl said. She sniffled a few times and then wiped her tears away with a coat sleeve.

"I love Big Brother for most times he's good to me," she said and looking down at the boy.

"I'm sure you did."

"Do you think he'll be hungry in heaven?"

"Oh, no. I'm sure he won't be."

"I hope he's not."

"What's your name?"

"Gracie."

"Gracie is a good name. I'm Alice. Let's go down stairs and sleep there."

Gracie looked at the boy and then at Alice. "I want my blanket."

"Yes, we'll need it to keep warm tonight?" Alice replied.

Alice removed the blanket from the still form of the boy.

"Alright. Let's go."

"What about Big Brother?"

"We'll find a policeman and tell him about your brother and he'll have somebody come and take care of him.

Gracie took hold of Alice's hand and held it tightly. "I'm really hungry. Do you have something to eat?"

"Part of a sandwich you can have. Tomorrow I'll find us more food." Even if I have to steal it, thought Alice.

She led Gracie down the stairs to the lower level where she spread their blankets on the wooden floor. She removed the sandwich from her pocket and handed it to Gracie, who hurriedly took it. She silently watched the little girl swiftly bite into the sandwich and begin chewing. Alice's empty stomach growled.

***

Alice awoke when first daylight came into the room of the deserted house where she and Gracie had spent the night. Gracie lay against her for both were wrapped in the same blankets. The girl appeared ill. Beneath the dirt smudges, her face was flushed. She coughed raggedly. Alice felt her cheek and found it hot.

Gracie roused at Alice's touch. "I don't feel good," she said.

"I know. I'll go and get us some food and then you'll feel better."

Alice climbed out of the blankets and tucked them in snugly around Gracie. She was anxious to go searching for food. She must be resourceful, daring in her hunt for they must eat. If that required her to be a thief today, then a thief she would be.

"You rest and keep warm, Gracie. I'll be back as quick as I can."

"I'll wait for you," Gracie said, a trusting expression lighting her hollow cheeked face.

"I won't be gone any longer than I have to."

Alice picked up her treasured items, a man's watch, a notebook with hand written poems and a picture tucked inside, from where she had placed them on the floor the night before and put them in her pockets. Her knife went into her right front pocket so as to be ready to her hand.

***

Alice shivered as the cold, blustery wind, swirling up scraps of paper and bits of dirt from the street, swept over her. She halted, lowered her chin down against her chest, pulled her coat tightly around her shoulders and waited for the gust of wind to pass.

The wind slowed and dropped its load of trash. Alice lifted her head and watched the street awakening to life in the early morning. Men, women and children all bundled up in coats and hats were coming out of the doorways of the two and three story aged, brick tenement houses and onto the street. Vendors with much used trucks loaded with their wares were setting up stalls along the edges of the street. Arriving last were a few horse drawn wagons with their beds full of produce from the farms and orchards outside the city. Several businesses, tucked into the bottom floors of some of the tenements, were opening their doors. The voices of vendors hawking their wares began to sound out along the street. A block away, blue uniformed young policeman moved along the street and swinging his club on its leather tether. He nodded to people as he passed by them.

Alice focused on the nearest vendor, a short, fat butcher with his meat wagon. He was removing smoked hams, sides of bacon and links of sausages from the bed of his wagon and hanging them on hooks fastened to a wooden frame where they could be seen by the passers-by. She shifted her view past the butcher to the bakery located not far away. The baker, a stooped, gray headed old man, was placing a loaf of fresh bread and half a dozen sweet rolls on a white cloth spread on the broad inside ledge of the front window of the bakery. The window was open half a foot to allow the aroma of freshly baked bread to drift out onto the street and so entice buyers. Alice should be able to out run both the butcher and the baker.

She lifted her face and breathed in deeply, smelling the tantalizing aroma of the meat and bread brought to her on the wind. Her stomach growled with hunger, her mouth moistened and she swallowed.

Alice looked beyond the bakery to the policeman moving away along the street. He was the greatest threat. He could quickly become the hound and she the rabbit. Should he catch Alice, Gracie would have no food and would die. Alice would be in the children's reformatory school. The policeman reached the corner two blocks distant and turned around it and out of her sight.

Alice was not alone in her keen evaluation of the events happening on the street. Two boys, street kids like herself for she knew this by their worn and soiled clothing, stood farther along the street and silently surveying the people passing by, and the vendors calling out the names of what they had for sale.

Nearer to Alice, two girls about seven years old came out from the narrow slot of an opening between two buildings. They stood on the sidewalk with their raggedy clothed shoulders touching as if each girl needed the others support to stay erect. They scanned the street. As Alice observed the girls, a well dressed man and woman approached the two tykes. One girl saw the adults coming in her direction and began to sing. The second hastily joined in, singing even louder than the first girl. As the man and woman drew nearer the girls' voices rose more strongly. Alice heard the words from a song she had heard before, "Big Rock Candy Mountain."

In the Big Rock Candy Mountains
There's a land that's fair and bright
Oh, the buzzin' of the bees in the peppermint trees
'Round the soda water fountains
Where the lemonade springs and the bluebird sings
In the Big Rock Candy Mountains

Still singing strongly, the girls held out their hands to the man and woman passing close by on the sidewalk. The pair halted and looked down at the pair of waifs. The woman spoke to the man and he took coins from a pocket and placed one on each outstretched dirty palm. The girls ran off squealing joyfully along the street.

The generosity of the man and woman and the happiness of the tiny girls, removed some of the weight from Alice's heart. Thank you, she silently mouthed the words for the girls who had forgotten to do that in their happiness with the money.

She turned back to the two boys. The larger one, half a head taller than his companion, was idly cutting shavings from a short piece of wood with a jackknife. Alice knew that like herself, the two boys were watching for an opportunity to somehow acquire something to eat.

A horse drawn wagon rolled by with its harness chains jangling and iron wheels rattling on the cobblestone street. Its wooden bed was filled with bushel baskets heaping full of red apples. The two boys came quickly alert. The larger boy leaned close to the smaller one and pointed at the wagon and said a few words. The lad nodded and darted out into the street and ran beside the wagon, and reaching over the wooden sideboard, grabbed an apple.

The driver caught sight of the lad stealing the apple. He twisted swiftly around in his seat and lashed out with his horse whip. The leather whip popped like a firecracker as it took an inch of skin from the side of the boy's face, barely missing an eye. The lad yelped with pain, and clutching the side of his face, jumped away from the wagon.

"You damned little thief, that'll teach you," shouted the man and grinned, pleased at the accuracy of his strike with the whip.

"You damned bastard," the larger boy yelled with high anger. "I'll teach you something." He sprang after the wagon, closed upon it with fast strides, raced past it and up behind the horse. The man slashed at the boy with his whip and caught him across the shoulders. The boy gave no sign that he had been struck. His right arm swung and he jammed the stick, upon which he had been carving, into the horse's rump.

The injured horse bolted away with a clatter of iron shod hooves and drawing the wagon along the street at a frightening pace. The driver hauled back mightily on the reins and shouting, "Whoa. Whoa." This had no effect on the runaway horse. People scattered, dashing for safety from the street and onto the sidewalk.

The tail gate of the wagon jolted loose and fell. Baskets followed and a tide of apples spilled and rolled on the street. Men, women, and children rushed from the sidewalk to the fallen fruit and hastily began gathering it up. The last Alice saw of the horse and wagon it was careening around a distant corner balanced on two side wheels.

Alice looked for the boys. They had disappeared.

She checked the butcher and the baker. Both men were watching the people milling about and talking loudly. Now was her chance and she must not fail. She sprang away along the street. As she raced past the meat wagon she snatched a foot long length of sausages from a hook. She dashed on to the bakery where she halted, reached in through the partially open window and grabbed a sweet roll. Clutching both items, she raced off with flying feet along the street.

Alice darted past people on the sidewalk. Many turned to stare after the fleeing girl. She came to a section of sidewalk without people and ran onward with all her strength. Behind her she heard the sound of heavy feet pounding the sidewalk in pursuit.

"Thief. Thief. Catch that little bitch." The angry cry of the butcher came to Alice.

From farther behind came the shouts of the baker. "Stop her. Somebody stop that girl."

Alice ran at the top of her strength, flying feet pounding the sidewalk. She sucked at the air and it made a cold, sharp stinging in her throat as it went down into the lungs. In the middle of the next block she flung a quick look over her shoulder. Her pursuers were far behind.

She came to an alley and veered into it. At the end of the alley, she slowed and hid the sausage and sweet roll under her coat. She must not draw attention to herself. She came out onto the street at a moderate walk and crossed the street to the opposite alley. There she broke into a fast trot along it. At the next cross street, she again slowed to a walk and turned left along it and merged with the few pedestrians.

Half a score blocks farther along, she turned to the side to step over a falling down picket fence, and onward across the weed choked yard to enter the sagging doorway of the house where she and Gracie had taken sanctuary.

Gracie opened her eyes at the sound of Alice's footsteps. "I was worried about you. Thought maybe a policeman would catch you."

"Everything's all right," Alice said and knelt by Gracie. "And I've got something good for us to eat."

She opened her coat and removed the sausage and sweet roll and held them out for Gracie to view. "How about this?" she said proudly. "Doesn't it look tasty?"

"I'm really not hungry. You eat it."

"You got to eat to get well. Which one would you like to eat first?"

"I can't eat. Really, I can't."

"Oh, please, Gracie. One bite at least. The sweet roll should be especially delicious. One bite now."

Alice put the roll to Gracie's mouth. "Do it for me, please."

Gracie took a nibble. She looked into Alice's eyes as she chewed mechanically and swallowed.

"No more. Please. I'll throw up." Her voice sank to a weary whisper. "I'll eat more later and get well."

Alice sat down on the floor and took Gracie's small, cold hand into hers. "Oh, Gracie, what am I going to do?" She feared for her little friend's life.

"I'll be all right so don't you worry. I think I'll sleep a little now." Her eyes closed.

Alice stroked Gracie's soft cheek. "Yes, sleep, Gracie. I'll be right here when you wake up." Alice began to sob softly and tears pooled in her eyes and overflowed and coursed down her cheeks.

Finally Alice stifled her tears of worry about her little friend. She began to eat the sweet roll.

She heard a sound on the floor behind her and whirled to look. The young policeman stood in the doorway. Alice leapt to her feet. How did he find her?

"You almost got away from me," said the policeman. "You shouldn't have stole those things for now I've got to take you down to the station house." He pointed down at Gracie wrapped in the blankets. "What's wrong with the little one?"

"That's Gracie and she's awfully sick. Her brother is upstairs. He's dead. I found Gracie and her brother last evening. With him dead, I decided to take care of her. The food was for her."

"Umm, I see" said the officer and rubbed the side of his face. "Well we can't just leave her here. And you say her brother is upstairs and dead?"

"Yes."

"What's your name?"

"Alice Childs."

"Well, Alice, I'll carry Gracie to the hospital where a doctor can care for her if you promise not to try to run off. What do you say to that?"

"Oh, yes, yes. I'll not run off." Alice nodded in quick agreement.

"You promise?"

"I promise with all my heart." With those words, she felt a dark foreboding as to what might happen to her at the station house.

The officer tossed aside the blankets covering Gracie, and scooped her up into his arms. "She weighs almost nothing. She sure needs some food got into her too. Now, Alice, you walk ahead of me where I can keep an eye on you."

"Yes sir," replied Alice.

"I'll send somebody for the boy." The officer motioned for Alice to move toward the door.

***

"Alice Childs, Mr. Jenkins here has made a complaint that you stole his sausage." The sergeant of police spoke to Alice from behind his desk in the police station. "Are you guilty of that?"

Alice remained silent as she watched the sergeant. He was going to send her to jail, she was certain of that. However Gracie was now at the hospital and a doctor was caring for her. That was sufficient payment for whatever punishment the policeman heaped upon her.

"Answer me, girl. Did you steal the man's sausage?"

"I wanted food for my sick friend, Gracie. She had to eat to get well."

"I'm sorry your friend is sick. But that doesn't excuse you from stealing."

"Yes, sir, I know that. But I had to do it for Gracie."

"Lock her up with all the other little thieves in the detention center," Jenkins said harshly from where he stood beside the arresting officer.

"Don't tell me my job, Jenkins," replied the sergeant. "You've made your complaint. So you can leave now. I'll take the proper action with this young thief."

"I don't trust you," growled Jenkins. "I've heard about you. I think you're going to let her off easy like you have some other little thieves."

The sergeant's face hardened at the man's accusations. "Jenkins, that's enough from you. You'd better leave before I arrest you for insulting an officer of the law."

"That's no crime when it's true."

"Go now, Jenkins, get the hell out of here."

"I'll report you to the chief," Jenkins fired back.

"You do that," the sergeant said in a challenging tone. He rose from behind his desk and glared at Jenkins.

"I'll report you. I sure as hell will." Jenkins stomped out of the room.

The sergeant stared for a moment at the door through which Jenkins had left. Then he spoke to the arresting officer. "Barker, go down the street to the Children's Aid Society and bring Sister Marie here."

"Right away," replied Barker. He smiled as he left with a quick step.

The sergeant spoke gently to Alice. "Miss, why don't you go over there and sit down and keep warm." He gestured at the four straight backed chairs arranged in front of the hot water heat radiator attached to the wall.

"You're going to keep me out of jail?" Alice asked hopefully.

"We'll have to wait and see."

"Thank you, sir. You're very kind." She felt a deep gratitude toward the sergeant.

"I'm not promising anything. Just go get warm."

Alice seated herself in the chair closest to the heat radiator. Please! Please! Don't send me to jail.

***

In the police station, Sister Marie spoke to the sergeant. "The orphanage is full. There's no space for even one more boy or girl. And still from what you've told me about this girl stealing to feed a sick friend, her crime isn't so terrible that she should be locked up. What possible good would that do? True friendship is a rare thing."

"That's why I sent for you," said the sergeant. "She should be given another chance. Can you take her out of the city on the next Orphan Train and find her a family to live with?"

Sister Marie examined Alice, frowning at the tangled hair, the dirt smudged face, the torn soiled coat, but mostly at her size. "She's older than most of the girls that I've taken west. Not many families would take her in except for the work she could do."

Alice had been evaluating Sister Marie as she listened to the conversation. The nun was a small woman with a long, thin face and blue eyes. She wore a nun's habit, a loose, black gown that swept the floor and a second piece of black cloth covering most of her head. Alice was no judge of an older person's age; still she knew the nun was many times older than she.

Alice must speak for herself. She crossed the room to stand near the nun and the sergeant.

"Sister, I must get out of the city. Please take me on your Orphan Train. I'll do what ever you ask of me. I'd work hard for any family that would give me a place to sleep and something to eat."

Sister Marie studied Alice for a moment longer. Then she turned to the sergeant and nodded. "All right."

"Then you'll take her on the next train?" asked the sergeant. "And find a home for her?"

"If I do take her, will you get in trouble with the chief?"

"No sister. The chief knows how bad it is for kids on the street, especially in the winter. In the past month we've found eight dead from hunger and the cold. Officer Barker said there's a dead boy, brother of the little girl Alice was feeding, that we've got to get. The chief appreciates the good work you and the church do for the boys and girls we catch pulling petty thefts."

"Very well then."

Alice saw a roguish glint come into Sister Marie's eyes, and she liked the expression.

"We have a train leaving tomorrow morning," continued Sister Marie. "It's full already, but I'll squeeze her on board. She'll be out of the city before Jenkins can take any action to stop me. There's something you should know, tomorrow's train will be the last one taking orphans west to find homes. With businesses failing and so many people out of work, donations are small and the church can't afford another train."

Sister Marie felt a deep sadness telling of the ending of the Church's huge effort with orphan trains. When the first train ran in 1854, it was estimated there were 30,000 abandoned or orphaned children living on the streets of the city. Their number swamped the orphanages. The Catholic Church took pity on the waifs and created the New York Children's Aid Society. Sister Marie had helped gathered up thousands of children and transport them across the land to distant farming town.

Most of them were taken in by families where they were accepted as full members and given love and an education. She knew that some children were taken in for the labor their young bodies could provide. She feared others might have fallen into the hands of people both brutal and vile and this caused her much sadness.

"Your Orphan Trains has helped a lot of kids," said the sergeant. "I'll tell the chief what you said about this one being the last one."

The sister nodded to the sergeant, then spoke to Alice. "Come along, Alice, I'm thinking you could use a bath, some clean clothes and a good meal."

"Yes, yes a bath," said Alice. She looked up into the nun's face and fastened on her eyes. "Sister Marie, thank you for keeping me from being locked up."

"You're very welcome, Alice." Sister Marie replied. The girl was young and vulnerable, and there was a wariness about her that had been earned from life on the streets. "Now let's hurry along."

Sister Marie led out of the police station. Alice followed. A great weight had been lifted off her shoulders. But this Orphan Train the sister and the sergeant spoke about, how far west would it take her? What would be the destination? Whatever it was, it couldn't be as bad as the past weeks had been.

Sister Marie walked swiftly her legs kicking her long skirt. Alice stretched her legs to keep up with the sister. It was pleasant to be walking beside her. She was tempted to catch hold of the sister's hand. She controlled the impulse.

Half a score blocks passed and they came to an aged brick, two-story building with many windows on a street lined with big elm trees. A sign over the door proclaimed this to be the Children's Aid Society. A trolley line ran down the center of the street in front. Alice heard the clang of a bell of a distant trolley. Sister Marie entered the front of the building through a thick oak door and Alice followed.

Deep inside the building in a tiny office, Sister Marie took out a thick ledger and recorded Alice's birthplace, age, and the name of father and mother, and adding that both parents were deceased. She then turned Alice over to Sister Evangeline, a slim, intense young woman.

Sister Evangeline guided Alice directly to a storeroom where boxes were filled with clothing, obviously used, but in good condition, and all clean and neatly folded. They searched among the clothing for the correct size to outfit Alice with garments from the skin out. A second set was chosen, to be kept fresh for "the inspection" as the sister put it. This would be when the people of the towns where the train stopped would come and choose a boy or girl to take into their family. This second outfit and a warm coat and hat were stowed away in a small canvas satchel. Alice silently thanked the good and generous people who had given the clothing to the Society. Alice put her treasures and the knife into the satchel.

Carrying her new clothes, Alice followed Sister Evangeline next door to the bath house. There the sister filled a tub with heated water from a faucet.

Alice stripped and stepped into the tub of warm water. She sat down, the water caressing her legs, hips, up to her breast. "Oh, how wonderful," she whispered. She took a bar of soap from the dish on the bath stand close by and made lather and began to wash her dirty body.

Sister Evangeline was examining Alice's raggedy clothing. "None of this is worth keeping," she said and tossed the lot into the trash bin in the corner of the room. She drew up the chair from the dressing table and seated herself in the doorway of the bathroom.

"You can go and do whatever you want," Alice told the sister. "I'll call you when I'm finished." She wanted privacy for her bath.

"I can't leave for I've been told to watch you and see that you don't run away," the sister replied. "If you run away, Sister Marie would be in trouble."

"But I won't run away. I want to go on the train."

"I believe you. But some kids do, especially the bigger ones who came from the police station. I'm going to do what Sister Marie told me to."

Alice could see Sister Evangeline would not leave. "All right. But I'd never do anything to hurt her."

Alice finished bathing, dressed in the fresh clothing and followed Sister Evangeline to the dining hall where the children were already at their noonday meal. The room was large and brightly lit by the sunlight streaming in through the four tall windows along a wall. At the near end of the space was a serving table with its pans and cauldrons of food, and a sister standing ready to serve. The rich aroma of food filled the dining air and Alice breathed deeply, savoring the delightful smell. The sister smiled as Alice drew near and handed her a bowl of soup and a plate containing bread, butter and a wedge of cake.

Alice turned to find a place to sit among the children. She estimated there were nearly sixty of them, about half girls and half boys. Their ages ranged from those barely able to dress themselves to early teens. All were neatly dressed, their clothes from the same source as hers, Alice believed. They were seated on benches at two long wooden tables, the boys at one and the girls at the second. Alice found a seat among the girls.

Alice ate with deliberate slowness, savoring the large bowl of warm vegetable soup and the thick slice of bread with real butter spread on it.

From all around her came the happy, friendly chatter of the children. That was suddenly interrupted by a roar of laughter erupted from many throats at the boys' table and Alice turned to see what caused it. A small, very thin lad of about six with black hair and fair skin was dancing and laughing and smiling and holding in his hand a piece of cake high above his head. His movements possessed a natural grace delightful to observe. He lowered the cake and took a bite. Then again he lifted the cake high, laughed in a high, childish voice and pirouetted, and smiled, always smiling with such a look of pleasure at the food that Alice could only smile with him. She had never seen anybody appreciate their food so much that they expressed it by dancing joyfully. Still Alice would dance for a piece of cake for Gracie.

The sister at the serving table started toward the boy. Alice thought she intended to stop the boy's antics. The sister halted and merely watched and smiled along with the children. However the lad had seen the sister start toward him, and with one last spin and a broad smile, quickly took his seat.

"That's Teddy," said the girl seated beside Alice. "He was starving on the street when they found him. Now he puts on a show at every meal that has cake for dessert. The sisters put up with him because he's so darn cute."

"He is cute," said Alice. "

"I'm Opal," said the girl. "What's your name?"

"Alice." She examined Opal, a plain girl with black hair and a large mouth with oversized teeth that protruded slightly. She was Alice's height and strongly built.

"You're new here, aren't you?"

"Yes. Just came today. Sister Marie brought me."

"She's a fine lady."

"She surely is. How long have you been here?"

"Nearly a week. Just waiting for the train to take us west. Hopefully to a new home."

"The sister said it leaves tomorrow."

"Yes," said Opal and smiled, and with her wide mouth and large teeth it was a huge smile. "And I'm anxious and ready to go."

Alice thought Opal's smile was a lovely thing. It brightened her face and mostly overcame her plainness. "Where's the train going to take us?"

"I've heard different places. Missouri, Kansas, maybe even farther west. We'll just have to wait for Sister Marie to tell us. I hope I'm taken in by kind people."

"I hope I am too," said Alice. "How do they find the families?

"The train carries us to towns out west where people come from all around and choose us and take us into their homes. I've heard they're mostly farm people who want children. Of course they expect us to work and earn our way. I'd work really hard for a home."

"I hope anybody who takes me in will let me go to school," Alice said.

"I heard that most families do let the kids go to school."

"That's good to hear."

"It's going to be a long trip," said Opal. "There's a library here and they'll let us take a book with us to read on the train. After we finish eating, do you want me to show you where it is and we can choose a book."

"Yes. I'd like to have a book of poetry."

"Poetry is okay. But sometimes I have trouble understanding what the poet is saying."

"Some poems are only for the poet who writes them to understand."

"I didn't know that. I thought poetry for was for everybody. Do you know a poet?"

"I once knew a wonderful poet," Alice said sadly.

***

Sister Marie stood beside Sister Evangeline at the doorway leading from the dining hall. She was studying the children filing toward her, some alone and silent, others in pairs whispering and smiling. The children looked up with awe and an obvious liking for her as they passed.

"There's the new girl from you brought from the police station, the one walking with Opal," said Sister Evangeline. "A bath did wonders for her."

"It certainly did," said Sister Marie and observing Alice as she smiled at something Opal said. It was but a half smile as if she didn't smile often. With her slender body, she appeared fragile. However, at the police station, Sister Marie had sensed strength in her.

"Even half starved she's beautiful," said Sister Marie.

"Yes she is," agreed Sister Evangeline.

Sister Marie put out a hand and stopped Alice as she drew abreast of her. She examined Alice closely, noting the smooth sweep of her forehead, the copper gold of her eyebrows and lashes, the fine straight line of her nose. With her golden hair and white, translucent skin rivaling alabaster in its purity, and those magnificence green eyes like gems, Alice was the most beautiful girl the sister had ever seen. Men would be strongly drawn to her, all sorts of men. Alice's great beauty could bring her great danger, thought Sister Marie.

"How long have you been living on the street?" Sister Marie asked.

"Since last April," Alice replied.

"I know that must have been a very awful time. But it's over now."

Alice doubted that the sister really did know how terrible it was to be on the streets and shoved aside, cursed and yelled at, to be preyed upon by those in the same dire straits but strong enough to take your pitiful possessions. For a girl it was very bad, for they had a special danger from the big boys, who would catch and fondle the private parts of your body. Sometimes they laughed as if they had captured a prize. Worst of all were the girls younger than herself, who in desperation, went into the dark alleys with men and laid down and sold themselves for a few silver coins with which to buy a little food to fill their empty stomachs.

Think of something else, Alice told herself and she shut off the picture. She spoke to Sister Marie, "Have you heard anything about Gracie at the hospital? Is she getting well?"

"I'll send somebody to the hospital in the morning before we leave to find out about her," replied Sister Marie.

"Thank you." Alice wanted to know about Gracie now and not later, but she must accept what the sister said.

"We're going to the library to get a book for the train ride tomorrow," Opal said.

"Go along then," said Sister Marie, and motioned the girls past.

***

Alice rested on a soft, warm cot near an outer wall of the girls' dormitory of the Children's Aid Society. The electric light at each end of the large room had been extinguished and darkness lay densely. Several rows of narrow cots completely filled the space, with each cot holding a thin cotton mattress, pillow and blanket. Every bed held a girl.

Alice felt safe among the girls, and by knowing Sister Marie and the other sisters were someplace close by in their own sleeping areas within the walls of the building. Tonight she would sleep soundly. For the first time in weeks, she was free of the constant fear that made her nights so tense and wakeful.

The conversations of the girls were a whispery murmur coming out of the darkness. A pleasant, sleep inducing quietness was settling as their voices dwindled. Then all talk ceased and a stillness fell over the dormitory.

Alice pulled the blanket up snuggly under her chin and closed her eyes. Her breathing slowed and steadied and her thoughts began to drift between reverie and sleep; circling, eddying, and drawing her backward. She surrendered to them, going back to memories of her earlier childhood, to events that could never be forgotten no matter how many years she lived.

Chapter Two

Wolves Of The Forest

Paul Douccard moved easily on snowshoes through the forest of tall pines and spruce and hard woods of northern Minnesota. A bulky pack containing his one-man tent and fur sleeping robe, food and other camping and trapping necessities was strapped upon his back. He was drawing near Head Lake that lay some eighteen miles south of Rainy River and the border with Canada.

Nearly a foot of new snow had fallen during the night and the limbs of the pines and spruce had caught mounds of it and now drooped in arches beneath the weight. The bare, leafless limbs of the hardwoods, the oak, maple, and birch made an intricate wickerwork pattern against the blue sky. Every tree stood motionless for the wind had gone off to some unknown place two days past. Though the January sun shone brightly, the deep freeze that had begun in December still held the forest in its frigid grip.

Paul carried a .30 caliber, Winchester rifle in his right hand, a much used gun that had belonged to his father until his death four long years past. His left hand held a tied bundle of fresh pelts, one from a mink, a martin, and two from foxes that he had taken from traps on this the first half of his sixty mile trap line. Three days were required to run the trap line and he ran it once a week. At the end of each day, he slept wherever the darkness caught him.

He was seventeen, lean and muscular. His eyes were gray and set far apart in a face that was somewhat broad, which gave it an open, yet a stern expression. He was dressed in woolen trousers, shirt and a long coat made of wolf fur. A woolen cap with a leather bill crowned his head. He moved warily, his senses alert. The forest was an old acquaintance of his and all the animals that made it their home were well known. Still there was danger should he come unexpectedly upon a wolverine, a cougar, a badger, or a pack of wolves.

On Paul's left, his long legged dog Brutus with his head held high kept pace through the snow. Brutus was a wolfhound with a gray pelt and black splotches on the sides. The coat was made of long, coarse guard hairs covering and protecting the fragile soft inner fur that was nearly an inch deep and provided protection from the cold. His head was longish with powerful jaws. His shoulders were strong, chest deep. His paws were large and round with arched toes and strong, downward curving claws. His dark eyes were set under bushy eyebrows. He was Paul's constant companion, and had been for all his five years of life.

Paul earned a living for his mother and himself by trapping fur and cutting ice in the winter and farming during the summer. The ice was sold to the Torgerson Ice Company located in the village of Diston some six miles west of his home. There it was stored beneath three feet of saw dust until needed in the summer. The furs were sold to a buyer also located in Diston. Paul and his mother raised wheat and tended a large garden on the farm that his grandfather and father had hewed out of the forest along the Rainy River. The river was the boundary between the States and Canada. Paul went to high school in Diston.

Paul slowed as he drew near the edge of the forest and Head Lake. In the last fringe of trees, he halted and swept his sight over the flat, snow-covered surface of the lake. It was some two miles wide and seven miles long and rimmed entirely by tall trees of the forest. Under the bright sunlight, the snow sparkled like a billion diamonds. Upon that glittering surface and several hundred yards away, a dark form, a wolf, was making its way in Paul's direction.

"Down, Brutus," Paul whispered and fell into the snow.

Brutus instantly crouched beside his master. He kept his legs bunched beneath him and waited, coiled for the next command. The tone of his master told him that something important had been seen. Brutus was ready to rush and attack, or steal silently back into the forest.

"It's Black Face himself," Paul whispered, staring out across the lake. "And he's coming our way. Now if he'll only come within gun range, all of our long hunt for him will end today." He chuckled softly with anticipation.

Brutus turned keen eyes in the same direction as his master. The wolf was but a black spot far away on the lake's ice.

Paul, moving slowly so as not to attract the wolf's sharp vision, slid his arms from the straps of the pack and placed it in front of him. He laid his rifle upon the pack to used it as a solid platform from which to shoot most accurately. He twisted about and removed his snowshoes. From a side pocket of his coat, he extracted a spyglass. He extended it full length and aimed it at Black Face.

In the 10 power magnified view field of the spyglass, the large, male wolf appeared to leap from 400 yards to but 40 yards distant. Moving easily the wolf made his way through the snow. Paul marveled at the strength of the animal, the dry, light snow seeming to be but fog through which he waded with little effort.

"He's too far off for a good shot," Paul confided to Brutus. "We'll have to wait a bit." As he lowered the spyglass, he noted a slight stirring of the top limbs of the pine trees as an unwanted wind came alive.

Paul again took up the spyglass and looked at Black Face. The predators, the hunters were the most intelligent animals in the woods. Of all of them, the wolves were the cleverest. They knew their home range, often encompassing a hundred and fifty square miles or more, like no other forest animal. Every hill and valley they knew, and the habits of every animal that lived there. Humans who entered the wolf's range were not exempt from being known by the wolves. The loggers, who spent much time in the woods, told of wolves spying upon them from but a few yards away. A wolf pack that trespassed upon another pack's range was not treated so benignly. Fierce battles were fought to defend a home range and thus save the deer and other prey for their own members.

Paul had known Black Face since he was a pup. He had come upon the female wolf's den made underneath the upturned roots of a giant pine tree that had been toppled by the wind. The five pups, believing the sound of Paul squatting down near them was that of their mother returning to the den, had whimpered and crawled toward him. Paul had drawn back for he didn't want to put his scent on the pups. Being newly born their eyes was of a pale blue color. A time would come soon when those eyes would be a fierce yellow with a black center.

One of the males, with a striking mixture of colors, was larger than the other pups. His nose was jet black. The blackness continued on along his head to encircle the eyes and the erect, pointed ears, and onward across the top of the head to merge with the black saddle that extended the full length of his body. The black graded into a reddish brown on his sides and that changed to a yellowish tan on his stomach. Paul promised himself that one day when the pup was full grown, he would take its pelt for sale. He had left with the wolf den undisturbed.

During the next two years, Paul had spotted the black faced wolf several times. Once he had aimed his rifle at the wolf and could have killed him, but held off to wait for him to reach full size. This past fall, the third year of Black Face's life, Paul had observed the pack pursuing a deer. Black Face had been the swiftest and had overtaken the deer and alone brought it down. Now in the dead of winter and pelts prime, Paul hunted the wolf with deadly intent, and had set traps to catch him. The animal had avoided all ambushes. Out of respect for the wolf's cunning, Paul had given him a name, Black Face.

At the moment, as Black Face trotted across the lake with his pelt rippling over his muscles and the bright winter sun upon him, the long guard hairs seemed to be on fire with dancing, red flame.

"Beautiful", Paul murmured. "Your pelt will bring a premium price."

Brutus whined, tensing, wanting to know what his master wanted.

"Just talking to Black Face," Paul said.

Brutus recognized only one master, Paul. When he spoke, Brutus responded without hesitation. Paul had been but a boy when Brutus first opened his eyes as a pup. There had been a man and a woman in the house at that time. However it became soon known to Brutus that he belonged to the boy. And it was the boy who taught him what was expected of him upon certain words and hand gestures. Brutus enjoyed the lessons for it gave him pleasure to do as ordered and to receive that gentle touch on his head, and sometimes a gentle thump on the ribs, that told him he had performed correctly. He had reached full size by the third winter, and at that time when he stood up on his hind legs he was as tall as Paul. Paul continued to grow and now stood six feet tall.

***

The black faced wolf stopped in mid-stride and stood motionless in the snow. His sensitive nose had caught the scent of his enemy on the wind. He lifted his head higher and sucked in another breath of air to be certain of his finding. The scent was present, both that of the man and the dog. He growled and dropped down on his stomach. Only the top of his head with the sharp eyes and his tufted ears showed above the snow.

He ranged his eyes out across the frozen lake to the forest that rimmed the shore and examined the openings between the trees, searching for the sight of the man and dog. The wolf feared nothing in his domain of forest and lakes except the men that lived and hunted there.

Two years before when he was but a curious yearling and innocent of the danger from a man, he had foolishly drawn close to the buildings of a farm to investigate a tantalizing odor coming from white animals in a pen. The farmer, to protect his sheep, had fired a rifle at the wolf. The bullet had punched a hole through Brutus's right ears. In pain, he had sped away from that hazardous place. He healed quickly as young healthy animals do. He had learned that man was dangerous and could reach out a long distance and hurt him.

Black Face judged this man hidden on the lake shore his special enemy for he had discovered him and the dog following his tracks several times. He breathed again of the frigid wind. This time it did not contain the scent of the man. Still Black Face was too wise to doubt those first whiffs of him. He was patient and would wait.

The man's dog caused Black Face little concern. When dogs were in a pack and chased after him, he easily out ran them. A dog by itself had always run away from him, except for one large dog that fought him bravely. Black Face was skilled in fighting. He fought to earn his status in the pack. He fought the bears and the wolverines to protect the pups. He fought to defend his pack's territory against the wolf pack from the river that sometimes stole into his territory to hunt. He killed to eat. The dog was strong; still Black ace had slain him.

The slow wind came again and it carried the scent of the man. In one fluid movement, the wolf rose to his feet, pivoted a quarter turn to the right and leapt away in long, lithe bounds across the snow covered lake.

***

Paul watched Black Face race away, the blackness of his body standing out starkly against the white snow. He seemed to flow over the lake and in seconds was only a black spot growing ever smaller.

He lowered the spyglass and spoke to Brutus over his shoulder. "Well he outsmarted us again." Paul felt no regret that the wind had blown his scent to Black Face and he had made good his escape. To Paul the hunt was mostly an interesting game, with some dollars to be earned by sale of the pelt. To Black Face, the hunt was not a game but a matter of life or death. He lived by his wits, avoiding man who would kill him. In turn he killed only what he needed to survive. As Paul considered the different values, he realized that the death of the wolf would create a sad and empty place in his life.

Every time Paul had spotted Black Face during this past year, the wolf had been traveling by himself. Was he searching for a likely female to start his own pack? He was a big fellow and obviously strong and could be the dominant male of a pack. A pack of wolves was to the south on the Red Lake Indian Reservation. A larger pack ranged the land along the Rainy River several miles north of Head Lake. Among the females of those packs, Black Face could find a suitable female. In two or three years, he and a fertile bitch could produce enough pups to have his own following. This possibility added to Paul's pleasure in not having killed the wolf.

He snapped the spyglass closed and slid it back into the pocket of his coat. He rose to his knees and stared out over the lake. Nothing marred the dazzling whiteness of the perfectly flat snow field.

Paul whirled abruptly, and growling fiercely, flung himself upon Brutus still lying in the snow. He wrapped his arms around the dog's rock-solid chest and rolled with him, kicking snow as his feet propelled them about. Still growling, Paul rolled them again.

Brutus began to growl even more savagely than Paul and kicked his legs as if trying to break free. He shoved his head close to that of his master's and began to snap his powerful jaws together with a clash of white fangs. Those teeth could have bitten off the side of Paul's face with ease. With their voices joined in a savage mock battle, they rolled again and again with first the dog on top and then Paul. The snow was crunched down in a wide area by their tumbling bodies, and hurled aside in white sparkling sprays by their thrashing legs. They crashed into the trunk of a birch, but neither of them paid the encounter heed. Snarling in a ferocious duo, they rolled in the virgin snow. From a distance, the mock battle between the man and big dog appeared to be a struggle to the death

Paul ceased flinging Brutus and himself about and lay on his back and began to laugh in high good spirits. Brutus crawled close and placed his head upon Paul's chest. He heard his master's heart throb and felt the vibration of that odd human sound he made after one of their false battles. Brutus sensed that his master thought all was right in his world. That made everything all right in Brutus's world. Unable to laugh, Brutus's eyes shone with contentment. He pressed his nose against Paul's chest and drew in a deep breath of his scent for it had an added and pleasant quality when he laughed. Brutus delighted in Paul's scent as he allowed it to drift slowly out past his marvelously sensitive nose to mix with the myriad of forest smells.

Paul stared up through the limbs of the birch tree under which they had ended the game. The limitless blue dome of the sky arched overhead. Nothing existed there, neither bird nor cloud. The emptiness of the sky and the silence of the forest brought peace to him. He placed his hand upon Brutus's head. The dog chuffed with pleasure at the touch. The day is perfect, Paul thought, so just let Old Man Time go by.

Paul's laughter softened and then stopped. The emptiness of the sky and the infinity that existed beyond it brought a new thought. If he didn't know better, it could be that the universe was his and Brutus's alone. What would his life be like if only he and Brutus existed? At that question, a feeling came over Paul that he had never felt before. Life was good, but not full, lacking something. He focused on his inner self and searched among his private desires. Nothing came readily forth. He probed more deeply for what might be missing, but again he found nothing. Still there was a stirring of an emotion, one whose identify just escaped surfacing to his full consciousness. He worried around the hidden thing for a moment longer and then let it go. Some of the pleasantness of the day had been lost

Paul pulled back to the here and now. The frigid temperature was working its way through his clothing, and snow was plastered on his face and had gotten down the neck of his coat. He sat up, with Brutus's head lifting away at his first movement, and looked west off through the forest. The sun was falling down its ancient sky path and drawing near the horizon below which it hid at night. In the dead of winter, the days were short and night came early to hide his path through the forest.

"Best we get traveling for it'll be dark in a couple of hours and we've miles to go," Paul said to Brutus.

Man and dog climbed to their feet and shook themselves vigorously and in unison to remove the snow plastered to their bodies. Paul strapped on his snowshoes, pulled the pack onto his back, took up the pelts and rifle and struck off across Head Lake. Brutus strode at his side.

***

From a mile distance, Paul saw the logging camp, a five acre clearing on the east shore of Head Lake. In the clear air, gray wood smoke rose in two vertical columns from a long, single story building in the camp. Paul knew the larger column would be from the chimney of the big heating stove in the barracks portion of the building, and the smaller one from that of the cook stove in the kitchen. Behind the barracks and towering above it was a huge barn that provided shelter from the severe cold for the horses and oxen used to drag the logs from the forest. It also held hay and grain to feed the animals. Many trees had been fallen and an enormous pile of logs filled most of the clearing. When the lake thawed, the logs would be dragged into the lake and gathered into huge rafts. A steam driven tug would tow the rafts to one of the saw mills at the northern end of the lake.

Paul increased his pace. He wanted to reach the camp in time for supper with the loggers. After two days of lean rations, he was ready for a meal prepared by the loggers' skilled cook. He was certain that Jack Dawson, the camp boss, would invite him to eat with the crew.

***

Paul placed his pack, furs and snowshoes on the snow near the door of the barracks, leaned his rifle against the wall, and entered without knocking. After the pristine air of the forest, the heat from the big, potbellied heating stove, odors of wood smoke, tobacco smoke and cooking food struck him powerfully. A cloud of tobacco smoke floated against the ceiling of the large room.

He glanced around at the twenty or so men clothed in heavy woolen pants and shirts and corked leather boots. They were all strongly muscled men from long days of hard labor pulling saws and swinging axes to fall the big trees. Mostly they were good sorts.

Paul knew most of the loggers, by sight if not by name. Half a dozen of them lay on wooden, double-decker bunks built against the walls. Other men sat at tables playing either cards or dominos. All wore full beards, some of them long and tangled. The men's voices trailed off as more and more of the men noticed Paul's entrance.

"Well, Paul, I thought it was about time for you to come by and stop to see us," said a big, rangy man as he rose from a chair at a desk near the right wall of the room. With a broad welcoming smile parting his reddish beard and showing his teeth, he came across the barracks toward Paul.

Paul motioned Brutus down into a stay position and went forward to meet the man.

"Good to see you, Jack," Paul said and grasped Jack Dawson's thickly calloused hand. He was pleased at the camp boss's greeting. Paul's father had been a logger and worked at the camp. He had been killed there. On a snowy, windy day while he was stacking logs by pulling them upon a tall pile with a team of horses, the bottom logs had slid on the snow and collapsed the mound. A falling log had crushed his father to death.

A voice called from the wide doorway leading into the dining area and kitchen. "Paul, you're just in time for supper. I bet you planned it that way."

"Two Doves, I ran the last five miles to get here on time to eat some of your delicious cooking," Paul replied to the smiling cook, a broad faced Indian woman from the Red Lake Indian Reservation. Paul had never seen Two Doves when she wasn't smiling, or looked as if she was ready to smile. She had been the cook for the logging camp for as long as Paul could remember, and that was back years when he first came to the camp with his father.

"We're having peach pie for dessert and everything will be ready in a handful of minutes." Two Doves said and vanished back into her kitchen.

"I've got some furs that I'd like to leave with my others in your cold room, if that's okay," Paul said to Jack. "I'll pick all of them up later at the end of the trapping season."

"Sure. You know where it is. Just hang them with your others. Take a chair and let's talk before we eat."

As Paul started to seat himself, a fierce snarl sounded from Brutus. That was instantly followed by a yelp of pain and a loud thump of some heavy object striking the floor. He whirled around to look. One of the loggers, a tall rail of a man with a bony face, was down on the floor on his back and Brutus had a mouthful of his leg just below the knee.

Paul jumped to Brutus and encircled his neck with his arms. The dog's body was rigid with every muscle and tendon taut and hard.

"Let go, Brutus" Paul commanded.

He felt Brutus quiver at the order. Still the dog kept his jaws clamped on the logger's leg, his teeth grinding on the bone.

Paul leaned close over the dog and spoke in a firm voice. "Brutus, let go." Paul kneed Brutus soundly on the ribs to show he meant to be obeyed. "Now, Brutus," Paul's tone was hard with impatience.

Brutus couldn't refuse his master's order. He opened his jaws and relinquished his hold on the man's leg. The taste of his man's flesh and blood in his mouth was good. With his eyes glittering threateningly at the man, Brutus allowed Paul to pull him backward a few steps.

Paul motioned Brutus into a stay position and turned to the injured man. Before he could speak the men shouted at him.

"Your goddamned dog is crazy. He almost bit my leg off." The man's voice was harsh and his hairy face was twisted with pain.

"What did you do to cause him to bite you?" Paul asked calmly. The man had done something to cause the attack. Brutus was gentle when stroked, but vicious when provoked.

"Not a damn thing. The dog is just plumb crazy. I was just going out the door when he jumped and bit me."

"Brutus doesn't bother anybody that doesn't bother him."

"He bit me, didn't he?" The man reached and pulled up his pant leg to examine his wound.

One of the loggers, Paul knew as Hank, had been playing dominoes close by. He spoke out. "Now, Oroville, that's not exactly the way it was."

"Stay out of this, Hank," Oroville shot back quickly. "I know how it happened. He jumped me for no damn reason and bit me."

"Paul and Jack need to know the truth." Hank said in a light tone. He turned to Paul. "Brutus was there just where you told him to stay. He was a little in front of the door, but still there was plenty of room for Oroville to go around him. But Oroville didn't want to walk around him and so made to kick him and make him move. Well the dog was quicker and just plainly caught Oroville's leg and took a bite of it."

"That's not right," Oroville quickly objected. "He jumped me."

Hank's mild expression turned to a scowl at Oroville's words. "Don't call me a liar for then I'll take a bigger bite out of you than the dog did."

Jack had come up and now spoke to Oroville. "You know Brutus is a one man dog. Only Paul could kick him and get away with all his skin."

"I'm sorry he bit you," Paul said. "If anybody is at fault then it's me. I had him on stay and he wouldn't move until I told him to."

"I'm going to kill that damned dog," Oroville said and cut Brutus a menacing look.

Paul opened his mouth to warn Oroville to never try to harm Brutus.

Jack spoke more quickly. "That's enough of that kind of talk. Go into the kitchen and let Two Doves treat the bite."

Oroville limped away toward the kitchen. Over his shoulder, he gave Paul a glare and called out. "I'm going to kill that crazy sonofabitch dog."

Jack spoke in a low voice to Paul. "I'll have a talk with Oroville and cool him down."

Paul nodded. "I don't want trouble with one of your men, but I'll not let anybody kill Brutus."

"Yeah, I'd feel the same way. Don't let it worry you too much. Have a seat and we'll talk a little before Two Doves calls supper ready."

Paul shook his head. "It's probably better that I take Brutus and leave. That'll give Oroville a chance to think things through."

"Maybe so. Maybe so. He'll need some time for he's the kind to carry a grudge. But you know you're always welcome to stop by the camp and eat with us. And spend the night if you want. We have a couple of extra bunks." Jack put out his hand.

Paul shook the offered hand. "Thanks. I'll put my furs in the cold room and be gone."

"Right. One other thing. You've grown fast this year. How old are you?"

"I'm seventeen."

"Then you should be graduating from high school this spring."

"Yes."

"After you're finished with school, come by and let's talk about working for me in the timber like your father did. That's if you can tend to your farming and work here too."

"Jack, I'd be glad to work for you this summer. I can use the ready cash for in the fall, I'm off to college in Winnipeg. Going to be an engineer and help build railroads."

"Glad to hear that you're going to college."

"Thanks again for the job offer."

Paul signaled Brutus to him and left the barracks.

***

Paul stood in the cold and snow outside the barracks and let the fresh, clean forest air clear his lungs of the smoke and smell of the barracks. He worried about Brutus biting one of the loggers. At the same time, he was proud of the dog for defending himself. Paul's work oftentimes put him in grave danger from large and savage animals and he needed a strong dog as a partner, one who would give his life to protect him. Brutus had proved that he was such a partner and carried a large scar on the right side of his head and neck from a fight with a wolverine. The attack had occurred when Paul approached the trapped wolverine. The snow had been deep and Paul could not see that the wolverine, caught by the rear leg in a steel trap, had nearly broken free. The wolverine made a powerful lunge at Paul, and in so doing had torn its leg from between the jaws of the trap. The animal struck Paul in the chest and knocked him backward and off his feet. As the animal leapt upon Paul to disembowel him with claws and teeth, Brutus attacked and a fight to the death had taken place. The wolverine's slashing claws had cut a deep wound.

Paul circled the barracks to the rear. To his right was the large barn made of hewed logs tightly fitted together to keep most of the winter winds from the draft horses and oxen. The roof was steeply pitched to force the snow to slide off and not accumulate to a weight that would crush the roof. To his left was the cold room, a log building of one modest size room. Its location had been chosen to keep it in the shadow of the barn and out of the sunlight and thus cold throughout the winter months. To enhance the building's capacity to stay cold, the loggers had piled snow against the walls up to the eaves of the building.

Paul carried his furs into the cold room. The air was heavy with the smell of meat; smoked hams and bacon, quarters of beef, skinned deer, bags of chickens plucked and ready for cooking, and all hanging on hooks attached to cords fastened to the ceiling joists and thus out of the reach of the woods mice and other hungry animals that stole into the room. All the meat was frozen and would remain edible for weeks. On the floor were metal containers of various sizes holding an array of food stuffs for Two Doves' pots.

In the corner farthest from the foodstuffs, he hung his furs on metal hooks with the others he had brought earlier in the winter. The furs must be kept frozen until he could find time to scrape off the flesh and fat and dry them. He left the cold room and with Brutus and struck out north across the clearing toward the lake where traveling would be easiest. He walked on his shadow lying long and thin on the snow. The day was fast ending and he must hurry and find a camping site.

Paul reached the north border of the clearing and came out onto the shore of the frozen lake. He halted abruptly. Brutus stopped quickly by his side. Both stood stock still and looked at the magnificently antlered stag that had left the forest and ventured out onto the ice. The stag, its tan skin making him stand out clearly against the snow, was gazing out across the lake. It sensed Paul's and Brutus's presence and turned to look in their direction.

Brutus, suppressing the natural urge of his kind to rush upon the deer, aimed his dark eyes up at Paul and whined urgently telling him that he wanting to be released to hunt. Yes thought Paul, you need to kill and forget the taste of man. He flattened his hand and thrust it at the deer in the signal to attack, and ordered, "HUNT."

The verbal command had not been required for at the first movement of the familiar hand motion, Brutus was leaping away in the direction of the deer. His padded feet and curved toenails gave him solid purchase on the snow and ice. In two bounds he was in full stride and at peak speed.

Reacting instantly to the dog's sudden movement, the stag wheeled in the direction of the shore and bound away toward the safety of the forest.

Paul remained transfixed as he watched the deadly contest between the powerful wolfhound and the sleek, swift stag.

Brutus adjusted course to intersect the stag in full flight and drawing ever nearer the forest. The stag made a mighty leap in a last frantic effort to reach the woods close ahead. Brutus sprang at the stag at the same instant and his one hundred pounds of bone and muscle struck the stag and they crashed down on the frozen lake. Brutus landed on his stomach and slid on the ice with the snow piling upon him. The buck fell and rolled, coming to rest on his side.

Brutus erupted from his snow drift and pounced upon the buck as it rose to its knees. His powerful mouth closed upon the slender neck of the deer, and he drove the animal down upon the snow. With a twist of his head, Brutus tore a gap in the tough hide. Another bite and his teeth sank deeply into the soft flesh of the neck, and there his fangs found the pulsing jugular and severed it. An explosion of blood filled Brutus's mouth as the buck's racing heart pumped it full.

The deer thrashed wildly about with its sharp hooves stabbing out like spears. Brutus twisted his body to the side to avoid the hooves. One blow could disembowel him. He lay panting and holding the buck pinned to the frozen lake as it kicked its life away.

A minute passed, then two. The buck ceased to move and Brutus surrendered his death bite. He stood, shook himself and looked at his master.

Paul came to Brutus and knelt down by him. "Good job, Brutus." He rubbed the dog's head in that certain manner that he used to show his approval.

Brutus chuffed with acceptance and wagged his tail

Paul took hold of one of the deer's front legs and dragged the animal back across the camp to the barracks. Frank opened the door at Paul's loud knock.

"Brutus gives this fresh meat as payment for the trouble he caused," Paul said and pointed down at the deer on the snow.

Jack eyed the deer and the wide, bloody tear in its neck. He gave Paul a joker's smile and said, "I'll have Oroville skin it for I'm sure it's meant for him."

***

Near the shore of the lake under the widely spreading limbs of an aged pine tree, Paul kicked the snow away to expose the thick carpet of needles that had accumulated over the decades. Upon that dry surface, he erected his tent that contained barely enough space for him to unroll his sleeping robe. With the evening shadows weaving themselves into night, he hurried to gather pine knots from a decaying tree and started a fire for light and warmth.

He laid out food for Brutus, and that worthy dog gobbled it in very short order. As Paul sat eating his food, he thought of the fine meal he had missed at the logger camp. It would have been good food without doubt for Two Doves was a master cook.

Brutus came and lay down beside Paul. Together they watched the fire. The flames burned into a pocket of pitch in one of the pine knots and heated it to a gas that exploded with a foot-long, hot lance of hissing flame. Brutus jumped at the noise. Paul laughed at the dog. Brutus looked at him with a quizzical expression. The dog's reaction to the flame and the laugh made Paul laugh even harder, and that brightened the dark evening.

***

41

Paul awoke to the sound of wolves running deer in the forest not far off. He sat up in his sleeping robe to listen. Brutus rose beside him and growled his dislike for wolves.

Paul opened the flap of the tent and poked his head outside to listen. Brutus shoved past him and went out and stood in the snow and stared off in the direction of the wolves yapping to each other as they pursued the deer. He growled again.

Paul looked up at the full moon floating in the center of the heavens and casting its silver light down upon the lake. A multitude of stars like diamonds flung across the ebony sky added their frail light. Ice crystals in the snow twinkled as brightly as did the stars. Paul's heart beat pleasantly at the sight for it was a fine night to be alive.

Brutus growled more fiercely as the wolves' noisy pursuit grew swiftly closer. Paul knew from the sound of the chase that it would pass very close. He reached out and pulled Brutus down beside him. He didn't want the dog to fight a pack of wolves. Though Brutus could kill any single wolf, a pack of them could tear him to pieces.

Wolves and cougars were the top predators of the forest and held the most interest for Paul of all the forest animals. The big cats were handsome animals, however their lives were secretive and mostly silent and rarely did Paul see one. Wolves were Paul's favorite of the two predators. They were different being clannish and running in packs, and very vocal with their barks and howls and yips. They gave the forest a voice to show it was alive.

A doe running for her life, exploded from the forest not ten yards from Paul's camp. She stumbled, exhausted, and almost fell. The plumes of her rapid breathing were white geysers in the moonlight. She gathered herself together and raced out onto the ice covered lake and onward toward the far shore.

A moment later, six wolves bounded from the forest and into view on the lake. As of one accord, they stopped and began to scoop their open jaws in the snow, mouthing a little of the frozen wetness to slack their thirst from the chase. Then seemingly forgetting the deer, they began to twist and turn and leap in silence, and their breaths smoking in the cold air as if they burned with some inner fire. One tackled another and they rolled in play. A third pounced upon the two and the three powerful bodies tumbled about in a tangle as would pups.

Paul watched, mesmerized by the splendid animals living for the moment in their friendly play. He knew they would all be of the same pack, and most of them relatives. After a minute or so of frolicking, one of the wolves lifted its muzzle and gave a series of yips in a clear tenor voice. All came instantly alert. The one that had given the signal sprang away on the trail of the deer. The others fell in behind. Running swiftly, they vanished from Paul's view.

Paul ducked his head and entered the tent. Brutus followed him. Paul wrapped himself in his thick sleeping robe and immediately went to sleep. Brutus lay down on a corner of the robe, sighed with contentment, and joined his master in sleep.

Chapter Three

The Emigrants

Alice was born in the coal mining town of Terryville located 60 miles west of Manchester, England. She and her parents lived in a rented cottage just outside town and between a dairy and a coal mine. Her father worked in the darkness of the mine far underground digging coal that was shipped by steam boat and barge along the River Mersey and the Sankey Canal to Liverpool.

The coal had made a deep impression on Alice because of her father who would return home in the evenings from work with his face covered with coal dust and only the whites of his eyes showing through the blackness. He would smile at her and his white teeth would flash as he laughed. That black face with the white eyes and white teeth was riveted into her memory. He would bathe and afterwards take her up into his powerful arms and hug her to him. With her heart ready to burst with her love for her father, she would snuggle against his broad chest and breathe him in savoring the familiar scent of him. Part of that scent was the smell of coal dust for it was ground into his skin.

Alice's mother began to teach her to read and write on her fourth birthday. That was the day Alice made the amazing discovery that a few squiggly lines written on a piece of paper made words, words that contained meaning and emotion when spoken in the right tone of voice. For the following Christmas, her parents gave her a thin dictionary and her mother showed her how to use its storehouse of many words. Mathematics was added to her studies and another miraculous avenue of knowledge opened for Alice. Her mother enforced rigorous study times, and pushed Alice to the limits of her youthful intelligence. Books on geography, history, and many other subjects were acquired from the rental library and Alice read for hours.

Her mother wrote poetry and kept them in a small notebook. Alice would hear her reading the poems out loud at the table where she worked on them and would quickly come to sit beside her. She was amazed by her mother's knowledge of words, and the quickness with which she could arrive at a word that propelled a poem onward to a rhyming ending that evoked a strong emotion, sometimes sad, but mostly a happy one.

Alice quickly grasped the concept of writing a poem, the necessity to choose the precise words to convey the story told in every poem.

A most enjoyable routine developed. Her mother would seat herself at the table with paper and pen. Alice would join her, and leaning close, read the words springing out from the nib of the pen and onto the paper. After but a few words, she grasped the story her mother was telling, and would close her eyes and search through her own reservoir of words. Most often her mother had written a word that perfectly fit before Alice could speak.

Alice's nimble mind began to arrive at words that her mother accepted as the best ones to carry the poem along and to bring it to a dramatic, rhyming conclusion that stirred the emotions of them both. When Alice won the unspoken contest, her mother would clasp her close and hug her.

The day the decision was made to come to America, her father had come home early from work. His shoulder was badly bruised. When her mother asked him what had happened to his arm, he tried to put her off with a smile and a nonchalant comment that it was nothing, just an accident. Her mother had insisted that he tell her the complete story. He explained that a section of mine tunnel roof had collapsed close to him and the edge of the slab of rock had struck his shoulder. "But I'm all right" he quickly assured her.

"You shouldn't work in the mine," her mother had said forcefully. "It hurts me when you're hurt."

"And what do I do if I quit. There's no other work here. I'm just lucky to have a job. There're a dozen men here in town who would jump at the chance to take my place below ground."

Both mother and father had looked at Alice. Nothing more was said about the accident.

In the night, Alice had risen from bed and was at the water bucket and drinking from the dipper, which she wasn't supposed to do, when she heard her mother's worried voice. Alice cocked her ear but could not make out the words. She crept to their bedroom door that was open a few inches and peeked into the room. The two were near the bed and facing each other.

"I don't want you killed," her mother said worriedly. "You've told me that it's a black hell down there in the dark with the coal dust so thick you can hardly breathe. And pieces of rock often fall from the tunnel roof. There were three men killed last year. All crushed to death. Do you remember that?"

"I remember. I helped dig their bodies out."

"I know that. Let's save money as fast as we can and go to America."

There was a long silence as her father looked into his wife's eyes. Then he spoke, "All right. I haven't heard any complaints from those who've gone over there. And I don't want Alice to marry a miner. And I think she'd like the adventure."

"Oh, yes, she would. I'll send off some of my poetry to that publisher in Liverpool. He bought those other ones and maybe he'll buy a few more of them."

An expression of love and desire came upon her father's face and he reached out and touched Martha's cheek. "You are the most beautiful woman in the world. And the best wife. How could I have ever won you?"

"Maybe I was the lucky one," her mother said.

He pulled her into his arms and kissed her. She returned his kiss and held him tightly to her.

Alice wanted to run into the room and throw her arms around both of them. But she could not for that would give away the fact that she had been eavesdropping. She was gladdened by what she had seen and heard. Her father's words were true; her mother was the most beautiful woman in the world.

***

The scrimping and saving began, a sixpence, a shilling were tucked into the beautifully old cream pitcher once used by Martha's grandmother. The publisher in Liverpool bought six of her mother's poems for six pounds and that went into the pitcher.

Two months later, Alice's world was shattered. Deep in the coal mine, a section of tunnel collapsed and killed her father and several other men. Every available miner was set to the task of clearing away the fallen rock to reach the men's bodies. The work was hazardous with slabs of rock falling from the ceiling and the miners barely avoiding being injured. On the fifth day, the mine owners and the government officials called a halt to the rescue effort, saying the tunnel was too hazardous. The dead would be left buried in black rock deep in the ground.

Alice and her mother wept in private, often together, hugging each other with their tears mingling.

***

Very early in a chilly, foggy April morning shortly after the rescue effort for her husband had ceased, Alice's mother came into her room and shook her awake. "Get dressed and pack your clothing. We're going to America just as we planned with your father."

"Really, mother?"

"Yes. We'll go to Liverpool and catch a ship to America."

"Do we have enough money?"

"It will depend on how much we can get from the sale of our furniture. Now you let me worry about that. Start getting your things together. Remember just pack those things you can't do without. And we must be able to carry everything"

"Yes, mother." Her mother was very brave to make the long journey to a foreign land with a eleven year old girl. She wished, oh, how she wished her father was alive to travel with them. With the three of them, the voyage would have been perfect.

***

Alice drew on a heavy coat against the cold and slipped away from the house as her mother packed. She hurried along the road to the gate in the woven wire fence that surrounded the mine. The guard, a Mr. Carrey that Alice had seen before on those times she came to walk home with her father, sat reading a newspaper in his watchman's shack. Alice crept past the man and onward across the black coal dust earth to the box-like lift with its wench and steel cable hanging over the shaft down which the men were lowered to the coal seam. She peered down into the narrow space between the side of the lift and the sidewall of the shaft into the darkness, the scary darkness of the earth that hid her father from her.

Strong hands caught her by the shoulders and turned her around. "Now what are you doing here, missy?" Mr. Carrey asked. "Kids aren't allowed on mine property. Now skedaddle home before I tell your parents you were here."

"But I must tell my father something."

"Tell him when he gets home this evening."

"He won't be coming home any more."

"What do you mean by that?"

"He's buried down there," Alice pointed at the mine shaft. "And I must tell him something very important." Alice stared into Mr. Carrey's face. He must let her do this thing.

"What's your name, missy?"

"Alice Childs."

"You're Benjamin Child's girl?" The man's expression had softened.

Alice nodded. "And I got to tell him goodbye before mother and I leave and go to America." Alice knew what she wanted to do was childish, even foolish. Still she must do this to honor her father.

Mr. Carrey looked from Alice to the mine shaft. "I knew Benjamin. He was a good sort. Big enough to whip any man in the mine, but never lifted a hand against anybody. You want to tell him from way up here?"

Alice knew from the tone of Mr. Carrey's voice that he wasn't going to laugh at her. "Yes. Do you think he could hear me?"

Mr. Carrey looked away from Alice and out across the piles of coal to the wooded hills far off. After a moment, he brought his eyes back to Alice. "Yes, he could hear you for the shaft and the tunnels guide voices real well for long distances."

"Even if I just whisper?"

"Miners have good ears. He'll hear you."

"May I tell him now?" Alice knew that Mr. Carrey and she were playing a game that both understood.

"Sure. Let me raise the lift a bit so that there's more room for you to talk down through."

49

Mr. Carrey pulled the lever that operated the wench. With a low growl, the wench turned and hoisted the lift until its bottom was above the surface of the ground and the full width of the mine shaft was exposed.

Alice had an instant feeling of being sucked into the gaping, black mouth of the shaft. She drew hurriedly back.

Mr. Carrey caught Alice by the hand. "Don't be afraid."

"Will you hold my hand?"

"I'll sure keep you from falling. Now just bend down and tell your father whatever it is you want to say."

"You won't listen, will you?" Play the game.

"No. I'll shut my ears."

Alice leaned over the black opening of the shaft. She felt the guard's hands tighten more firmly on hers. She liked that.

She whispered,

Father, I've come to tell you goodbye.

Mother and I are going to that distant land.

Just as you and she and I made our plan.

I love you dearly and I grieve.

Father, I tell you goodbye as I leave.

Goodbye, father, goodbye, goodbye.

Alice looked up at Mr. Carrey. His eyes were moist as if he was near to crying. He was a kind man.

"Thank you, Mr. Carrey. Thank you very much."

Alice hurried across the black coal dust earth to the gate. There she broke into a run along the road toward the cottage.

***

Martha and Alice sold their household possessions and added that money to the sum that had been saved. They packed their clothing and personal treasures in two pieces of luggage. The most valuable items were a picture of Benjamin and his pocket watch. In the picture, Benjamin was dressed in his Sunday suit and standing and smiling as he looked directly at them. Alice had always thought the expression in his eyes said I love both of you. The pocket watch had a silver case, a white face across which rotated the jet black hour and minute hands, and an eight inch silver chain. Her father kept the watch fastened to his vest when they went to church.

The keys to the cottage were given to the owner. Then carrying their luggage, they walked to the railroad station.

"We must be very thrifty with our money," Martha whispered to Alice as they boarded the train that would carry them to Liverpool. "We'll have enough for the voyage. After that we'll have only a few pounds to live on until I find work in America. It's going to be very difficult making enough money to live on without your father."

"I've saved almost seven shillings," Alice said and held up her purse for Martha to see.

"We may need it later."

"What kind of work would you like to do?"

"Work for a book publisher. That way I could earn money and learn more about writing. Maybe someday I could write a book of poems."

"You already have enough for a book."

"Yes. If all of them were good enough to be published."

"I think they are."

"I have much more to learn."

"You can write more poems while we cross the ocean to America."

"And you can help me."

"I'd like that."

***

In Liverpool, Martha and Alice hired a cab to transport them from the railroad station to the waterfront. They found it a noisy place with a throng of people bustling about and nearly every pier lined with ships. Gangs of stooped stevedores carried big loads on their backs up and down gangways. Noisy clanking cranes hoisted heavy pallets of cargo off and onto ships. People dressed for travel and carrying luggage were winding a path through the hectic activity from ships recently arrived, or to vessels scheduled to soon sail.

At the Cunnard Steamship Company they purchased two second class tickets on the Pannonia for the long sea voyage. The ship was scheduled to depart the following day in mid-morning. They spent a quiet night in a hotel near the waterfront. Early in the morning, they carried their luggage to the pier where the Pannonia was tied with thick hawsers.

Upon sight of the Pannonia, Alice stared in awe. The ship was hundreds of feet long and towered six stories high. The hull was painted a light gray color from five feet above waterline to the main deck. The three story superstructure was a brilliant white. Below the main deck, three horizontal rows of round portholes extended along the Pannonia's side from the stern to near the bow marking the location of three lower levels of the colossal ship.

She and her mother queued up with other arriving passengers and climbed the gangway to the purser, a slender man with a short, full beard and immaculately dressed in a starched white uniform with a billed hat.

The purser focused on Martha, and smiled broadly. "Welcome aboard the Pannonia," he greeted Martha. "My name is Mr. Stoddard."

He continued to smile at her for a moment, and then lowered his head to check their tickets and note their arrival in his log.

He brought his sight back to Martha and handed her a brochure. "This will tell you about the ship, and how to find your way about her." His eyes lingered upon Martha's face.

The purser's expression angered Alice. That was the same expression that her father had when he looked at her mother just before he took her into his arms and kissed her. Only her father had the right to hug and kiss her mother. Alice felt like yelling at the purser to stop looking at her mother.

The purser turned away from Martha to the group of boys of fourteen to sixteen years of age, stewards and all outfitted in neat blue uniforms and caps. He motioned at one of the smaller boys and spoke, "Townsend, we have these lovely ladies Martha and Alice Childs traveling to New York with us. Take them to B 86."

"Yes, sir, Mr. Stoddard, B 86," Townsend replied, and came toward Martha and Alice.

Alice studied the boy. His complexion was fair with a smattering of freckles across his nose and cheeks. His hair and eyes were brown. His face had an openness about it that caused Alice to think that he would be somebody with whom she could talk.

He spoke to Alice and Martha in a pleasant voice. "Ladies, please follow me and I'll show you to your cabin."

The boy picked up the two pieces of luggage and led off across the deck. He spoke over his shoulder as he led onward. "The Pannonia was built in 1913 in Glasgow. She is four hundred and eighty seven feet from stem to stern. Her width is fifty nine feet. She can accommodate forty first class passengers, and eight hundred second class passengers."

He fell silent and led them down a wide metal stairway, made a half right turn and down a second flight of stairs, and along a narrow passageway showing doors set into the iron bulkheads. He stopped at B 86.

"This is your cabin." He opened the door with the key already in the lock, shoved the door open and set the luggage inside. He stepped back into the passageway and handed the key to Martha.

"My name is Andrew Townsend. This is the part of the ship I'm assigned to serve. If you need anything once we're underway, you can find me with the other cabin boys in our waiting room just starboard of the dining room. Or if you want to signal me to come to you, press this button here inside the door and a light with your cabin number will show in the steward's waiting room." He pointed to the button. "I'll come soon as I see your signal."

"Thank you," Martha said and gave the boy a coin, and hoping the amount was proper.

"Thank you, mam." He looked away from Martha and to Alice, then back to Martha. "After the ship gets under way, I'll be free of toting luggage. Then I can come and go as I want. It would be my pleasure to show you about the ship."

"Yes, mother, let him show us the ship," Alice said. "I want to know how everything works. What makes the ship move?"

Martha suppressed a smile at the obvious interest the two young ones showed in each other. She spoke to Andrew. "We accept your kind offer. We'll be on the main deck watching the ship sail."

"I can find you easy." said the boy. He gave Alice a quick look, touched the bill of his hat, and left with hurried steps.

"He seems to be a nice boy," Martha said and looking at Alice. "And quite handsome in his uniform. Don't you think so too?"

Both mother and daughter broke into smiles.

"Mother, let's go back up on top. I want to see the ship sail away."

"I do too, but first we'll take care of our luggage.

Alice and her mother entered the cabin, a small room furnished with a bed for two with blankets and pillows, and a small table and two chairs. A door opened to a tiny bath. A porthole provided daylight for the cabin. A single electric light bulb was in a small, white globe in the center of the ceiling.

"It appears we'll be sleeping together," Martha said and gesturing at the bed.

"That's okay by me," Alice said. She enjoyed being near her mother, especially now after her father's death.

They hung their clothing in the closet, as much as the cramped space would hold, and placed the remainder of their luggage at the foot of the bed. They returned to the main deck. The sky was cloudless and a slow wind blew. To the west, a black haze of coal smoke hung over Liverpool. Alice smelled the acrid smoke and it reminded her of her the smoky days in Terryville. She missed her father and wished with all of her heart that he was here beside them on the ship that would carry them to the fabulous land of America.

They joined the many passengers gathered on the port side of the ship overlooking the pier. An even larger crowd had assembled on the pier to watch the ship's departure. The air was filled with laughter and shouts and waving of hands and calls of goodbyes. Alice saw expressions of sadness on the faces of some of the people.

On the dock, longshoremen moved to the hawsers that held the ship tied to the pier, lifted them off the cleats and dropped them into the water. Seamen on the ship speedily dragged the dripping hawsers aboard and began to coil them neatly on the deck. The ship's steam whistle gave a loud blast. Alice felt a slight vibration of the deck as the powerful steam engine in the bowels of the ship rumbled to life. The big iron propeller started to turn, its three blades churning the quiet water of the bay. The ship pulled away from the land that had been but a temporary place to halt.

Alice looked up at her mother to see if she too felt the joy of beginning the voyage. To Alice's surprise, there were tears in her mother's eyes.

"What's wrong, mother?"

"Alice, my love, I don't believe I'll ever see England again. I feel it here." Martha touched her breast.

"But aren't we leaving England because America is a better place?"

"I hope it is. But I'll miss being close to where your father is buried."

"So do I." Alice was disturbed by her mother's sorrow.

"America will be a better place for us," Martha said stoutly. "But it would have been so much better if your father was here with us." She caught Alice's hand and held it tightly.

"When we become rich, we'll come back for a visit," Alice said and trying to lighten her mother's mood.

"Yes, we'll do that when we are rich. Come, let's take a walk."

They had taken but a few steps when a man called out behind them. "Mrs. Childs."

Martha and Alice turned to look in the direction of the voice. The white uniformed purser Stoddard was approaching them. He smiled pleasantly and touched the bill of his hat.

"I see you two ladies are exploring the Pannonia. May I offer my services to escort you? I know the ship very well for I have sailed on her these past four years."

"Andrew is going to show us the ship," Alice said and glad that it was true for she didn't like the man.

"Andrew Townsend the steward?" Stoddard said and his face tightening with a frown.

"Yes, the young man who carried our luggage to our cabin," Martha replied.

"Mother, we must keep our word," Alice said.

Martha gave Alice's hand a little squeeze to show she understood. "Yes, we must keep our agreement with Mr. Townsend. But thank you for you offer, Mr. Stoddard."

"Townsend has duties to perform," Stoddard said. His frown was evolving into an expression of anger. "I shall speak to him about them."

"Are we not part of Mr. Townsend's duties?" Martha spoke in a soft voice that Alice recognized as the one she used when angry.

"Yes, of course you are," Stoddard said hurriedly.

"Then there is nothing more to say, is there, sir? Come along, Alice. We shall look for Mr. Townsend."

As they walked away, Alice looked back at Stoddard. The man was staring at them with a baleful glare. Had she by insisting that Andrew be their guide, brought trouble down upon him from Mr. Stoddard?

They had gone but a short distance when they found Andrew hurrying through the other passengers on the deck. He saw them at the same time and waved.

"I told you that I'd find you," Andrew said and his face beaming with pleasure. "Are you ready to see the ship?"

"We are, but first there is something we should tell you," Martha said. "Mr. Stoddard asked to show us about the ship. He seemed angry when we told him that we had agreed to see the ship with you. He said he would talk to you about your duties. Have we caused you trouble with him?"

Andrew's face tightened. "He's a hard man to work for." Then he grinned. "But I can handle whatever he hands out."

"Even so, Alice and I can see the ship by ourselves and you won't be caught in a situation where your boss might have it in for you."

"No. I want to show you. Don't you worry about Mr. Stoddard."

The time passed pleasantly as Andrew led Alice and Martha in a stroll forward along the starboard side of the ship's main deck, with the tall white superstructure on their left and the blue ocean close on their right. The deck extended from stern to bow and was wide enough for eight people to walk side by side. A waist high metal guardrail provided safety from falling overboard.

Near mid-length of the ship, Andrew guided Alice and Martha to the dining room and inside to view its scores of tables and chairs. The tantalizing aroma of food made Alice's mouth water.

They left the dining room and continued along the deck past the stairs leading to the upper decks. There Andrew pointed at the topmost deck. "The forward part of that is the bridge where the captain does the navigation and guides the ship. Only important passengers are invited on the bridge."

"I'm important," Alice said with a laugh.

Andrew smiled with agreement.

He led them to one of the many lifeboats all snugly covered with canvas and resting on their davits just above and outboard of the ship's safety railing. Pointing as he spoke, he explained how a boat could be lowered into the water by use of the cables and pulleys to which each was attached.

Andrew glanced forward along the deck. "It's best that I go and see if any other passengers have asked for my help. Or Mr. Stoddard has something for me to do."

"Thank you for showing us about, Andrew" Martha said. She noted the worry in the young man's eyes. "Is there anything I can do for you regarding Mr. Stoddard? I'm still bothered with the thought that he might do something to hurt you."

"No, mam. I'll be just fine." Andrew gave Alice a last look and turned away along the deck.

"I hope Andrew isn't in trouble," Alice said.

"Yes. Let's wish no harm comes to him because of us."

They made their way back along the main deck to the bow of the ship and there, standing close together, stared westward toward America. Behind them, the land shriveled and sank below the wet horizon. Ahead there was nothing but the empty blue, green ocean. After a time, the April wind became damp and chilled and drove them off the deck and below to their cabin.

***

During the first days of the voyage, the weather held fair and Martha and Alice donned their prettiest dresses, tied their long hair with ribbons to control it in the wind created by the Pannonia's eighteen knots speed across the gentle sea, and roamed the ship's decks. They encountered many men, women and children out and about on the decks and they would nod polite greetings, but rarely spoke to them, feeling self-sufficient unto themselves.

One of their favorite places to pass the time was at the stern of the ship where flocks of birds followed and fed off the waste created by the hundreds of passengers. There were several species of birds, but the seagulls with their gray and white bodies and bright yellow bills were the most numerous by far and dominated the feeding. Uttering their raucous calls and wheeling agilely about the stern, the birds searched for food below. Spotting a tempting morsel, they dove down to pluck the object from the swirling water left by the ship and its spinning propeller. Then rising, the birds ate on the wing. Now and again, one of the seagulls would sail down within a few feet of Alice and Martha, and fluttering their wings to hold station on the two humans, evaluate them with sharp black eyes.

On one of their excursions about the deck of the Pannonia, Alice chanced to glance behind. The purser was following several steps behind. His sight was fastened intently on Martha. He seemed to feel Alice's focus upon him and he caught her eyes, and then quickly looked away.

Later in the day, Alice again saw the purser looking at them, or rather watching her mother. That was too much for Alice. She caught her mother by the hand.

"Mother, that Mr. Stoddard is following us. And I've seen him doing it before."

Martha looked back over her shoulder. The purser was leaning on the ship's railing and looking out across the sea.

"He's not looking at us," Martha said.

"Maybe not now. But he really was looking at you, and I've seen him doing it before. I don't like him."

"Why don't you like him?"

"Because of the way he looks at you."

"And what way is that?"

"Like father sometimes looked at you."

Martha laughed lightly. "How did he look at me?"

"Like he wanted to hug and kiss you. And then lay down on the bed with you."

Martha ignored the comment about lying down on the bed. She and her daughter had discussed such man and woman loving. "I liked for your father to look at me that way. I miss him so terribly."

"I miss him too." Alice cast a hard eye at the purser. "I want that man to stop following us."

"I really don't think he is."

"I do," Alice said with conviction.

***

On the fifth day of the voyage as Alice and Martha lazed about with scores of other passengers on the forward deck of the Pannonia, a dark storm cloud appeared rising out of the watery, western horizon ahead. The cloud grew as the day wore on, climbing and broadening. By the middle of the afternoon, the cloud had risen to block the sun and gray streams of rain fell from the storm's swollen bottom and onto the ocean.

Alice felt the first gust of the storm's frontal winds that came rippling the top of the low ocean waves. Looking farther ahead, she saw the waves were angry, rising tall and ridged with white frothy crowns. The white capped waves seemed to advance with unnatural swiftness and in only a handful of minutes were upon the ship with the wind blowing half a gale. Alice was fascinated by the mass of churning clouds rushing at her with the rain now cascading down in wide, gray curtains.

Martha caught Alice by the hand. "Run," she shouted.

Caught up in the wild energy of the storm, they fled across the open deck. Cold rain drops struck them upon the head and shoulders as they darted through an open hatchway and into the ship's interior. They stared out onto the rain washed deck with its scuppers running brim full of water, and beyond that, to the rain lashed waves of the sea. She saw no birds. Where did the poor birds go to find shelter during a storm at sea?

Alice watched the waves grow in size and violence as the Pannonia plowed ever deeper into the storm. Torrential rain hammered the deck.

The ship rode up and over the huge black waves. Now and again the bow crashed into a mountainous wave and sent salty, chilled spray to mix with the hard driving rain flooding the deck. Wind eddies formed

61

around the ship's superstructure and swept some of the cold water into the space where Alice and Martha huddled.

Alice felt her mother's hand stroke her hair and it was a comforting feeling. The hand stopped on her shoulder and squeezed it gently as was her mother's way.

"Let's go below to our cabin," Martha said.

"I am getting cold," Alice replied.

They walked cautiously; placing their feet carefully on the deck being heaved this way and that way by the rolling and pitching ship struggling across the stormy sea. Holding to the banister of the stairway leading down to the lower decks, and then to the wall of a passageway, they made their way to the cabin.

***

Darkness filled the cabin. The porthole in the outer hull of the ship was barely visible with the storm clouds and rain obscuring the heavens. Martha flipped the switch to the electric light and its rays flared and drove the blackness out through the porthole to the wind swept sea.

"Why don't we write some poems until it's time for supper?" Martha said.

"All right, if you want to," Alice replied. "But the way the ship is bouncing around every which way is starting to give me a headache."

"Maybe the game will take your mind off it."

"I hope so."

Martha picked up the notebook containing her collection of poems from the table. She removed the picture of her husband from between the notebook's pages and laid it carefully aside. Then with pencil in hand, she reclined on the bed. "We'll write a poem and forget the storm," she said.

"Why not write about the storm?" Alice said.

"Yes, we could. Or about the sun that we can't see."

"Or the moon."

"Or about anything that pops into our heads?"

"You start it."

Martha moved to the far side of the bed and patted the space beside her. "Come and lie beside me."

Alice lay down upon the bed and scooted closer until their bodies were touching. The love she held for her mother lifted her heart and it beat pleasantly. Did a mother feel the same emotion when near a daughter? By the expression in the eyes gazing at her, Alice was confident that this mother did.

"I'm ready to begin," Alice said.

Martha was silent for a moment. Then she spoke. "Look, there's a spider hanging from the ceiling."

"I see it. I didn't know there would be spiders on a ship at sea."

"I suppose they can be found anyplace. Let us begin the poem. We'll call it 'Spider'." Martha paused, then, "I spin webs impossibly fine."

Alice hastened to discover the story that her mother wanted to tell by use of her first few words. But then it might be more fun to turn those words into a story Alice wanted told. She spoke. "Until one web slips its reel."

Martha was silent for a few seconds, then, "And that stops the spinner's wheel."

Alice was ready. "That made it so gosh darn real."

Martha spoke, "Until the last rhyme line."

"So what do we have when we put it all together?" Alice said.

"We have this," Martha said.

Spider

I spin webs impossible fine,

Until one web slips its reel.

That stops the spinner's wheel,

That made it so gosh darn real

Until the last rhyme line.

"That's a foolish poem," Alice said with a laugh.

"But a good way to start. Now let us try one with more feeling." Martha was looking at Benjamin's watch lying on the table where she had placed it. The short silver chain was hanging over the edge and swinging to the movement of the ship.

"How about a poem about your father's watch and measuring time? After all, we are only marking time until we reach America."

"I like that. I can see him now pulling the watch from his vest pocket and looking down at it."

"So can I. How about 'Father's Little Clock' for the title," Martha said.

"That's a good title," Alice agreed. "You start."

"All right, then. Father's Little clock."

Martha:	For us the little clock ticks.
Alice:	Ticking and tocking.
Martha:	Clocking our future.
Alice:	Clocking our past.
Martha:	Timing our present.
Alice:	The day and the night.
Martha:	Beginning our A.M.
Alice:	Ending our P.M.
Martha:	For us the little clock ticks.
Alice:	Ticking and tocking.

"Oh! Mother, I like that one." Alice was pleased they had brought thoughts of her father into the poem game. She turned and hugged her mother very tightly.

"I do too. I'll write it in my notebook and keep it for just us two."

***

Alice lay on the bed in the cabin and pressed against her mother's warm body. In this way she braced herself to prevent being rolled from the bed by the rise and plunge of the ship battling the enormous storm waves. She felt the Pannonia shudder each time its bow struck a wave head on. Then the ship would rise and right itself as the waves rolled beneath her keel and slid along her sides. Now and again the stern of the ship would lift clear of the water and Alice could hear the propeller whine with increasing speed, for then with its blades no longer restricted by the clutch of the sea water, its revolutions increased swiftly.

Her mother had slept, a miraculous accomplishment to Alice considering the constant motion of the ship. She had lain listening to Martha's gentle breathing. Now she felt her mother stir as she came awake.

Martha rose and went to the porthole and looked out at the night, the storm clouds black and solid and pressing down heavily upon the heaving, wave tossed world.

She spoke over her shoulder to Alice. "It's stopped raining. But the wind is still blowing hard and the waves are just as big." She picked up the watch and checked the time. "It's supper time and the dining room will be closing soon. Let's go and eat?"

"I've got a headache and don't feel like eating. Doesn't the motion of the ship give you a headache?"

"Just a bit of one. Nothing serious."

"Well it does me."

"That's too bad. But surely there'll be something to eat that will appeal to you."

"No, thanks. I'll just wait for you here."

"All right. It's a long time until breakfast so I'll bring you something back should you change your mind later."

"If you want to."

Martha climbed from the bed and pulled on her coat. "I won't be gone long. Bolt the door after me."

"Yes, mother." Alice rose from the bed and stood by the door.

Martha stepped out through the doorway, gave Alice a last look, and turned and went off sliding her hand along the steel wall of the passageway to keep her balance upon the moving deck.

Alice closed the door and shoved the locking bolt into its socket. She again lay down upon the bed, closed her eyes and willed the headache to go away. Maybe she could eat a little. She drifted off to a light, shallow sleep as she waited for her mother to return.

***

A knock sounded on the cabin door. "Hello, this is Andrew. I didn't see you or your mother at the dining room and have come to escort you there."

Alice was pleased to hear Andrew's voice. She rose from the bed and opened the door to Andrew's smiling face.

"Mother already went to eat."

"Then I'll escort you."

At the invitation, Alice felt her touch of seasickness lessen dramatically. "I would like that. If we hurry, maybe we can catch up with mother."

She went into the passageway and locked arms with Andrew, and the solid feel of him gave her a comfort that here was a true friend. They hastened along the passageway with Andrew always able to anticipate the next movement of the deck and keep them steady on their feet. They climbed the stairs and came out onto the Pannonia's open main deck. Immediately the storm winds roared out of the darkness and struck them, staggering them and flaring their coats. Andrew hurried them forward toward the stairs that led up to the dining room.

Alice checked the deck ahead. It was visible for a short distance ahead due to the meager illumination provided by the low wattage electric lights spaced at wide intervals. She felt a chill that wasn't just from the cold spray that the wind tore from the sea and carried up and over the guardrail to strike her. She sensed something menacing in front of them. She shivered.

Andrew tightened his arm around Alice's and struck out along the deck. Alice matched his stride.

They had progressed but half a hundred steps when ahead on the poorly lighted deck, Alice saw a woman struggling with a man. The man, dressed in black, had his arms around the woman and pinning her arms. He was dragging the woman toward an open hatchway. She was kicking and twisting wildly as she fought to break free.

"Mother," Alice cried and raced forward.

Andrew ran beside Alice. She heard his angry shout. "That bastard Stoddard has her."

Before Alice and Andrew could reach Martha, the Pannonia struck a huge wave at an angle and rolled steeply to port. The ship's movement flung Alice and Andrew against the steel side of the superstructure. A sharp pain ran through Alice's right wrist as she broke her fall with a hand. She shoved erect just as Andrew reached out to help her regain her footing. They turned back in the direction of the fighting man and woman.

Stoddard and Martha had also been thrown against the metal bulkhead. The collision had broken them apart and Martha now backed hastily away from Stoddard. She seemed half stunned and did not move quickly enough and Stoddard lashed out with his fist and struck her and knocked her reeling. He leapt upon the dazed woman and seized her by the shoulders and shook her savagely. Still holding her, Stoddard pivoted and took three long steps to the safety railing. There he hoisted Martha up above the railing and outward over the black sea.

Alice rushed at Stoddard. She saw him look into her mother's face and shout something. Alice couldn't make out the words, but their angry tone and the fierce expression on the man's face showed his hate and intent to kill. With a last shout at Martha, he flung her into the darkness hiding the sea tens of feet below.

At that last instant as Stoddard released his hold on Martha, her hands shot up and grabbed him by the front of his jacket. As she fell into the blackness, she yanked him against the guardrail with the upper part of his body bent far out over the sea. He made a grab for the iron railing with the curved talons of his fingers reaching desperately for a hold to stop his fall. The fingers missed the railing and for a moment Stoddard hung there leaning over the water. Then the full weight of Martha's falling body tore his feet loose from the deck and they kicked wildly at the heavens as he up-ended over the guardrail. With legs and arms flailing, he vanished into the darkness and the sea with Martha.

Alice ran to the guardrail where Martha and Stoddard had vanished. "Mother! Mother!" she screamed in anguish down at the sea.

She hastily climbed upon the guardrail and leaned precariously far over and stared down at the sea. Nothing was visible in the blackness of the night except a now and again a glimpse of the white cockscomb of one of the giant storm waves reaching up. Her beloved mother was down there in the brutal sea and enduring unimaginable agony. With that blood-chilling thought, Alice senses were flooded by the sea's odor; its wetness, the tang of salt, the smell of rotting things that had died in that watery world.

"Mother! Mother! Mother!" Alice shrieked her torment down at the sea. The grief from the loss of her mother cramped her heart and it beat weakly against its cage of ribs. The world was a terrible place. How could something so awful happen to her mother? How could Alice ever survive without her loving, caring mother being near to hug her, to speak lovingly to her?

A whispering voice came to her. She leaned farther over the railing and cocked her head down at the water and listened more closely. The whispering rose and fell in volume and the tone was such that she couldn't tell if it was that of a man or a woman. She felt a palpable force in the voice drawing her toward the darkness. What was that the voice said, come and join her mother? Yes, thought Alice, it would be the best to jump into the sea and die along with her mother and escape the cruel world. Would there be much pain as she died?

As she hesitated considering the rash act, the identity of the sound registered in her sorrow-filled mind. It was but the noise of the storm waves rising and sliding along the Pannonia's steel hull. Alice hastily caught hold of the top bar of the guardrail with both hands and clutched it to her bosom. Her mother and father would be ashamed of her for surrendering so easily the life they had given her. She must guard that gift with all her strength.

Andrew, fearing Alice might jump or fall into the sea, sprang forward and caught her firmly around the waist. "Come down off there before you're thrown into the water," he said and pulled her off the guardrail and down onto the deck. He put his arms around her and pressed her quaking body against him.

"She's dead," Alice sobbed on Andrew's shoulder. "My mother is dead. That horrible man threw her into the ocean."

"By God, she took him into the drink with her," Andrew said with awe.

"She's gone! Gone! What'll I do without her?"

"The ship is moving fast so let's hurry and tell the captain. He'll stop and look for your mother."

"She can't swim. Andrew, she can't swim. She'll drown."

"Come on and let's hurry and tell the captain," Andrew locked arms with Alice and they rushed off toward the ship's bridge.

***

Captain Adams was a broadly built man wearing a blue uniform. His face hardened and his full, gray beard bristled as he listened intently to Andrew and Alice rapidly describe Stoddard's murder of Martha and her last act of pulling him into the sea with her. He knew by the expressions on the faces of the two young people that they told the truth. Damn Stoddard to hell for his murderous deed.

The captain turned to Alice and caught her trembling hands in his huge ones. He lowered his bearded face and peered into her large eyes moist with tears.

"I'm sorry for your loss, Alice," he said speaking gently. "You expect me to turn the ship around and go back and look for your mother. I'd like to find her, and catch Stoddard. But the ship has traveled three, maybe four miles since she went overboard. With the sea rough and a strong beam wind striking the ship, it would be impossible to find the exact location where she might be. If by chance I could find the spot, I

70

wouldn't dare put men in small boats onto the water in a storm with twenty foot waves to look for her."

Upon hearing the captain's words there would be no search, Alice knew he was pronouncing the certainty of her mother's death. Though she knew it was unfair, she was angry at the captain for not trying to find her mother. Her tears broke free and she sobbed. She pulled her hands free of the captain's and wiped her tears away, and fought back the new ones welling up.

"Do you have relatives in New York, or anyplace in America?"

Alice thought quickly. What would they do with an orphan in the strange city? Put her in an orphan's home? Not that. Never. "I have an uncle in New York," she lied.

"Will he let you stay with him?"

"I've never seen him. But I'm his niece so I don't know why he wouldn't let me."

"I would think so too," said the captain.

"What's his name?"

"Harold Tyler." Alice replied using the name of a neighbor in Terryville.

"Do you have his address?"

"Yes."

"Good," said the captain. He spoke to Andrew. "Mr. Townsend, move Alice's possession to one of the vacant first class cabins nearest the bridge. Then find the assistant purser and tell him to have one of the senior maids stay with Alice during the night and until we enter New York harbor tomorrow. Now see that she gets safely back to her cabin." The captain gave Andrew an intent look that told him to be diligent with his duties.

"Yes, sir," Andrew acknowledged the orders.

Andrew held out his arm to Alice. She took hold of it and they left the bridge together.

***

Alice lay in the black night on one of the two beds in the first class cabin on the upper deck of the Pannonia. She held her mother's book of poems with her father's picture inside it, and her father's watch pressed tightly to her breast. They were all she had left of her beloved parents. She would keep them with her always. She stroked the cover of the poem book and gripped the watch and spoke into the darkness, "Oh, mother, oh, father, I feel so terribly lonely without you."

Alice shivered as the last view of her mother's death came again. Her white hands gripping Stoddard's black jacket as she pulled him over the guardrail and down into the watery darkness with her.

Alice had always thought there was order and predictability in the world for her earlier life had led to that conclusion. That ordered life with her parents was gone forever, torn from her by their deaths.

She knew now that the world held murderous people, and deadly events that nobody could control. Even someone as powerful as the captain of the huge ocean going Pannonia, had been made weak and helpless to rescue her mother by the incalculable power of the sea and wind.

She felt overwhelmed by the knowledge of the limitation of men and women to control their destiny. Had her parents known how fragile life was? They had given her no sign that they did. Still they must have recognized this truth and simply forged ahead showing no fear.

Alice must not allow her deep grief for her parents to make her weak. She, like they, must use her strength and courage to forge a path through the unknowable world that lay ahead of her.

***

The night spent itself with Alice unable to sleep and sitting in a chair in the cabin and staring out into the blackness lying on the sea. In the wee hours of morning darkness, the Pannonia steaming at full speed escaped from the storm with its winds and a black sky studded with a million stars unrolled across the heavens. With the winds gone, the tall waves weakened and the ship rode more smoothly. The sun hurrying westward, overtook the Pannonia and burned away the night with its brilliant stars and turned the sky pale blue.

A time later, Alice saw a long, thin fringe of dark gray become visible stretching across the ocean horizon far ahead. That must be the land of America, she thought. The sight of America caused her spirit to rise a little.

In the cabin near Alice, the maid that had been assigned to stay with her during the night, stirred in her blankets. After a few minutes, she rose from the bed and came up beside Alice and peered out the window.

"We'll be entering the harbor soon and I should go see about my duties. Will you be all right by yourself?"

"I'll be just fine. I'll wait here until we reach America."

"Then goodbye. I'm really sorry about your mother."

"Thank you." The maid left the cabin, quietly closing the door behind her.

Alice again faced the window and stared ahead as the Pannonia drove ahead with the two headlands of the harbor rose up out of the ocean and embracing the ship.

A time later, a knock sounded upon the door. Alice stepped to it and found Andrew with a worried expression upon his face.

"I thought you might want someone to talk with," Andrew said and examining Alice's face closely.

"Come and sit with me," Alice said.

Andrew pulled a chair up beside Alice's and sat down.

"Are you all right," he asked with concern in his voice.

"Yes, thank you." She was glad he had come to be with her.

"We should be docking in an hour or so."

Alice laid her hand upon Andrew's arm. "I don't want to talk about that. I know nothing about you. Tell me about yourself. Where are you from?"

"I'm from Australia. My folks have a sheep station about fifty miles north of Sydney."

"Then how in the world did you ever get here on the Pannonia?"

"Three years ago we hit a bad drought and the grass didn't grow and the sheep were starving. My parents had to sell most all of them, just kept a few for breeding when the rains would come again. My brother and I decided to leave home and earn money to send to them so they could hold onto the land for it's their life. I got this job as steward on the Pannonia. My brother got a job in Sydney. We've send every penny of our money that we don't need to live on home to them. But now they've written me that the drought has ended. The Pannonia is sailing next to Sydney and I'll get off there and go home. I've really missed them these past years and will be glad to see them again."

"What do you plan to do once you're home?"

"I like the sea. I'm going back to school and study to become a ship's officer. But we need to talk about you. What are you going to do now that we've arrive in New York? Do you really have an uncle there?"

"No. I lied for I didn't want to be sent to an orphan's home. I'll make my own way."

Andrew nodded his understanding. "How old are you?"

74

"Twelve. Be thirteen in April"

"If you strike out on your own, you'll need money. How much do you have?"

"I found thirty two pounds in my mother's purse."

"That's about seventy American dollars for the exchange rate is about two to one. That's not much but you could live several days on that if you were careful how you spent it."

"I'll find work. I'll tell people that I'm fifteen or sixteen so they'll hire me. I'd work hard."

"I don't think you could pass for that age, maybe for fourteen. I've heard tales of how bad it is for orphans in New York. There are thousands of them on the streets and people treat them like dogs."

"Why would there be so many?"

"Most people going to America aren't like you and your mother with a cabin to live in while crossing the ocean. Most are too poor to pay for one and sleep in the bottom of the ship. Once they reach America, many of them can't find work to make a living for themselves and their kids. Some of them just walk off and leave the kids on the street. And parents die of sickness in those terrible immigrant ships where the people are jammed like pigs in the holds. Some are even murdered. That leaves kids without any grown ups. They end up begging on the street."

"My father and mother decided to come to America. Well I'm here and I'll find work and make a living, somehow."

Andrew shook his head. "I don't think you know just how dangerous it'd be for a pretty girl like you."

"You think I'm pretty?"

"Yes. Too pretty to live on the street for things happen to pretty girls."

"I'll make out."

"All right. When we dock and after I've brought all the luggage of my passengers ashore and collected my tips, I'll come and help you with your luggage. And we'll get your pounds changed to dollars. The captain has a money changer on the ship to give his passengers a fair exchange, a much better trade than anyone on shore would give.

"Thanks, Andrew, for all your help."

"You're sure welcome."

Alice wanted to do something for Andrew to show her appreciation for his friendship. What could it be? An idea came to her. "Andrew, I would like to give your mother a present for having such a good son. Would she accept my mother's clothes as a gift? Most of it is new, bought just for this trip. They are much too big for me to wear."

"A gift for mom?" Andrew beamed. "She'd be tickled to get new clothes. With times tough, getting clothes for herself would be the last thing she would buy. The first thing would be to buy sheep and then something for dad."

"Good. Then it's settled. I'll pack them in that biggest suitcase and leave them for you."

"Thank you, Alice."

Andrew gave Alice a huge smile. "I'd better leave and see about my passengers."

He left, closing the door behind him.

Chapter Four

City of Orphans

Alice stood with Andrew on the street in the cool wind. They had left the Pannonia, and with Andrew carrying her suitcase, had walked along the pier to the quay and onward to the nearest street. Evening was upon them with the sun low in the west and the buildings casting dark gray shadows that filled the street.

People flowed past from the waterfront and into the city; somber; silent peddlers and dock workers hurried to their homes, and uniformed ship's crewmen talked and laughed as they headed out for a night of freedom and pleasure on the town. Alice noted that among the crowd were children, boys and girls of various ages and wearing dirty, tattered clothing. Some were silently drifting along with the migrating throng, others stood against the walls of the buildings, or in recessed doorways, or in the mouths of alleyways. The faces of the children held a weary, dejected expression that deeply touched Alice. They had to be some of the many orphaned and abandoned children that Andrew had told her about.

Alice was much saddened at the plight of all the children. She touched the small bulge of American dollars that she had pinned inside the bosom of her dress. She never wanted to have to beg.

She reached out and took hold of Andrew's hand. His fingers immediately tightened upon hers.

"Are you sure you'll be all right?"

"I'll be just fine," Alice replied.

"I hope so. Don't trust anybody. And don't let one living soul know that you've got money."

"I won't."

"Then I guess this is goodbye," he said in a sad voice.

Alice dreaded parting from Andrew for he was a fine friend and she would sorely miss him. A handshake was not sufficient to match her feelings. She brushed his extended hand aside, and stepping close, kissed him, a brief touching of her lips upon his. She hastily drew away, pivoted about and walked away carrying her suitcase.

***

In the dusk of night, Alice slowed her step along the sidewalk at sight of the faded wooden sign hanging over the sidewalk and labeling the business beneath it as Sandoval's Cobbler Shop. The sign brought memories of the cobbler's shop in Terryville, and the old cobbler with whom she had become great friends over the years that she had brought the family shoes to him for repair.

She halted and looked in through the window to the interior. Under a single electric light bulb hanging on its cord from the ceiling, an ancient relic of a man sat behind a work bench that spanned most of the width of the narrow room. His white head was turned down as he labored on a shoe. She wondered if this cobbler like the one in Terryville would be friendly. She hoped it ran with the trade.

She ranged her sight over the shop. All the cobbler's tools with which she was familiar were present. On the work bench to the left of the cobbler were different sizes of iron lasts used when nailing on soles and heels, and a small belt sander, and a sewing machine for leather. To his right were knives of different shapes and other assorted cutting tools, and small cans that most likely held polish of various colors. Shoes were arranged in two neat and separate groups, those awaiting repair and those waiting for their owners to come, pay and retrieve them.

***

Eduardo Sandoval raised his weary head to get the kinks out of his aching back and looked toward the window that provided him a view of the street. He jerked with surprise for peering in through the window glass at him was a very beautiful young woman. Her face held a pensive, questioning expression. Their eyes touched and he expected her to turn away from him as other people always did when he caught them looking at him. However this girl held his eyes.

Eduardo was an ugly man and knew it. He had known it since early in childhood when the boys of his neighborhood gave him the name Ugly Eduardo. The knowledge was reinforced when he began to notice girls and found their difference from boys most interesting. Their reaction to him was hurtful for when they caught his eyes upon them, they would hastily look away. If they had a girlfriend with them, they would giggle and talk between themselves. He knew they were laughing and talking about his ugliness.

Eduardo could have allowed the agony of the ugly man to make him resentful and jealous of others that had been gifted with a fair face and body. He refused to allow himself to fall into that useless emotion. Instead he found great pleasure in looking upon beautiful people, and beautiful animals, and any and all objects manmade and natural that had splendor of form and color. His love of beauty was so intense that sometimes he cried upon viewing something truly outstanding. He felt that urge to cry now as his sight rested upon the girl holding his eyes through his shop window, for of all beautiful things in the world, he most enjoyed the beauty of young women.

Never in all of Eduardo's seventy two years, had he seen a more lovely girl than the one framed by his window. She could be an exquisite painting by a master artist. Had she actually been one, Eduardo would have tried to buy it. He had to give a sign of his appreciation of her beauty. He lifted his hand to the girl and nodded his approval of the rare gift she was giving him by merely existing and allowing him to look upon her for this moment of time.

To Eduardo's surprise, the girl raised her hand and nodded back at him. She stood there with her hand up and her eyes reaching out and touching his. Then the hand lowered and the girl stepped from in front of the window and the wall of the shop came between her and Eduardo.

As Eduardo felt an instant ache from the loss of sight of the girl, the door of the shop opened and the little brass bell fastened near its top, chimed out as the clapper struck upon the bell's body. The girl came inside. She wore a gray jacket over a pale blue dress, and a little hat of the same color as the jacket. She carried a suitcase. The suitcase surprised Eduardo.

"Good evening, young lady, what can I do for you?" Eduardo wanted to hear the voice of the girl. Would it be as lovely as she?

"Kind, sir, do you have work that I could do?"

"Work?" Eduardo said in astonishment. Never before had a girl asked for employment. Now and again, a man or boy entered the shop and ask for employment. Eduardo always told them no and sent them on their way. He could with his own labor repair the number of shoes and boots that came to the shop.

"Yes, sir. I'm strong and would work very hard."

Alice studied the aged, white headed cobbler. His body was narrow and boney and stooped. His head was large and much outsized for his thin body. His face was broad and deeply wrinkled with his years. His mouth was wide with lips but mere lines beneath a straight, sharply ridged nose. The two halves of his wide face were somewhat unbalanced, the left side being set somewhat lower than the right which caused that portion of his mouth to droop and gave it a leering twist. However, one feature of that misshapen face held a magnificence that, to Alice, made all the ugliness dwindle too little importance. The cobbler's eyes were large with a wide band of white surrounding dark brown pupils. Though the eyes showed age, they were eloquent, and at the moment were shining brightly with the intensity of their emotions, kindness she thought, and perhaps awe though she did not know why there would be awe. There was something else, the eyes seemed to hold a bit of the innocence of a youth, which was very odd in one obviously quite old. She immediately liked the old gentleman, even if he should have no work for her.

"I would work just for a place to sleep tonight," Alice said pressing her need and hoping. She had been unsuccessful in obtaining a room at any of the boardinghouses she had passed, and feared sleeping on the street. Her mother had told her that very old men and women were most often gentle and kind and so she was ready to take a chance with this old cobbler who sat and watched her so intently. "I'd sleep on the floor. And I have a little money and can buy my own food."

New emotions began to flow across the cobbler's expressive eyes. Alice wished she could read the thoughts that were creating them.

Eduardo knew that he could never turn the girl away. "Well, now. The shop does need a good cleaning. The floors and windows haven't seen soap and water and a scrub brush for some time. And there's leather to cut for repairing the shoes and boots. But I can't pay you. I have plans for all the profit I make."

Alice smiled with thankfulness and relief. "Oh, I will work very hard and you won't be sorry."

"I believe you," Eduardo said and basking in the girl's smile. "We can fix you up a pallet there near the heating stove." He pointed at the little gas burning stove. "You'll be warm there when the night turns cold."

"That would be just fine." Alice's good fortune wouldn't allow her to stop smiling.

"Then we have a bargain. Maybe tomorrow we can talk about a permanent job." Eduardo climbed down from his stool and came around the end of the workbench to Alice and held out his hand.

"I'm Eduardo Sandoval."

"I'm Alice Childs." She accepted the offered hand stained with brown shoe polish. The hand was muscular and the grip firm. She noted that she was nearly as tall as the cobbler.

"That's a nice name." Eduardo glanced down at the suitcase and back up to Alice's face. "But I must ask, why are you out on the street?"

"I just arrived from Liverpool today. My mother died on the way to America. I couldn't find a room for tonight."

Eduardo had seen the pain of the girl at the mention of her mother's death. There was a story here but he would wait for the girl to tell it. "I've heard that it's hard to find a room. I have an apartment back there where I live," he said and pointed at a door set into the rear wall of the shop.

"As far as you buying your own food, that won't be necessary. That will be part of your pay." Eduardo admitted to himself that to set across the table from Alice and have a meal would be more than fair pay for any amount of food she might eat.

"I'll close the shop. Then we'll fix some food for I'm starving." Which wasn't true for Eduardo ate sparingly. "Then we'll fix you a bed for the night by the stove."

***

Early in the first night in the cobbler shop, Alice awoke from sleep, a shallow and uneasy sleep due to the strange surroundings and the unknown character of the cobbler close by in his tiny apartment in the rear. She sat up and listened for what had awakened her. She heard the sound of the cobbler talking. Who was he talking with? She arose and crept to the door of his apartment and pressed her ear against the wood paneling. The first words she heard told her that he was saying his prayers and thanking God for the favors that had been given to him during the day. He ended his prayer with the surprising words, "And thank you, All Mighty, for sending me Alice Childs to delight my old eyes and drive away my loneliness." The words relieved Alice's worry about the character of the cobbler. She stole back to her pallet and fell into a sound sleep.

During the first day with the cobbler, Alice cleaned the shop with fervor and thoroughness, and by the middle of the afternoon, it was spotless. She had also removed the jumble of tools and other odds and ends piled about on the benches and shelves and arranged everything according to Eduardo's directions.

Eduardo complimented her on her work. He then left and returned with a fold-up cot and used it to replace the blanket pallet by the stove. With that obvious sign, Alice knew that she had been accepted to continue working for the cobbler.

Alice's days working for Eduardo passed pleasantly one after another and for he was a jolly man, always ready with a pleasant word and one of his lop-sided smiles. She called him Uncle Eduardo. When someone asked who Alice was, Eduardo proudly told them that she was his niece.

They had settled into a comfortable routine of working together during the day. After the shop closed, they ate together in the kitchen of his apartment. He insisted on doing the cooking and served up delicious food. Upon finishing the meal, they drifted off doing their own private chores and entertainment.

Eduardo was a zealous reader of both the New York Herald Tribune and the New York Times. He would sit and read in detail the financial section of the papers. Sometimes he would chuckle, but never offered to say why. Rarely, he would sigh.

Eduardo always left the shop for an hour or so every morning, Monday through Friday. He would simply tell Alice that he had a little business to do downtown and she should mind the shop. She did not ask what type of business drew Eduardo away. She reasoned that he would tell her if he wanted her to know.

Eduardo's business increased with Alice's presence and the cleanliness and neatness of the shop. He noticed that young men began to appear with shoes for repair and would linger to talk with Alice. Some young fellows brought shoes that would have been quite serviceable for several more miles. Not just the young men found conversation with Alice pleasant. Most all of his customers would smile and dawdle for a few moments to talk with her on even the most simple of subjects. He recognized Alice's value to draw new customers and assigned her to greet and serve all who entered the shop.

Summer arrived and Alice and Eduardo were kept busy repairing shoes and boots. She learned to cut patterns from pieces of tanned cow hide, how to use the sewing machine to fasten the pieces together to form the upper part of a shoe, and to nail on soles and heels. There was always a good feeling when she finally applied a thick coating of polish to the shoe and buffeted it to a glistening shine.

The hot days of the New York summer passed and the cooler days of September arrived. One evening as they ate supper together, Eduardo told Alice that the shop was more profitable now than before she had come. With that compliment, he told her that she would receive a wage of two dollars a week.

Alice saved most of the earned money and added it to what she kept pinned inside her dress. With her growing savings, she felt more secure. She also felt more secure in another manner; she had had her thirteenth birthday and had grown an inch taller since beginning to work for Eduardo.

On the last Thursday of late October, Eduardo returned from his trip downtown with his body more stooped than usual and his face strained. He said not a word to Alice, just silently sat down at his usual stool and began to work fitting a sole to a shoe. She felt saddened at his worry, whatever that might be. In the afternoon, he again left for downtown, which was very unusual. He returned late in the day with a New York Times special edition. Alice caught sight of the headline. In huge bold letters it read, Stock Market Crashes. Investors Lose Millions Of Dollars. Eduardo went into his apartment and closed the door and did not emerge the remainder of the day. Alice was quite worried about Eduardo. She walked two blocks away along the street and ate the evening meal at a restaurant.

Alice heard Eduardo arise on Friday and leave just as the sunlight came in through the shop window. She opened the shop at the usual time and tended to the customers. Eduardo did not appear as the day wore on.

Five o'clock arrived and Alice prepared to close the shop for the day. She was worried about Eduardo for it was so unlike him to miss a full day of work. As she started to shut the door, a black sedan pulled up in front of the shop and stopped. A tall man in a gray suit climbed out of the car. He signaled for Alice to not close the door. The man wasn't one of their customers and Alice's concern for Eduardo surged.

Alice backed away into the shop to allow the man to enter. He came inside, cast a quick, appraising look over the shop and then settled his attention on Alice.

He spoke to Alice. "My name is Earl Whittaker. I'm a lawyer. Eduardo Sandoval was one of my clients. He once told me a niece had come to stay with him. Are you that niece?"

Alice nodded, and wondering at the same time if she should tell the man the truth of her relationship to Eduardo. Before she could resolve the question, the man continued speaking.

"I have bad news for you. Your uncle is dead. He died about an hour ago in my law office."

"Dead?" Alice said disbelievingly.

"Yes, I'm sorry to say. The stock market fell steeply today, even steeper than yesterday. He came to my office to tell me that he had lost all his money and couldn't pay me what he'd borrowed on this shop. And that the shop now belonged to me. Then he just keeled over dead right there on the floor." Whittaker shook his head. "I warned him not to invest all his money in the stock market, but he was a stubborn man. He was old and not in good health and his heart just couldn't stand the loss of all his savings."

Whittaker noticed Alice's intense sorrow. "Miss, I've known Eduardo for several years. We met soon after he came here from Spain and started this cobbler shop. I liked him. But he was too much of a gambler and brought this trouble on himself. And there are thousands of others in the city and elsewhere around the country in the same sorry straight. They all went crazy believing the market would climb to the sky and they would become millionaires. Damn fools.

"However, Eduardo did plan ahead in one regard, he had placed enough money with me to ship his body back to Spain when he died. He wanted to be buried in his home village among his relatives. I made him a promise that I'd do that. And so I will."

Whittaker cast a look around at the tidy shop. "I see that he had a nice little business here. I should get my money back when I sell it."

Whittaker turned to Alice. "Can you run the shop by yourself? Long enough to give all the people back their shoes?" He gestured at the several pairs of shoes on the workbench.

Alice nodded, unable to speak through her misery. She had liked the old cobbler very much.

"Then I'll give you a week to find the customers and return their shoes. You can keep all the money you collect. I'll send Mrs. Rodriquez around late next Friday to collect the keys and lock the shop up until I can get it sold."

Whittaker abruptly left. Alice watched through the front window until the black car pull off along the street. She was all alone again.

***

In the cobbler shop, Alice waited for the appearance of Mrs. Whittaker. Her suitcase was packed and sat by the door. The day was ending, the light fading. A cold November wind blustered along the street. The people passing by on the sidewalk were bundled up in heavy coats and hats.

An older woman dressed for the cold passed in front of the window and entered the shop, ringing the little brass bell on the door.

"I'm Mrs. Rodriquez. Mr. Whittaker sent me to collect the keys and lock the shop." The woman gave Alice a friendly smile.

"He told me to expect you. Here are the keys."

Mrs. Rodriquez accepted the keys. She started toward the back of the shop, but then halted and watched Alice pick up her suitcase.

"Do you have a place to stay?"

"Yes. I've rented a room on Calloway Street."

"That's a long ways off. Especially to carry a suitcase."

"I'm strong and I'll be okay."

"Be careful for you've got to go through a bad neighborhood to get there. It'd be especially risky for a girl in the dark like it's getting outside."

"I'll be careful. I'd better get going."

"Watch out for the gangs of boys. They're the worst. Mugging people and stealing what they've got that's valuable. Now I'd better see that everything is locked up and get home myself."

"Goodbye," Alice said.

"Better hurry for it looks like rain," Mrs. Rodriquez said and moved toward the rear of the shop.

***

Alice hastened along the sidewalk through the deepening night and the rain that had begun to fall shortly after she left the shop. Her coat was buttoned tightly to her chin and her hat was pulled low over her head. She leaned into the stiff, chilled wind that blew directly into her face. She was getting wet and so too was her suitcase, and there were still several blocks to travel to reach her room on Calloway Street. The rain had driven foot traffic indoors, and except for a vehicle passing now and again on the street, she was alone.

Her thoughts were gloomy. She was friendless in the strange city. She touched the packet of bills pinned inside the top of her dress. The money must be spent frugally.

She stopped on the curb of a cross street and waited for a car to roll by with its two yellow headlights fighting the rainy darkness. The big raindrops were visible falling through the beams of the headlights. She proceeded on and had progressed half the next block when a man came up behind her and passed by, his raincoat flapping in the wind and shedding water. He slowed and glanced back at Alice and then down at her suitcase. She had a sudden concern that he was going to turn back toward her. However he faced about in the direction he had been walking and continued on. Alice breathed a sigh of relief. A girl in the night carrying a suitcase could be in danger for it might signal that she was a stranger and by herself and unprotected. She shivered and not just from the falling rain penetrating her thin coat and pressing cold against her skin.

Ahead of Alice in the middle of the block, two people, blurred, ghostlike forms in the night, left the sidewalk and took shelter from the rain under an awning over the entryway of a store, the store closed and dark. She made out the two turning to face her. A fiery red eye opened in the face of one of the murky figures and glared at Alice. She knew the eye was but the burning end of a cigarette. Her step faltered for she sensed danger. She moved off the sidewalk and continued her course on the street.

As Alice drew even with the two figures, the larger one leapt across the sidewalk and upon her. His arm swung and a hard object crashed into her head. Alice fell heavily upon the brick pavement. With stars exploding in her brain, she looked up through the falling rain to see a big boy kneel over her. She struck up at his face and hit him on the mouth. She twisted to the side and started to roll away so as to get to her feet and run. The boy ignored the blow and reached out and caught her by an arm and pulled her down and captured the other arm. Alice screamed and tried to bring up her legs to kick him.

The boy leaned closer over her and clapped a rough hand over her mouth. He called out to the second boy. "Hurry, damn you and help me pen her down!"

The second boy sprang close and caught Alice's thrashing legs with strong hands. Both boys leaned their weight on Alice and pressed her down upon the street on her back. Their foul stinking bodies intensified her fear and anger. Were they going to rape her?

"Now search her and see what she's got hidden on her," said the first boy.

The second boy speedily ran his hands into the side pockets of Alice's coat and found nothing. He moved his hands to her legs and worked upward to her crotch, hesitated there his fingers probing for the cleft between her legs. Alice squeezed her legs together. He pinched her leg painfully, but moved on and ripped her coat open, breaking lose all the buttons. His hands slid up her waist and then over her youthful breast, stopping there, lingering to rub and finger their firmness and the nipple.

"She got some nice tits. You want to feel them?"

"We've got no time for that," the first boy said nervously. "Hurry up and find what's she got hid on her."

The second boy's hands moved off Alice's breast. He cried out with discovery. "Found it, sure as hell. It was pinned between her tits. And it's a thick wad too." The boy jerked the money loose, tearing Alice's dress.

"Make sure there's no more money somewhere else on her."

"I felt everywhere and I got it all. Let's get the hell out of here before somebody comes and sees us."

"There might be something we can sell in the suitcase."

The boys sprang to their feet. The larger boy snatched up Alice's suitcase, and following his companion, raced away along the dark street.

Alice struggled to her feet. She trembled, shaken by the violent blow to her head and the boy's hands on her private parts. She felt the inside pocket of her coat that the boy had missed in his search. The treasures of her mother's poems and her father's picture and watch were safe. She ran her hand under her hat and explored the lump on her head caused by the boy's blow. The wound would heal. However the money that she needed for survival was gone. The room on Calloway Street was paid up for a week. After that she would be just another penniless orphan on the perilous streets of New York.

A hot anger burned through Alice. Damn those two to hell. She should have carried a weapon with which to fight them. She knew where to get one. She pulled her torn coat closely around her and began to retrace her steps toward the cobbler shop. The blustering wind heavy with rain pushed against her back and lengthened her resolute stride.

***

Alice left the street and entered the alley and onward to the rear yard of the cobbler's shop. She looked warily about at the pale squares of light from the rear windows of the nearby buildings. Nobody was out and about. The only sound was the wind and the falling rain. She opened the gate to the yard of the shop and stole to the door and tried the knob, finding it locked.

She moved to the kitchen window made of two sashes, each containing six small panes of glass. Searching about on the muddy ground with her hands, she found a loose brick among those that made the pathway across the yard. She hoisted the brick and struck a pane of glass that broke with a sharp crack and a tinkle of falling shards.

Careful of the jagged edges of broken glass, Alice reached through the window and undid the latch. The sash lifted easily and she crawled out of the rain and into the kitchen of the cobbler shop. She drew the blind down over the window and turned on the electric light

She lit the gas kitchen stove and with it burning and casting off heat, undressed and hung her clothing over the backs of chairs to dry. The book of poems and the picture within it had become damp even though she had done her best to protect them. She opened the book midway and laid it and the picture in the heat of the stove to dry. A can of green beans and one of corn and a packet of crackers were taken from the almost empty pantry. She ate directly from the cans.

Alice went into the shop with all it familiar its odors. She glanced about. Never again would she see the stooped old body of Eduardo bent over a shoe, or hear the rapid clicking of the sewing machine or the whisper of the sander. Her heart felt lonesome. She shook the sad thoughts away and moved to cutting tools. She chose a pocket knife that she could carry. She tested the blade by stabbing it through a thick piece of leather and slicing a long cut. She smiled grimly, never again would she allow herself to be harmed without fighting back.

With weariness heavy upon her, Alice set up the cot and spread two blankets upon it. She wound her father's watch, as she always did every evening before she slept, and placed it and the knife within easy reach on the floor. She slid naked underneath the blankets. Cautioning herself that she must be gone from the cobbler shop before daylight, she went to sleep.

Chapter Five

Orphan Train

In the girl's dormitory of the Children's Aid Society, Alice awoke from her sleep with its dreams and memories. That journey through her past life had caused her to sleep fitfully and she felt un-rested and troubled by the lingering emotions. A sense of loss, of aloneness lay heavily upon her. That brought thoughts of Gracie in the hospital. She hoped fervently that her little friend now in a doctor's care was recovering from her illness.

The other girls in the dormitory still slept. In the far end of the room, a tiny voice spoke in a babble that Alice couldn't decipher. Nearer to her, a child whimpered. The orphanage with all of its strangeness and now the journey to some unknown destination was worrisome for Alice. For the little girls, it must be terrifying.

She felt restless, and shoving aside the blankets, quietly rose to sit on the edge of the cot. The room was chilled, the wooden floor cold to her bare feet. The rectangle of the close by window was visible and she knew the day was breaking. She stood up and stepped to the window and placed her hand upon one of the glass panes totally covered with frost of a thousand crystal forms. Using her fingernails she scratched the frost from a small area of glass at eye level. Under a darkly overcast day, the sidewalk and an elm tree were in view, and farther away was the brick paved street with the trolley rails. A snowflake, a quite large one that appeared to be partially defying gravity by the slowness with which it drifted downward, passed in front of the window. A second fell. Then more snowflakes followed, quickly increasing in numbers.

Alice heard somebody come up beside her. She turned to see Opal.

"What's happening out there?" Opal asked as she scratched at the frost on the window.

"It's starting to snow."

"So I see," said Opal and peeking out through the small opening she had made. "It's going to be a cold day for traveling."

"That's all right with me for I want to get out of this orphanage."

"Me too."

The door at the end of the dormitory opened and Sisters Marie and Evangeline entered. Sister Marie flipped the switch and the electric lights flared to life.

Sister Marie lifted a little brass bell and shook it three jingling times and called out, "All right, girls, rise and dress. We've a long journey ahead of us. The train won't wait so hustle yourselves. You big girls help the little one you've been assigned to care for. See that they get washed and dressed. Breakfast is ready and waiting. Soon as everybody has eaten, then off we go to the railroad station."

Sister Marie turned to Sister Evangeline. "See that the little ones are properly taken care of. Find dry clothes for those that have peed themselves."

"Yes, Sister," Sister Evangeline replied.

Sister Marie turned and left the dormitory. Sister Evangeline moved in among the cots and began to pull blankets off those children slow to rise. Little voices began to cry, complaining at being hastened from their warm beds.

Alice washed and dressed and followed Opal into the dining room that was warm due to its nearness to the cooking stove in the adjoining kitchen. The aroma of the food was a fine welcoming to the day. At the serving table, a nun handed each girl a plate containing a bowl of porridge, two generous slices of bread covered with butter and a mug of hot tea.

Alice sat with the other big girls and watched the boys appear and accept their breakfast and carried it to the same tables they had used the evening before. Alice saw Teddy with his plate of food. She noted some of the older boys looking at the girls.

Alice finished her breakfast and was directing her steps back to the dormitory to pack her belongings when Sister Marie intercepted her and caught her by the arm.

"Come with me," said Sister Marie.

"How's Gracie," Alice asked quickly and sensing the sister had news. "Is she all right?"

"Just come along," said the sister in a non-committal voice and walked toward her office.

"Is Gracie all right?" Alice asked again as she followed behind.

Again Sister Marie did not reply, but led onward and into her office and closed the door. There she turned to face Alice. "Gracie is dead, Alice. She died during the night."

"Oh! No! My Gracie can't be dead." Her grief was too much and she began to sob.

"I tried to take as good care of her as I could," Alice said through her sobs.

"It wasn't your fault. It was God's will."

Alice focused her tear blurred vision on Sister Marie. "God's will that Gracie died? No, it was because she was starved and weak and with the cold and everything else, she died."

"It was all his plan for Gracie."

"Plan?"

"You don't understand."

"No, I don't understand." Alice was angry at God and at the sister for defending him. "Do you?"

Sister Marie clasped Alice in her arms and hugged her closely. Though her mouth was almost touching Alice's ear, her words were barely audible. "No, dear Alice, I don't know why innocents are allowed to die."

They stood wrapped in each other's arms for a moment and then Alice pulled away. "I'm alright," she said

"Then go pack and get ready to travel. We're going to Minnesota which is far off to the west."

"Yes, Sister Marie," Alice said and left the office.

As Alice entered the dormitory, she came upon Sister Evangeline talking with Opal and several other larger girls. Opal beckoned to Alice.

"Sister Evangeline has just told us we're going to Minnesota."

"I know," Alice replied. "Sister Marie told me."

"I don't want to go to Minnesota," said one of the girls. "It's cold and snowy there." She shivered.

"I've heard there're wolves and bears in the woods that eat people," another girl said.

"I've heard there're panthers too," said a third girl.

"God will protect all of you," Sister Evangeline said stoutly.

"He hasn't protected me in my life," Opal said. "And that's why I'm here."

Opal spoke to Alice. "Has God protected you, Alice? Will he protect us in Minnesota?"

"God didn't protect my friend Gracie and she died last night."

"I'm sorry your friend died," Opal said in a sympathetic voice. She paused. "Maybe there isn't a God," she said and her voice rising.

"Don't blaspheme," Sister Evangeline exclaimed in a frightened and scolding tone. "God will strike you down."

"God doesn't protect girls living on the street," another girl said angrily. "He didn't protect me when that gang of boys dragged me into an alley and did hurtful things to me. When I fought to make them stop, they hit me and hit me. Nobody came to help me." She turned her face down and stared at the floor.

Opal spoke to Alice. "Do you think there's a God now after Gracie died?"

"The nearest thing to God that I've seen in America is Sister Marie," Alice said harshly, and ignoring Sister Evangeline's warning that she could be struck down.

"You shouldn't say that," Sister Evangeline said quickly.

"What? That Sister Marie is a good person?"

"No, not that. That God doesn't exist."

"For you maybe he does exist." Alice wanted to ease the harshness of her remark.

She didn't want to talk any more. She stepped past the sister and went toward her cot to prepare for the train journey to that land called Minnesota with its snow and bears and wolves and panthers. She didn't like the feel of that future.

***

From her seat in the passenger coach of the train hurrying westward from New York, Alice watched out of the window at a land battered by a powerful blizzard. Snow covered the roofs of the farm house and barn, and the wide fields with their fences. In one field she saw three horses standing with their rumps turned to the storm. The thick winter hair of their backs carried a blanket of snow. Huge drifts were forming at the base of the fence paralleling the railroad tracks. The frigid scenes made Alice shiver. She was glad for the coal burning heating stove radiating its warmth from the center of the coach.

The train consisted of the engine and two coaches, one for the passengers and the second for dining. The passenger coach was shared by the boys and girls, the girls having the front half. A curtain was drawn to separate the two halves. Now and again Alice heard boys shouting and wondered what had caused it. The girls were subdued and talked in muted voices.

The seats were in pairs and faced each other. Alice and Opal occupied one seat and two other larger girls, Bertha and Jeanine, the opposite seat. Their small pieces of luggage were stored below their seats. The girls had talked together at first. Now Opal read a book and the other two sat silently and watching the countryside.

They had eaten lunch in the dining car. As for sleeping, Sister Marie had explained that when night came, a bed now folded up against the ceiling would be lowered half way down, and a second bed would be made from the pair of seats. Curtains would enclose the beds. Two girls would share each one. Alice knew that with food and a bed provided for each boy and girl the cost must be substantial. She remembered Sister Marie telling the policeman that this was the last train to take orphans west due to lack of money.

She closed her eyes and listened to the clickety-clack of the coach wheels. Every clickety-clack meant she was being carried ever closer to a place where unknown people would decide her future. Oh, how she wished that her mother and father were still alive. She stood up, and opening her satchel lying on the rack above the seat, removed the poem book. Adding a verse to the book might make her feel a little closer to her dear mother and father, and to Gracie. She seated herself and began to write.

Alone.
By and with just one.

The first number after none.
Will there ever be two,
Me and you?
Or always alone?
Alone.

"What are you writing?" Sister Marie asked. She had come close without Alice having noticed. "Or is it personal?"

Alice broke from deep concentration on her writing and looked up at the sister smiling down at her. She didn't want to show the poem for it expressed her private feelings. However the sister had been kind to her. She held the page up for the sister to read.

Sister Marie read the words and her face saddened. She leaned close to Alice and whispered. "Too much sorrow is bad for the body and soul. You will have a fine life, Alice. God will see to that."

Sister Marie turned away and went back through the coach.

Alice stared after the sister. You are the one that may have set me on the path for a good life, Alice thought. She dozed off.

"Alice, I have somebody who could use your help."

Alice roused to see Sister Marie with a little girl three to four years old with black hair, very pale skin and a lovely bow shaped mouth. Her eyes were soft brown, and at the moment were shadowed with worry about what was happening to her. She clutched her canvas satchel holding her inspection clothing and stared bashfully at Alice

"This is Della, "Sister Marie said. "She needs some older girl to see that she is properly cared for. Would you do that for her?"

"Yes, oh, yes, Sister Marie. I'd be glad to." Alice was pleased that she had been chosen to tend to the girl. She gave the tyke a smile and reached out and pulled her close. The girl came willing.

Alice spoke softly to Della. "I don't have a little sister. Would you be my sister and we'll ride the train together. We'll talk and tell stories."

Della nodded and pressed her face against Alice's breast.

"She'll have to sleep with you and Opal," Sister Marie said.

"That's all right, isn't it Opal?"

"I just hope she doesn't pee on me," said Opal.

Della looked angrily at Opal. "I don't pee the bed," she said proudly.

"That's telling her," Alice said and liking Della for her spunk. "Hop up here on the seat between Opal and me."

Della climbed into the seat and scooted away from Opal and close to Alice.

"Will I always be your sister and live with you for always"

"We'll have to see what happens when we get to Minnesota," Alice replied.

"But I want to know now," said Della and frowning.

"I know, but I can't answer you now,"

"I don't like to wait," Della said looking up into Alice's face. "Would Sister Marie know?"

"I don't think so. It'll depend on the people who choose us."

"Maybe if I wish real hard, that'll help us live together."

"You do that," Alice said, not believing wishing made any difference in what would happen in the future. She caught hold of Della's hand and it snuggled in her larger hand like a little, warm animal. That trusting action make Alice feel stronger.

Chapter Six

Black Face's Quest

Black Face lay resting in the snow near the trunk of a birch and studied the members of the wolf pack that ranged along the Rainy River. From his home range, Black Face had traveled twenty miles north through the forest lying along the Rapid River. He had crossed the river on its frozen breast near its junction with the Rainy River. Then he had journeyed for nearly another twenty miles searching for this most unfriendly band of wolves. He had found them lazing about in an opening in the forest after killing a deer and feasting. His arrival was now an hour past. He was savoring the scent of the young female with the brown and gray coat and the unusual marking of a white patch on her throat. She was standing a few body lengths away and intently watching him.

Black Face had made his appearance openly and drawing close enough to easily see and scent the Rainy River wolves. There he settled down to evaluate the females of the pack. The dominant male, a big, gray coated wolf, had wanted none of Black Face's presence and had come toward him with hackles raised and growling threateningly and ready to fight and drive away the interloper. Black Face stood his ground, made no sound and held the eyes of the pack leader. He would fight if it became necessary; however he would not be driven away until the purpose of his long trek was satisfied. With but a distance of a long leap separating them, the gray wolf had changed his mind about fighting the large stranger by himself and instead had led the other males of the pack in a charge upon Black Face. Knowing the group of wolves could and would rip him to pieces, Black Face had raced away through the forest.

He gave them a speedy, three mile chase, and all the time gradually circling back toward the place where it had started. Each time he chanced to pass through an open area, he looked to the rear to check the nearness of his pursuers. He played with them, allowing the swiftest to draw close, then putting on a burst of speed and putting safe space between them.

Black Face returned to the exact starting place of the chase and stopped and waited for his pursuers. When they appeared, he moved off a short distance along the previous path of the chase, and faced about to see if they wanted another run over the same ground.

The leader of the River Pack gave Black Face a hostile stare, but did not approach. After eyeing Black Face for a short time, the leader made a threatening growl, turned about and guided his followers back to the females lying and observing the action of the males.

Black Face returned to his original place of observing the wolves and, after standing alert for a few seconds and watching the pack leader, sat down in the snow and turned his attention to the young female. The dominant male and female kept wary eyes upon him, and so did the other adults. None came out to challenge him. The young quickly lost interest in the motionless stranger and began to frolic in play.

The wind had carried the scents of the eighteen wolves making up the pack to Black Face. He now had each wolf identified visually and by his or her distinct scent. He separated out and concentrated on the scent of the dominant female. His instinct told him that she was too old for the purpose of his plan and so she did not interest him. His attention had shifted to this handsome two year old female. She had detached herself from the others and come a few steps in Black Face's direction, where she now stood and looking at him. Her ears were pricked forward and her tail wagged slowly showing friendliness.

Black Face breathed in her smell, and admiring her sleek, shiny coat. The instinct that had told him the dominant female was too old, now told him that this female was healthy and strong.

The pack leader made a threatening growl at the young female. She did not respond to the warning and continued to stare at Black Face and wag her tail. The leader growled more fiercely. The young female's tail stopped wagging and she sank down to lie on her stomach in the snow. She still showed her interest in Black Face and their eyes talked across the distance separating them.

Black Face broke eye contact with the female and checked the remaining members of the pack. There were fewer of them than had been present a few minutes before. Some of the males were missing. Black Face rose and ranged his sight through the woods behind him. It was a wolf's practice for a portion of a pack to get between its prey and its safety before the remaining members attacked. His enemies were closing off his escape route.

He again looked at the alluring female and drew in her scent one last time. He gave her two friendly "woofs" a promise that he would return. With that statement of his intention, Black Face broke into a run toward his home territory.

After running a short distance, he flung a quick look over his shoulder and saw four males had come out of the forest and onto the path that he had just crossed over. They were no danger to him. He slowed to a trot that he could maintain for all the long distance to his home territory. A pleasant sense of anticipation warmed his wolf's heart. Regardless of the danger from the males of the River Pack, he would soon come again and take the young female from them and start his own following of sons and daughters.

***

Half way back on his journey to his home range, Black Face came to the frozen Rainy River. As he trotted out onto the ice to cross to the opposite side, he saw two humans on the ice just upriver a few hundred feet. On the shore near them, a black horse stood hitched to a sled. A dog lay on the front of the sled. One of the humans was bending at the waist and then straightening, and repeating the motion again and again, and always moving very slowly backward. The second human was shoveling snow off the ice. The nearness of the humans and their movements brought the wolf to a stop.

One of the humans appeared familiar to Black Face and he tried to catch his scent, but the wind came from the wrong direction. Held by his curiosity regarding the actions of the humans, Black Face sat down on the ice and lingered, watching them.

***

Paul worked steadily, bending at the waist and straightening and performing the motion again and again as he pulled the six foot ice saw up and down at a steep angle with most of its length first in the water and then most of it in the air. He was cutting blocks of ice from the half foot thick sheet of it floating on the Rainy River near his home. The saw was made of iron and wood, and designed to cut the ice into blocks of a size that could be lifted from the water. The iron part of the saw was forty two inches in length with teeth an inch and a quarter long. Bolted to the upper end of the saw was a wooden handle shaped to be held by both hands. Paul kept the teeth of the saw very sharp for easy cutting. The saw had been passed down from his grandfather to his father and now Paul.

He had selected a section of the river for ice harvesting where a section of the current had splintered off from the main flow and eddied and ran less swiftly and so the ice had grown thicker than in other places. To allow the ice to grow an even greater thickness, his mother was shoveling the newly fallen snow off the ice close by. Snow insulated the water from the air that was below zero.

The block upon which Paul had been sawing came loose from the ice sheet. He grabbed up the ice hook lying nearby and snagged the block and with a strong heave, hoisted the block out of the water and upon the rigid sheet.

He turned to his mother, Heather, bundled up in the winter clothing. She had recognized the sound of the block coming out of the water and had halted her shoveling and was looking at him. Her lovely face displayed a fine flush from the cold and the exertion of the shoveling. She gave him one of her delightful mother's smiles.

As always, Paul couldn't help but smile back. He admired his mother very much. She had worked side by side with his father and now by Paul's side. More than her willingness to work alongside her men folk was her wisdom.

That first winter when there was but the two of them, she had taken fourteen year old Paul, and from the combined knowledge the two of them had acquired by working with his father, they had reestablished his trap line, setting the steel traps and the snares made with steel wire and the deadfalls made of logs. The bait, usually a portion of a rabbit, was placed in such a location as to entice a desired fur bearing animal to come to a trap to find a meal, and there be caught. The work of setting the traps was hazardous, the running the trap line and harvesting the pelts was even more so. A trapped animal in severe pain from its injury, would strike out with claws and teeth. During that frigid first winter, they had taken the pelts of several animals. In the second and following winters, Paul ran the trap line by himself.

Paul did some quick calculation and decided his mother was thirty six years old. What did she think about during the long days when he was gone off on the trap line, or away at school? Did she get lonely? Wasn't she too young to spend the rest of her life on the farm without a husband? What about when he left and went away, and he would be leaving in the early fall to study at the university in Winnipeg? They had saved nearly enough money for the first year of schooling.

Maybe there was a situation developing that would answer the questions about his mother. When he had arrived home from the trap line the following evening, he had observed that she had had a visitor who came in a horse drawn sleigh. The visitor had remained for a substantial period of time. Paul knew that from the amount of snow that had been packed down by the hooves of the horse where it had been tied to the garden fence. Paul counted the number of sleigh tracks and found four and knew that not only had the visitor stayed for s spell, but had gone for a sleigh ride and returned.

Mr. Torgerson, the owner of the ice company, had a high stepping pacing horse that could cover five miles an hour, and so the trip from Diston would have taken but a little over an hour. Paul had seen the man and his mother talking together in Diston, and from their expressions, the conversation seemed to be a pleasant one. So if the man was Mr. Torgerson, then his mother would have certainly been on the sleigh ride with him. Paul hoped the ride behind the pacing horse along the wooded lane and on the country road with the farm houses and fields had been an enjoyable time for her.

His mother had not mentioned the visitor, which was all right with Paul. He wanted her to be happy. He knew that his father would also have wanted her to be happy.

"Mom, it'd be a nice day for a sleigh ride," Paul said to show her that he knew and approved.

"It was a nice day yesterday for a sleigh ride also," Heather said.

Paul laughed and knowing that a complete understanding had occurred between them.

"It looks like you've cut about enough blocks for a load and I've got the snow shoveled off the ice," his mother said. "So I'll go and start supper."

"All right, mom."

His mother carried the shovel to the river bank and there stuck it upright in the snow ready and handy for the next snow storm. As she passed the sled where Brutus lay watching the action of the two from a pallet of straw, she stopped and leaned down close and rubbed his powerful jaws with both hands. She whispered to Brutus. "You big rascal, always take good care of my son." She playfully thumped the dog on his ribs with both hands. Brutus was pleased at the touch of Heather's hands and gave her a "Woof". He watched after her as she hastened away toward the house and barn which sat some hundred steps away upon a bluff above the river and out of its reach during the spring floods from snow melt and rains. She was the only human, other than his master, that Brutus allowed to lay hands upon him.

Paul took up the last block of ice in his gloved hands, braced it against his thick wool coat, and carried it to the sled and placed it with the others there. He backed up and eyed the stack of ice blocks and estimated that he had accumulated at least a ton. The sled was strong being constructed of tough hickory and oak and had runners of strips of iron that slid easily on snow and ice.

On Paul's side, Brutus made a low warning "Woof". Paul pivoted around to see what had caused the dog's alarm. Immediately his hunter's eye caught sight of Black Face on the ice down steam from him. The wolf sat motionless and staring at Paul. "Well, I'll be damned," Paul muttered. His rifle lay on the sled but he didn't reach for it. He copied Black Face and froze into stillness and stared back.

The tableau of wolf and man and dog appraising each other held for a quarter minute. Then Black Face rose nonchalantly to his feet and trotted to the far shore and vanished into the forest.

Paul noted Black Face's direction and knew it led to his home range and the members of his pack. That told him the wolf had come from the territory of the River Pack. "Have you been searching for a pretty lady wolf?" Paul asked silently. "I'm sure you were and that's good for it means another pack of wolves in three or four years."

Paul retrieved his ice saw and hook and placed them on the sled. He untied the reins from one of the wooden uprights and called to the horse. That willing beast leaned into its harness and the sled slid forward on its iron runners with Brutus riding the top of the pile of ice blocks and staring ahead.

As was Paul's routine, he would take the ice laden sled along the short lane that ran from his home and along the river to the main road running north and south. From that location the main road continued north for a short distance and over a bridge into Canada. Paul would leave the sled beside the road on the south end of the bridge. The ice company truck came by once a week to pick up the ice. Payment would be credited to his and his mother's account.

Chapter Seven

Taken In

The locomotive towing the coach full of orphans came to a stop with a hiss of steam at the railroad station in Bimiji, Minnesota. The steam froze in the frigid air and fell in a rain of fine crystal onto the cinder covered ground.

Deputy Sheriff Sam Horton, from two blocks distant in the Beltrami County Courthouse, saw the train stop at the station. Sam was a slender man twenty six years old and slightly less than six feet tall. He kept himself in top condition by long runs, competing in snowshoe races in the winter and canoe races in the summer.

He spoke over his shoulder. "Sheriff, the Orphan Train has just pulled into the station."

County Sheriff Oscar Taggert, seated at his desk and reading the top sheet of paper from a pile of them, raised his face and aimed pale brown eyes at the back of Sam's head. "Horton, how in hell could I not know that with all the noise it makes?" He said sarcastically. "You talk too damn much."

Sam's face tightened with anger at the rebuke. He was just making conversation and any reasonable man would have known that and accepted it in that spirit. But not Sheriff Taggert, he had a mean streak. Sam would have enjoyed walking over to Taggert, telling him to stand up and then knocking him flat on his back. Two things were wrong with that idea. Sheriff Taggert was a large man, thick boned and heavy muscled, and immensely strong. In all of Beltrami County, there might not be one man who could knock him off his feet, if they dared try. Sam wasn't one of them. Secondly, such an action would get Sam fired and he liked being a lawman with the pay and prestige that went with it.

He knew first hand that Taggert was a talented detective and relentless in pursuit of a criminal. Sam had been with him when they trailed a thief through the forest to Canada, and without contacting the Mounties, drag the man back across the border into the States. Taggert was tough on the convicts locked up in his jail, striking a prisoner with his fist for simply being slow to answer a question put to him, or merely giving the sheriff a sour look. Once released from jail, the prisoners knew to stay clear of Taggert and to keep their mouths shut about their treatment while behind bars. Taggert had also demonstrated his willingness to shoot to kill. He had gone to arrest two men suspected of a robbery. He had come back with their bodies, stating simply that they had resisted arrest. The two men were known and there was talk among the people that they were not the kind to resist arrest. However, nobody openly questioned the sheriff's word.

Sam often wondered why Taggert had hired him to be deputy sheriff. Sam knew he was a good lawman; however men with more experience had applied for the job back in April when the previous deputy sheriff, Jan Johansson, had been killed. He hoped the sheriff had not hired him due his aunt Matty, Matilda, being married to Cole Taggert, the sheriff's brother.

The gunman who had shot and killed Johansson had never been caught; the only unsolved crime in the county in the nine years Taggert had been sheriff. When Sam came on duty, Taggert turned the case over to him to try his hand at solving it.

As Sam reviewed the case file, he found that Taggert had documented in much detail every step he had taken in his investigation of the murder. Deputy Johansson had been found dead with three bullets to the chest and lying on the road beside his sheriff's cruiser along Highway

72. The bullets extracted from the body had led nowhere. Among other avenues, Taggert had questioning all previous inmates of the jail that had been locked up there while Johansson was alive. That avenue had provided nothing, with all ex-cons having alibis.

Sam started all over, viewing the scene of the killing, but after nearly a month, and two heavy rains, there had really been nothing to discover. He had again questioned the ex-jailbirds, who fortunately still lived in the county. Somewhat to his surprise, he found that the convicts had considered Johansson a proper lawman, as opposed to Taggert which they heartily disliked. One ex-convict stated bluntly that it should have been Taggert instead of Johansson that had been killed.

Taggert had made a final comment in his report, "That it was considered most likely that Deputy Jan Johansson had been killed by a transient motorist he had stopped passing through the county". Sam could add nothing to that.

Taggert rose from his desk and stretched hugely with arms flung out widely. He took his broad brimmed lawman's hat from the tree stand and placed it squarely upon his head. He positioned his holstered pistol just so on his hip, and drew on his heavy uniform coat.

"Come along, Horton, we're supposed to be present when the folks make their selection of the orphans. Do you know of anybody in the county who we shouldn't allow to take one?"

"No" replied Sam.

"Neither do I."

Taggert strode swiftly from the office, forcing Horton to grab up his coat and draw it on as he trailed behind.

A two minute walk on the sidewalk, covered with several inches of snow from yesterday's storm, brought them to the railroad station. There they gathered with George Sherrod, town mayor, and Father Joseph Brannan, the local catholic priest, and fifteen or so men and women who had braved the frigid cold to come to the station to view the orphans as they came off the train.

A door on the passenger coach opened and Sister Marie dressed all in black attire descended the steps and stood on the station platform. She looked expectantly at the group of people. The priest followed by the mayor went forward to meet the nun.

The priest smiled broadly and caught the hand of the nun in both of his. "Welcome, Sister Marie, we've been expecting you." He shook her bare hand gently. He seemed on the verge of hugging her, but stopped and simply held her hand for a second before releasing it, before saying. "This is Mayor Sherrod."

"Oh, yes, I remember Mayor Sherrod very well from our trip here back in the spring," said Sister Marie and extended her hand to the mayor.

Sherrod clasped Sister Marie's bare hand with his gloved one. Sister Marie forgave him this lack of manners with the glove, for after all, it was terribly cold with the low temperature and the wind.

"Everything is arranged, sister, just as we agreed," said the mayor.

"I hope there are many people willing to take children. I want every one of them to find a home."

"Father Brannan and I have been busy finding homes for them," said the mayor. "The people who chose children during your last trip have told their neighbors that they are very satisfied with the children."

"Based upon that favorable report, we do have a list of interested people," added Father Brannan. "Mostly farm families same as during your last trip."

"Because of the terrible cold, I've arranged for the inspection of the children to be held in the school gymnasium and the people are waiting there," said the mayor. "The school is just along the street three blocks from here."

Sister Marie swept a look over the snow covered town lying under a low, dark overcast sky. She would have preferred a sunlit day for she had found that people were more generous when the sun shone. She turned back to the mayor. "That was very thoughtful of you. Give me a minute to be sure my children are dressed for the cold and I'll bring them off the train."

***

Alice had gathered with the other girls and boys pressed against the coach windows and watching Sister Marie talk with the two men. One was dressed like the priest she had seen in Terryville.

Alice's stomach felt odd and her chest was tight. She didn't like the thoughts of being inspected by strangers and judged to see if she was worthy of being taken into their homes.

"I'm scared," Della said in a tiny voice. She clutched Alice's hand in a tight grip.

"Don't be scared, honey," Alice said. "Nobody will hurt you."

"How do you know that?"

"They're all good people in this town."

"Are you sure?"

"I'm sure for Sister Marie wouldn't talk with people who would hurt a little girl. So don't you worry."

"All right, Alice."

***

Sister Marie climbed the three steps and came onto the coach in the girls' end. The curtain had been drawn back between the two halves and she could see all the boys and girls. Everyone turned from the windows and looked at her. Most faces held expression of doubt and anxiety. Some held fear. A few of the oldest boys showed outright anger at what was happening to them.

Sister Marie moved to the center of the coach so that all could hear her. "Boys and girls," the sister avoided calling them children, "Father Brannan and Mayor Sherrod have found people who have said they're interested in having a new girl or boy in their home. Some will want a little one and some a big one. All of them will want pleasant children so stand up straight and smile, show them that you aren't a sourpuss." Sister Marie smiled as she said sourpuss. "If people talk with you, answer politely and say yes mam or yes sir."

Alice didn't feel like smiling. She didn't think many of the other children would be able to make a smile.

"It's a little walk to the school where the people are waiting. Now you big boys and girls help the little ones put on their coats and hats and get them all buttoned up for its very cold outside. The snow is deep and little feet will need help, so help them along. Bring your satchels with your old clothes for if you are chosen, you'll leave with your new family."

Sister Marie swept a compassionate look over the half circle of worried, wary young faces regarding her so very attentively. "Now don't feel badly if you aren't chosen here in this town for we have other towns to visit. Now get ready quickly."

There was a flurry of coats being donned and buttoned and satchels taken in hand. Then all the boys and girls turned and looked expectantly at Sister Marie. She nodded and led them off the coach.

The snow crunched under Alice's feet as she stepped down onto the station platform. A large quantity of the cold crystals fell into the tops of her low cut shoes and lay against her ankles. She hastily lifted Della up out of the snow and into her arms. The child wrapped her legs and arms tightly around Alice and nestled her head against her shoulder.

"It's really cold," Della said.

"Yes it is," Alice replied. "But we should soon be where it's warm."

Holding Della close in her arms, Alice joined with the other children following Sister Marie, the priest and the mayor. The people that had come to the station came last. The procession was too large for the sidewalk and the priest and mayor led the people along the snow covered street. Small voice complained of the snow and cold.

***

Inside the entryway of the school gymnasium, Alice sat Della down upon her feet, but continued to hold her hand. She commenced to examine the Bemiji folk that had gathered to view the orphans. More than a hundred men and women, and a few children not yet of school age, mostly filled the end of the gymnasium. They stood silently with their eyes running over the orphans. Many of the men's faces were weathered by sun and wind and reflecting their outdoor occupations as farmers or workers in the forest. Standing off by themselves were two men in uniforms with badges.

A table and four chairs had been placed in the center of the gymnasium and the mayor and the priest led Sisters Marie and Evangeline directly to them. The children followed, pressing close about the sisters as if afraid to let them get far away.

The mayor spoke to Sister Marie. "Sister, would you please line the children up for inspection?"

"Certainly."

Sister Marie spoke to the children. "You boys start a line there and extend it back toward the door. You girls start here." She pointed at locations on the wooden floor. "And take off your coats and hats so that the people can see you better."

The children, their faces holding a mixture of worry, and of hope that they would find somebody who would take them in, somebody they could call family, hastened to obey. Alice took a place in line with Della by her side. Opal took a position on Alice's other side. Within but half a minute the boys and girls were in line. Thin and nervous, they stood quietly with their eyes searching the faces of the town's people. Della clutched Alice's hand tightly.

The mayor motioned for the nuns to be seated behind the table, and he and the priest claimed the remaining two chairs. Sister Marie opened her ledger and sat waiting and watching the gathering of people. Even though she had brought the children here to find homes for them, she felt a loss at their going, and she admitted to a concern that they might not be treated kindly and fairly. She knew the largest boys would be chosen first for they would be cheap labor for the farmers or tradesmen. The girls would be chosen based upon both their size and prettiness. Sister Marie recognized the human nature of this.

Della tugged on Alice's hand and whispered to her. "Please, Alice, make them let me go with you."

"I'll try my best," Alice whispered back.

As she returned to observing the four people at the table, the two lawmen came to stand near the mayor. The mayor nodded at the officers. He then said something in a low voice to Sister Marie. She gave the lawmen a short scrutiny.

Mayor Sherrod called out in a loud voice. "Ladies and gentlemen, please give me your attention." He waited until the people quieted, then continued to speak. "Sisters Marie and Evangeline have brought these orphans girls and boys all the way from the streets of New York City with the hope and prayer that they will find homes among the good folks of Minnesota, and especially the generous people who live in and around Bemiji. Now I have a list of those among you who have expressed an interest in choosing a boy or girl. If there are others here who have not signed up with me but have an interest in a child, you are also welcome to look them over. Please be gentle with them. They have had more than enough ill treatment in their short lives.

"As we have in the past, proceed down the lines and look at the children. When you see a boy or girl that you think might fit into your family, you can take him or her aside and talk privately. Should you decide to take the child, come to Sister Marie here at the table and she will record the information about you and the child. You must agree to treat the child as a member of your family and not as a servant. If it comes to a situation later that you find the child does not fit into your home, you must turn the child over to Father Brannan."

At that moment, Alice saw Teddy, who was in the boy's line across from her, hand his coat and hat to one of the boys beside him. He stepped into the open space between the lines of boys and girls and faced the assembled people of Bemiji. He made a deep bow and held it for a moment. He straightened, and gave them a huge smile from his pale, thin face. He began to dance. Supple as a new blade of grass, Teddy's slender body spun in charming pirouettes with arms outstretched. He spun left for a dozen times and then, without the slightest loss in the smoothness of his steps, reversed to spin right. He pirouetted with his arms making elegant movements and always with that lovely smile upon his face. His pirouettes slowed until he was hardly turning and his arms and hands began to pantomime in marvelous, fluid motions. First he imitated a butterfly, his hands and arms making the slow beat of its wings and his steps moving to mock its customary erratic flight; he abruptly stiffened his body and his hands performed the rapid, precise flutter of a hummingbird's wings, and then the speedy dive of a hawk upon its prey. At least that was the way Alice interpreted Teddy's movements. He danced on returning to his pirouettes, performing not as a showoff, but with a child's innocent joy of dancing obvious upon his young face and thus making it all so very wonderful. With a last whirl with arms outstretched, Teddy ceased moving and stood very still with that magnificent smile directed at the people. He gave them a deep bow, held it for a moment, and then stepped back into line.

The crowd had stood transfixed as the boy danced. Now a great flash of smiles showed and someone clapped. The clap was instantly taken up by the other people and the gymnasium filled and echoed with the clamor of many hands.

Even before the clapping stopped, Alice saw two different couples of a man and a woman break from the gathering and hastened in Teddy's direction. Teddy, you have won a home, thought Alice. And good for you.

Alice felt Della's hand tighten on hers as the entire group of people came alive and moved in a wave toward the children. Their faces held a look of expectation and an urgency to have first choice from among the children. As the people drew closer, Alice saw a young man and woman had their eyes on Della.

The two drew close and stopped in front of Alice and Della. "Is this your sister?" the woman asked Alice in a soft voice.

"No. She's my good friend."

"I want to stay with Alice," Della said hastily for she understood the purpose of the question.

"We have a very little house and room for just one little girl," said the woman as she knelt in front of Della. The man knelt beside his wife. The woman spoke, "We'd like to talk with you about being our little girl. Would you talk with us?"

Della looked up at Alice. "Do you think it'd be all right for me to talk with them?"

"I think you should for they look like very kind people and you would be their only little girl. And I don't believe there will be many people willing to take both of us."

Della thought about that for a moment. Then she turned to the kneeling woman and studied her eye to eye for a few seconds. "Would you take me to see Alice?"

"If she stays close by Bemiji, I certainly would."

Della looked up at Alice. "I'll talk with them." She turned to the woman and put out her hand. The woman clasped it tenderly.

"We'll go over there just a little ways where we can talk in private," said the woman.

The young man and woman led Della away.

As Alice looked back along the line of girls, a man and woman were approaching with quick steps, the woman on the man's side and a step behind him. The man's sight was fixed on Alice. He spoke over his shoulder to the woman and she began to smile. Alice thought the smile forced.

The woman was nearly as tall as the man and thin. Brown hair framed a narrow face with small eyes, a nose too large, the lips thin. She possessed none of the rounded curves of breast and hips of a woman. A very homely woman, some might even call her ugly. Alice had made the appraisal, but the woman's body was not her fault, only the uncaring hand of fate.

The man was strongly built with a broad chest and a broad face that reminded her a little of her father, but lacking her father's outstanding tallness. As the couple drew closer, Alice saw the similarities of the man with her father diminish to but minor sameness. This man had a hard face. His eyes were of a peculiar light brown color.

The man stopped in front of Alice and the woman halted by his side. "I'm Cole Taggert," the man said and his eyes running over Alice from the crown of her head to her feet. His eyes came to rest on Alice's face. "This is my wife Matilda. We call her Matty. What's your name?"

"Alice Childs.

"Well, Alice, we're interested in a girl about your size to help Matty around the farm. Could we talk a little?"

She recalled her mother's words that a woman could tell by the expression in a man's eyes what he was thinking about her. She had had much practice with strange males during the past few months, as with the Pannonia's chief steward, her friend Andrew, the generous old cobbler, and the rough boys on the city streets. However she could read nothing in this man's eyes for it was like trying to glean information from puddles of mud. What thoughts lurked in their hidden depths? She was receiving conflicting emotions about the pair. Her intuition told her to be wary, and yet the man's soft words together with the smiling woman were sending a different message.

"Cole, this girl will be stronger and can do heavier work," said the woman and pointing at the sturdy Opal.

Cole gave Opal a brief head to toe inspection. Then without looking at the woman, he spoke in a voice that brooked no argument, "No, Matty, we should choose this other one if she is willing to come home with us."

Cole faced back to Alice. "We have cows and horses, and a large pond for skating in the winter and good for fishing and swimming in the summer," said the man. "Best of all, you would have your own room."

The man's outburst of information about his farm surprised Alice for it seem that he was trying to persuade her to accept them instead of the other way around.

"She could start school at once, isn't that so, Matty?" The man's voice demanded an affirmative answer.

"Oh, yes, at once," the woman said hastily. "I was born and raised on the farm and went to school from there. The school bus comes past the lane to our house."

The thought of being able to go to school and living on the farm where the woman had grown up, decided Alice. To have a home was worth taking a chance on them. And further, if the people and their home didn't turn out to be the correct one for her, she would leave and go to Father Brannan.

"I must go to school," Alice said.

"You have our promise," said the man and he smile broadly. "You'll find we have a nice farm. Now let's go pass Sister Marie's inspection and then we can all go home"

Taggert led the way toward the table where Sister Marie sat with Sister Evangeline, Mayor Sherrod, and Father Brannan. As Alice and the man and woman drew close, Sister Marie gave Alice a look that asked if she was satisfied with the man and woman who had selected her. Alice read the expression for what it was and gave Sister Marie a slight nod.

Sister Marie entered the information into her ledger that Matilda and Cole Taggert had taken the fourteen year old female Alice Childs into their home under the conditions as described. Matilda and Cole signed their names at the proper location on the page.

As Alice and the Taggerts were about to leave the table and Sister Marie, Cole caught the eyes of Sheriff Taggert and spoke to him. "Oscar, come out to the farm on Sunday and have dinner with us."

"I'd like that and I'll be there unless a case comes up that Horton can't handle."

Sam ignored the Sheriff's comment. He had seen Cole Taggert select the pretty blond girl from the line of girls. He had also been present when Cole had chosen a girl from the Orphan Train back in April. That girl had stayed with Cole and aunt Matty only a few days before she ran away. Sam had ridden with the sheriff searching for the girl, but had found no trace of her. He knew Cole treated Matty badly. Had he also treated the girl in the same manner and that had caused her to run away?

Sam saw a special look pass between Cole Taggert and the sheriff. There was something in the trade of looks that seemed almost conspiratorial, a secret between the two. Surely Sam must be wrong about that.

Sam watched Cole, his aunt Matty and the blond girl make their way toward the exit of the gymnasium. "Cole has chosen another pretty girl to take to the farm. He must work them hard for they soon run away."

"What was that you said?" the sheriff questioned, his head snapping around.

Sam silently cursed himself for he had spoken his thoughts out loud. "I merely said that Cole has taken another pretty girl home."

"So what, Horton? What in the hell is that to you?"

"Absolutely nothing. I was just thinking."

"Keep your damn thoughts to yourself."

Sam remained silent and wishing mightily that he had indeed kept them to himself. By speaking, he had inadvertently crossed a line that only the sheriff knew about.

"I've told you before that you talk too goddamn much," Taggert continued. "Some day that could get you into a hell of a lot of trouble."

Sam flashed angry for he recognized the expression and the tone of the words from previous outbursts by the sheriff. They had always led to somebody getting hurt, usually a prisoner in the jail getting a smashed face or a cracked head, and sometimes with a suspect of a crime who was reluctant to answer a question. Through Sam's anger, he felt a prickle run along his spine. He wasn't a prisoner; however he wasn't sure how much protection that gave him from the quick fists of the sheriff. The thought came to him of the death of Deputy Johansson. Had Johansson said something that had enraged Taggert to the degree that he was killed? Sam didn't like being threatened. He would think on the question of why the sheriff had taken so much offense at Sam's simple observation of facts about the new girl.

***

Alice turned back at the door of the gymnasium and looked at the lines of boys and girls. There were empty spaces in the lines where children had been drawn from them by folks for private conversation. Opal stood alone in the spot where she had been when the inspection of the children had begun. Her face held shame and disappointment. She had been examined and judged, a demeaning experience by itself, and then rejected. Poor Opal, thought Alice. She lifted a hand in farewell to Opal, who raised her hand in return.

There were other girls and boys still standing silently in the broken line. A few held expressions of hope that someone would yet come to talk with them and find them not too ugly and take them into their home. Alice blinked to keep from crying. She wished with all her heart that Opal and all the remaining children would be chosen at the next stop of the train. She tried to hold back her feelings, trying not to be hurt too much by the sadness so openly expressed, but she could not. The picture of the orphans standing so forlornly would remain with Alice the rest of her life. She left the gymnasium with the Taggerts.

***

Under the dark, low hanging clouds, the black Ford Model A farm truck droned on and on slewing and sliding and spinning its wheels on the snow packed road that twisted and turned and dipped into hollows and climbed the hills. The wind came up through a crack in the wooden floor boards to freeze Alice's feet in their low cut shoes that were wet from wading snow. She wiggled her toes and could barely feel them. The Taggerts were dressed in winter clothing and boots and gave no sign they felt the cold.

Alice sat between Cole and Matty in the single seat of the truck. The bed of the truck was empty except for a spare tire. Cole drove, steering left and right to correct the skids of the truck, and shifting to low gear to plow through the snowdrifts that the wind had built across the narrow country road. Alice tried to keep track of the distance traveled. She gave up after a time simply knowing it was a very long distance from Bemiji.

Cole reached in his usual gesture to shift gears. Instead of grabbing the gearshift extending up from its mount on the floor boards, he caught Alice by the leg and gave it a quick squeeze, before releasing it and taking hold of the gearshift and shifting.

Alice hastily moved her legs away from the gearshift, and looked at the woman to see if she had seen what her husband had done. Matty looked steadily ahead, seeming not to have observed the man's groping hand. She appeared totally turned inward to her private self. Alice moved away from Cole as far as she could on the short seat and close to Matty. She could still feel the man's calloused fingers upon her leg and hated his touch.

***

Several additional long, cold miles had passed under the rolling wheels of the Ford when Cole spoke. "We're almost home" He pointed ahead at a metal mail box mounted on top of a post on the right side of the road.

Alice made out the name Taggert on the side of the mail box. The paint of the name appeared new as compared to the rusty condition of the mailbox, and that caused Alice to wonder how long Cole Taggert had lived on the farm. Matty had said that she was born and grew up here. Were they newly married?

Just past the mail box, Cole steered the truck into a lane that showed one set of tire tracks partially covered with snow drifts. Large oak trees, their limbs frozen and stripped bare of leaves by swift winds, bordered the lane. The widely spreading branches of each tree reached out over the lane and intertwined with those of the tree on the opposite side.

Alice stared out through the windshield at the tangle of limbs. She thought the opposing oaks seemed to be battling each other for space, and it came to her that they really were battling each other for space in the sun. Just as she was struggling to find a place to survive under the sun. Even a cold winter sun

The farm house came into view ahead, a single story frame structure of moderate size painted white and with a steeply pitched roof, as all building seemed to have in this land of snow. As the truck plowed further along the lane through the snow, a fair size barn came into view to the right of the house. Its wooden sides were weathered to a dark gray from enduring many years of storms. Four cows and a team of horses were in a fenced area attached to the side of the barn. On the right of the barn was a broad field of snow with the blond stubble of wheat stalks showing above the whiteness. A dense wood lay beyond the wheat field. Alice wondered what size farm the Taggerts owned.

Cole brought the truck to a stop beside the house. "Your two go on inside and get the fire started," he said. "It looks like it's going to snow so I'm going to put the truck in the barn. I'll feed the livestock and milk the cows while I'm out there."

Matty made no response. She opened the door and climbed out. Alice, anxious to put distance between Cole's hands and herself, scrambled out after Matty. The deep snow, reaching far above her shoe tops, poured in around her frozen feet. She must not complain. She would not. She clamped her jaws together and waded through the snow behind Matty.

As they drew near the house, two black and tan hound dogs of medium size bounded off the porch and rushed out to meet them. The dogs centered on Matty, dancing about her with joy. One began barking a greeting to her. The second joined in and the two gave the woman a choral medley of welcome.

The dogs quieted and turned their attention to Alice and came close sniffing and nosing her. She felt no danger for she noted their wagging tails and the friendliness of their eyes. She reached out and petted and rubbed their long, floppy ears. The tails wagged more swiftly.

"Well now, how about that?" Matty said. "They usually don't take to strangers."

"Dogs just seem to like me," Alice replied.

"I believe that from what I see."

Matty continued on toward the house, to halt at a large stack of wood covered with a tarpaulin. She spoke to Alice. "Put your bag inside the door and then come back and help me carry wood inside to fill the wood boxes."

"Yes, mam," Alice replied.

"Call me Matty," the woman said in a voice that for the first time held some warmth.

"Yes, Matty."

"Just shove the door open for it's always unlocked."

Alice stepped upon the porch and to the door that opened upon the turn of the doorknob. She leaned inside the house and placed her satchel on the floor beside the door. This was the kitchen with table and chairs and a large cast iron cooking stove. To her left was a wide room with furniture and a big, round heating stove in the center.

Alice hastened back to the wood pile and filled her arms and followed Matty into the house. After several trips by Matty and Alice to the wood pile and back inside, the wood boxes of both stoves were full.

Alice stood shivering and watched Matty kneel in front of the heating stove, and using an iron poker, move aside the ashes that had been used to bank the fire. Live coals glowed red as the air struck them. Matty carefully placed kindling of slender pieces of wood upon the coals.

Matty spoke over her shoulder. "Do you know how to start a fire?"

"Yes. At times I started the fire at home in Terryville. Except we used coal instead of wood."

"I'd like to hear about your home. When we get settled, you must tell me about it."

"I'd like to."

Matty placed larger pieces of wood upon the blazing kindling and closed the iron door of the stove. As she rose to her feet, she noted Alice's low cut shoes and her shivering body.

"Dear mother in heaven, you're freezing. Drag up a chair and put your feet close to the stove. I'll fix you a big mug of hot chocolate."

Matty turned away toward the kitchen. She pulled off her coat and hat and draped them on the back of a chair as she left the front room.

Alice was pleased to comply with Matty's direction. She carried a chair near the stove, sat down, pulled off her shoes and socks and placed them on the wood box to dry. She put her bare feet close to the metal side of the stove that was warming from the fire within. Ah, how wonderful to be able to feel her toes again. They began to tingle as the blood flowed more strongly. She looked into the kitchen where Matty was preparing food with swift and practiced movements. Alice should be helping Matty, but she was just too cold.

In but a few minutes, Matty came into the room and handed Alice a steaming mug of chocolate. "Supper will be ready in half an hour," Matty said. "Until then just you stay warm." Matty hastened back to the kitchen.

The outside door swung open and Cole came into the house carrying a pail of milk. Without a word, he handed the pail to Matty. He turned back to the door and picked up Alice's satchel from beside the door and carried it into the front room.

"It going to be a bitch of a night for the temperature is falling fast," he said to Alice and handed her the satchel. "Come and let me show you your bedroom."

Alice followed Cole through one of the doors and into a room with a full size bed, a wooden wardrobe, and a straight backed wooden chair. Close beside the bed was a nightstand with an oil lamp and a small glass holding matches for lighting its wick.

"There's a thick pile of quilts on the bed so you should keep warm," Cole said.

Alice glanced around at the room. She felt she had to say something. "It's very nice."

"There's plenty of things your can do here to earn your keep," Cole said. He led the way back into the living room.

Alice quickly retook her seat by the heating stove. Then to her dismay, Cole drew a rocking chair up in front of the stove and seated himself. He took a plug of tobacco from a shirt pocket and bit off a piece. He opened the door of the stove, and staring at the flames, began to chew the tobacco.

Alice made no sound, no movement, her eyes focused on the stove. She was a penniless stranger in the house and had earned no right to be here, and such outsiders kept quiet for they knew they should by instinct.

Cole often looked at the silent Alice as his jaws worked methodically chewing the cud of tobacco. After a time, he leaned forward and spit a squirt of tobacco juice at the fire, where it hissed into steam and was sucked up the chimney. He began to chew the cud again.

Alice was revolted by Cole's chewing and spitting and the sound of it hissing in the fire. She was glad when Matty called softly from the kitchen, "Supper's ready."

"The only thing she's good at is cooking," Cole said. He tongued his cud of tobacco into his hand and tossed it into the flames. "Let's go and eat."

Alice was angry at the man for his criticism of Matty. She followed him into the kitchen for she was starving, having had nothing to eat since a small breakfast on the train.

***

The three ate in silence, and that was just fine by Alice. She concentrated on the food on her plate, the boiled potatoes and beef that was cooked and seasoned to perfection, the hot cornbread spread lavishly with butter that melted upon it, the fresh milk was the sweetest Alice had ever drunk. A bowl of chocolate pudding waited beside her plate. Food was often on Alice's mind since she had arrived in America.

Cole's eyes were often upon Alice as she ate, examining her openly. He spoke abruptly "How did you come to be on the Orphan Train?"

Using as few words as possible, Alice described her home in Terryville, the voyage across the sea and the events in America leading up to her arrival in Bemiji. Cole asked questions about the coal mine, how many men worked in it, how deep underground it was and where the coal was sold? Alice relayed the facts she knew from what her father had said.

Matty asked a few questions in her soft, hesitant voice. She would wait until Cole fell quiet as he considered Alice's last words and then ask hers. Sometimes Cole overrode Matty before she could get the full question spoken. His disregard for Matty caused Alice to feel sorrow for the woman.

It was obvious Cole owned Matty. Alice recalled Cole's touch of her leg. Was he planning to own her also?

Matty rose from the table and started to clear away the dishes. Alice hurriedly joined her in the chore. There would be safety in the kitchen with Matty. Alice wanted to get through the remainder of the day without talking to Cole and then rest alone in her room.

Without a word passing between them, Alice and Matty worked slowly and thus prolonging the task of washing the dishes. Matty washed and Alice dried and put them away in the cabinet.

"You two going to be in there all night?" Cole shouted from the living room.

"We'd better go in," Matty said hastily.

She led into the front room where Cole sat chewing a cud of tobacco in front of the open door of the stove. Alice found a seat by the stove. Matty went to the Victrola that sat by the wall and wound the spring of the instrument by turning the projecting handle. With the turntable spinning, she placed a record upon it and then gently set the needle. The music of a waltz filled the room.

With a broad smile, Matty held out her hand to Cole, inviting him to dance. He shook his head and spit into the flames of the stove.

Matty's smile vanished and her shoulders sagged. Then she straightened and held out a hand to Alice, who hesitated but a second before moving to her. They joined hands and danced to the music, swinging and turning and promenading to the rhythm. Alice enjoyed dancing with the homely woman, who had a fine ear for the rhythm of the music.

Cole tossed his cud of tobacco into the stove, shut its door, and climbed to his feet. "Time for bed," he called out above the music.

Alice and Matty ceased dancing. After a moment of hesitation, Matty turned off the Victrola.

"We go to bed early around here," Cole said to Alice as he rubbed the front of his britches in the heat of the stove.

Alice looked at Matty. The woman's face was strained with anger.

"Alice, let's get your bed ready," Matty said.

"All right," Alice said, much saddened by Cole's treatment of Matty,

Matty led into Alice's bedroom and there struck a match and lit the lamp. "Cole will keep the fire burning all night for its cold outside. If you leave your door open some of the heat will come in here."

"I'd rather have my door closed," Alice said.

"I understand," Matty said. "But there's no key for it. It's been lost for years. You can prop the chair under the door knob though."

Alice didn't like that information about the key. She would use the chair as Maddy suggested. "I need to go outside," she said.

Alice went quietly through the house and out the door into the yard. She wanted to run and run and put distance between Cole and herself. But that could not be for where would she run to wearing but a thin dress and the night black and frigid.

Turk came and stood but a few feet distant and quietly watched her.

'Go away, Turk. This is private business."

Turk but wagged his tail.

"Alright, you peeping Tom. No, you're a peeping Turk. Watch if you must."

Alice squatted in the cold darkness and peed on the snow while looking up at the far away stars. The twinkling stars seemed to whisper that the universe was an empty place. To that, Alice silently added, and a heartless place for one such as she. A heavy loneliness draped itself over her. Unless she made a family of her own there was no one to mourn her when she died. Did she possess the bravery and the strength to live long enough to become a woman and find a gentle man like her father for a husband and a protector?

"Yes," she answered herself out loud.

With that pronouncement, she stood up, gave Turk a disapproving look and reentered the house.

***

Alice closed the door to her bedroom and wished the key had been present to lock it. She leaned the chair against the door with its back beneath the door knob. With all her strength, she wedged the chair's rear legs tightly against the wooden floor and in this manner jamming the back of the chair firmly up beneath the door knob. She pulled on the doorknob and could not make the door move.

Alice wound her watch and laid it on the nightstand beside the knife. She pulled her dress up over her head and hung it in the wardrobe. Wearing her petticoat, she blew down the globe of the oil lamp and snuffed the yellow flame. In the darkness, she climbed into bed and pulled the covers up to her chin.

Alice was weary to the core for the day had been long and cold and filled with a flood of emotions. Alice hated Cole's treatment of Matty. She hated his hand upon her leg. Would he try to come into her bedroom? The chair must hold the door closed and protect her through the night.

Alice lay quietly and unmoving as she listened for a sound to come from the door should Cole try to enter. The minutes passed and she heard nothing except the now and again muted groaning of the walls of the old house as the temperature fell ever lower and fought to come inside. Finally sleep overwhelmed Alice and she drifted off with her last thought that of Opal standing so awfully forlornly in the school gymnasium and waving goodbye.

Later, a length of time that Alice couldn't judge, she came awake to the rattle of the door knob being turned back and forth. Her heart began to thunder in her bosom for she knew it was Cole trying to get into her bedroom. The rattling stopped and silence held for a moment. Then the door creaked as heavy pressure was put upon it. The door held. Alice could imagine Cole standing on the other side of the door and wondering why it wouldn't open. Please, please, let the door keep him out of her bedroom.

Something heavy struck the door with great force, as if Cole had thrown his entire weight against it, and immediately came the sharp crack of wooden panels breaking. The scrape of the legs of the chair against the floor sounded and then a clatter as the chair fell to the floor. The door opened and Cole stood framed in the doorway, his broad body dimly silhouetted by the faint glow coming from the flames in the heating stove. He laughed low and guttural.

Alice, her senses sharpened by her great fight, could smell the man, smell the danger he brought. She feared what he was going to demand she surrender to him, and if she didn't give willingly, then take from her by force.

Unless she fought him and won. She flung off the quilts and scrambled from bed. Snatching up her knife from the night stand, she sprang into the closest corner. She crouched there with her back against the wall, and held the knife in a fierce grip and ready to thrust at Cole's stomach when he came within striking distance.

Cole crossed the room with four long strides and fell upon the bed. His hands searched for Alice, tossing aside the covers, knocking the pillow to the floor, sweeping the length and width of the bed with hooked fingers.

"Where are you, you little bitch," he said in a hoarse voice. He swept his eyes over the room. They found Alice crouched in her white petticoat in the corner.

"So there you are. Come and be nice to me and nobody will get hurt."

Alice remained silent with her knife ready. Her thundering heart was ready to explode from her chest. She had known fear before, but her fear of Cole touched a deep primitive level where nothing had ever touched her before. Father, my big, strong father, why aren't you here to protect me?

"Come here, girl. You and me'll have a little fun on the bed. Then everybody'll be happy. Especially me."

Alice doubted her ability to cut Cole badly enough to stop him from what he planned. Where was Matty? She had to have heard the sound of the door breaking and the chair falling.

"Matty!" Alice screamed at the top of her voice. "Matty! Matty! Help me! Come help me!"

"Shut up, you little bitch," Cole snarled. He lunged at Alice.

Alice dodged below Cole's outstretched arm. As she passed by Cole, she struck at him with the knife. Her reach was short and the knife missed.

Cole spun and rushed at Alice. She leapt up on the bed, almost falling as the springs sank under her weight, but caught her balance and jumped down on the far side. She must get out of the confining walls of the bedroom. She pivoted toward the doorway. As she prepared to make a dash for the opening, it filled with light and Matty came into the room carrying a lamp.

Cole whirled toward Matty. "Get the hell out of here," he roared.

Matty flinched at Cole's shout, but stood her ground. She held the lamp high and looked at the bed stripped of its quilts and at Alice on the far side, her face strained with fear and her hand holding a knife.

A wave of thankfulness swept over Alice at Matty's appearance. She would protect Alice from her husband. Even as the thought came to Alice, she noted Matty's expression was changing from one of alarm at the loud noise to something else. What was the woman thinking? Surely she wasn't going to leave Alice in Cole's hands.

"This doesn't concern you, Matty, so get the hell out of here." Cole said in a savage, commanding voice.

"Everything that happens in this house is my business," Matty said and stepped through the doorway and into the room.

Alice was intently watching Matty's face and knew the woman had come to some silent conclusion about something more than Cole coming into her bedroom. Matty's eyes had widened as if coming more awake.

Matty spoke in a calm voice to Cole. "Oscar won't like this. You'd better leave her alone."

"I don't give a damn what Oscar likes," Cole shot back.

"Yes you do," Matty said in a firm and knowing voice. "You've seen how mean he can get when somebody does something he doesn't like. So you'd better wait for him."

Cole's eyes swung from Matty to Alice and back to Matty. "To hell with Oscar, I can't wait," He took a step toward Alice, then halted and turned back to Matty and they stared at each other for what to Alice seemed a very long time.

Make him leave, Matty, Alice pleaded silently. Make him leave.

"Goddamn you, woman," Cole snarled and came close to Matty. He lashed out and slapped her a stinging blow across the face.

Matty staggered back and collided with the wall and leaned there half stunned. The hand holding the lamp sagged so as to almost topple the globe. She shoved away from the wall and stood upright. Blood oozed from her split lip. She wiped at the blood with the sleeve of her nightgown.

Matty spoke, her voice holding that same calm tone. "I'll going to kill you the next time you hit me."

"You've sad that before," Cole said and gave her a smile that said she didn't worry him. He stomped out of the bedroom.

"I mean it this time." Matty said to the empty doorway.

Alice hurried to Matty. "Here let me have that," she said and took the lamp from the woman's unsteady hand.

She owed the woman a great debt. "Thank you, Matty. Thank you very, very much?"

"I couldn't let him hurt you."

"I'm sorry that I caused you to get hit."

"That wasn't the first time. But it's the last time." In the lamplight, Matty's eyes glittered like frozen spheres. After a brief pause she spoke again. "We've got to be very careful until we figure a way to deal with Cole."

"What're we going to do?" Alice asked, and wondering what the woman meant by dealing with Cole. Did she intend to kill him soon as she found a way?

"Wait here," Matty said. "I'm going to wash the blood off and get something."

Matty hastened from the room. A minute later she returned with a long bladed carving knife.

"We'll sleep together tonight," Matty said. "Then tomorrow we'll figure out what to do."

"Who is this Oscar that you mentioned to Cole?"

"He's Cole's brother and the county sheriff."

"Cole is afraid of him?"

"He surely is. You saw how he acted when I mentioned Oscar. And there are many others who're afraid of Oscar. Now help me move the wardrobe to block the door so that it'll make a noise if Cole tries to move it to come in here. Then we'll make up the bed and try to get some sleep."

"I don't think I'll sleep very much."

"I don't think I will either." Matty said, gripping the long knife.

***

"Wake up," Matty said and shook Alice by the shoulder.

Alice sat up quickly. "What? What?" she said, startled by the abrupt wakening. She flung a hurried look around the bedroom for Cole.

"He's left and we've got things to plan. I'm fixing us a quick breakfast. Hurry up and dress. Put all your clothes on, coat, everything." Matty hastily left the bedroom.

Alice was surprised that she had slept. That could have been dangerous. She sprang from bed and hurriedly drew on her clothes. She pocketed her knife and her treasured picture, poem book and watch. She would leave the farm soon as possible.

Alice came up beside Matty frying bacon at the stove. The smell of the sizzling bacon made her realize that she was ravenously hungry. Her body wanted to be fed regardless of the danger she was in.

"Where did Cole go?

"He took the truck and went to buy some grain for the livestock. We had a short hay crop this past summer."

"How long will he be gone?"

"He said a couple of hours."

"Then I have time to leave before he gets back," Alice said, much relieved. "Why don't you come with me?"

"I'm never going to leave for this is my home. It's been in my family for three generations, counting me. I worked the farm by myself for three years after mom died, dad had died a couple of years before, and no man ever came to visit me. Then Cole came calling and after a few weeks asked me to marry him. I knew he was marrying me because I have a good farm. I didn't care for I thought the marriage would work out. I'm an ugly woman and I know it. But like any woman, I wanted a husband and kids. And he was so very nice to me before we married. Afterwards he changed to his real self, the cruel bastard he really is. So I got a bad husband and no kids. But I'll not be driven from this house, not off my land," Matty ended angrily.

Alice put her arms around Matty to comfort her.

"You're the one in most danger," Matty said and pulled free of Alice's arms. "You've got to get away from here this very morning. Soon as you get some food in you."

"How far away is the nearest neighbor?" Alice asked.

"That'd be the Tillson's. They have a farm about two miles off in that direction," Matty said and gestured with the fork she held. "Soon as you get something to eat, I'll take you there and ask them to drive you to Bimiji."

"I saw your face last night and heard what you said to Cole. You know something about him and Oscar. What is it?"

"I'm not going to say any more except that you've got to leave right now and get to Father Brannan. I'll give you a note explaining things to the Father. He'll keep you safe until he can find a proper home for you."

"How can I do that? I don't have warm clothes and I'd freeze if I tried to walk."

"I'm sure that I can fit you out with a warm outfit. My mother wasn't much bigger than you are and I kept some of her clothes. You tend the bacon while I go find you something warm."

Alice felt the weight of the danger like a shroud over her. Matty was correct, Alice had to get far away from Cole. From what Matty had said, she must also stay clear of Cole's brother Oscar Taggert the sheriff.

Matty returned with an armload of clothes. "These are all heavy winter clothes for mom worked outside a lot with dad, and then with me after he died. Here, try on this outfit and see how it fits. Just put it on right over your other clothing for you can't get too warmly dressed on a day as cold as this one."

Alice kicked off her slippers and pulled on a heavy pair of blue pants and a heavy shirt of the same color. She cinched the pants snugly around her lean waist with a leather belt. Then she drew on thick socks and a pair of leather boots with the tops reaching half way to her knees. The boots were slightly large. "With one more pair of socks, they'll be a good fit," she told Matty.

"We have that. Take off the boots and put these on."

Alice removed the boots and pulled on a second pair of socks and again drew on the boots. That makes a good fit," Alice said.

"Good. Finish dressing with these."

Alice put on the heavy wool coat with a red check design, a matching thick wool cap with ear flaps and a bill, and wool gloves. The garments were only slightly large. "I feel warm and toasty," she told Matty.

"You look like you'd be warm. Now while you're all dressed, go out to the chicken coop and get us some eggs to go with the bacon. The chicken house is on the far left side of the barn."

Matty went to the cupboard and retrieved a small basket and handed it to Alice. "Chicken's don't lay eggs often when it's really cold but you should find a few. Hurry for we've not got much time."

Alice left the house and crossed the porch and went into the yard. With the two dogs frolicking around her, she hastened through the snow toward the barn.

She entered through the open door that was wide enough for a large wagon load of hay to pass through. The rank smell of horse and cow manure, and the more pleasant odor of hay lay on the quiet air within the barn. She looked into the deep interior, a half lit, gloomy place. The barn had a ground floor and a loft. Five hand-hewed wooden columns evenly spaced ran down the center of the barn. The roof rested upon the tops of the columns and the loft was attached to their sides.

The main floor of the barn was made of earth packed solid by the tromping of feet and hooves and by rolling wheels, and now frozen in the deep cold. A passageway for a wagon or truck to pass through extended the full length of the barn. A large wagon with iron rimmed wheel sat empty in the far end of the passageway. On the side of the barn opposite the doors were several stalls. Two of the stalls each held a horse. They watched her with large, liquid brown eyes.

The loft level extended the length of the barn but occupied only half the width. Hay filled a third of the loft. A waist high pile of hay lay on the dirt floor below the edge of the loft floor. A pitchfork was stuck into the hay. Alice thought the hay had been tossed down from the loft in preparation to feed the horses and cows. Two sets of horse harnesses with their leather straps and iron trace chains hung over a low railing near the pile of hay.

She hastened toward the distant end of the barn and the chicken house. Both horses nickered to her as she passed by them. She unlatched the door of the chicken house and entered. She counted nine hens, all white and very noisy with their clucking and cackling. Attached to the inside wall of the chicken house were four nests to hold the hens while they lay eggs. One nest held a squatting hen. From the other nests, Alice took four eggs and placed them in her basket.

Above the noise of the clucking hens, Alice heard Cole's truck drive into the barn. Why was he here? Matty had said that he would be gone two hours. She hastily scanned the chicken house for a second way out. There was none. She was trapped.

She thought of the knife buried in her coat beneath the coat Matty had given her. The knife had been of no benefit against Cole in the night. She thought it would be of even less use in the daylight where it could be seen. She must get out of the barn and run to Matty.

She peeked out the door and saw the truck parked in the center of the barn near the pile of hay. Cole climbed out of the truck and began to unload sacks of grain from its bed, lifting the bulging sacks easily and stacking them near the mound of hay.

Alice had to get out of the barn without Cole seeing her. She stepped quietly out of the chicken house. She intently watched Cole, timing his movements, and each time he had his back toward her, she stole three or four steps along the wall toward the door. When he dropped a sack of grain and turned toward the truck to get another one, she froze against the boards of the wall and became stillness itself. She wished that she could fade into the wooden boards and vanish. Hugging the wall and taking a few steps at a time, she drew ever closer to the open door and the outside world where she could run to Matty.

She had almost reached the barn door when the nearer horse turned from watching Cole at the truck and saw Alice. It nickered to her. She instantly knew her danger. She bolted for the open doorway.

Cole glanced over his shoulder at the horse and saw Alice running. He dropped the sack of grain he held and sprinted to head Alice off from the door. He arrived first and spread his long arms out to block the opening.

Alice tried to halt her all out flight, but failed and slid into Cole. As his arms closed around her, a black shadow fell across her mind and she thought she would faint with fear of the man.

Chapter Eight

The Fight For Life

"Well now, how about finding you way out here," Cole said and holding Alice tightly against him. He began to chuckle with immense pleasure. He moved his hands to Alice's shoulders and held her out at arm's length and stared down at her. "This's sure my lucky day for there's no ugly Matty to interfere."

He shook his head in a disbelieving manner. "I've thought of nothing but you ever since I saw you in that line of girls in Bemiji. And that damn fool Matty wanted me to take that ugly one. But I didn't and now you're all mine."

Through her fright, Alice remembered Matty's words about Cole's brother. Struggling to get the words out, she said, "Your brother Oscar won't like it if you hurt me. You'd better let me go."

"To hell with Oscar. I can't wait. Damn it, I won't wait."

Cole lifted Alice off her feet as easily as lifting a doll, and hugging her tightly to his chest, carried her kicking and thrashing toward the pile of hay.

"That's right, girl, fight me. That always makes it sweeter."

Cole knelt in the hay and laid Alice down on her back. He straddled her and whispered. "Keep fighting me, girl, keep fighting."

He caught Alice's wrists in one of his hands and stretched her arms overhead. With his free hand, he caressed her face, tracing the outlines of her mouth with his finger tips, running them across her clenched lips, over her cheeks and across her forehead. "My, God, how smooth and soft you are."

"Let me go," Alice pleaded. Cole's touch upon her face sickened her. "Please let me go."

"I see Matty gave you some of her old clothes," Cole said as he took hold of the buckle of the belt that held Alice's trousers.

"No! No! Don't do that. Please don't do that." Alice cried out and squirming and thrashing with all her strength. Her movement brought her fingers into contact with cold iron and she recognized the iron chains of one of the horse harnesses hanging on the railing.

"You're going to be a good one." Cole said coarsely. The belt of Alice's pants came free of its buckle. He shoved the pants down to her knees. With his attention focused on tearing Alice's clothing off, his grip on her wrists loosened slightly.

With terrible fright giving strength to her arms, Alice tore her wrists free of Cole's grasps. She grabbed hold of a two foot section of the iron harness chain with both hands and lifted it high and brought it down upon Cole's head with all her might. Cole shuddered at the blow and sank down on top of Alice. He shook his head and pushed upward with his arms. Desperate, Alice hurriedly raised the chain and again struck Cole upon the head, and then again. Cole collapsed upon her.

Sobbing with fear, Alice caught Cole's limp, heavy body by the shoulders and managed to shove it partially off her. Scooting on her rump, she tore free. She climbed shakily to her feet, pulled up her pants and buckled the belt. She looked at Cole. Had she killed him?

Cole gave out a groan and his chest began to rise and fall. His eyes opened and he stared weakly around. His sight fell upon Alice and recognition of what had happened flooded across his face.

"I'm going to wring your neck," he said hoarsely, his face twisting with rage and the sure and certain intent to kill Alice. He rolled to his stomach and struggled to his knees.

Alice wanted to run, but there was no place to run and be safe from Cole. She reached for the knife in her pocket, but then halted as her eyes fell upon the pitchfork sticking in the pile of hay. The pitchfork with its strong wooden handle and five long sharp steel tines would make a better weapon. She leapt for the pitchfork and grabbed it up. Gripping the pitchfork handle fiercely, she aimed the tines at Cole and rushed at him.

Cole saw Alice and the pitchfork bearing down upon him. He came to his feet and turned to jump aside. Still half weak from the blows of the chain, he failed to move quickly enough. The slender tines penetrated his muscular side.

Cole gasped at the vast explosion of pain. He swiveled his head and saw the pitchfork imbedded in his side. His eyes jumped along the handle to Alice staring at him with fear filled eyes and clutching the pitchfork with both hands. He twisted and reached for the pitchfork to pull it from his body. His movement swung the pitchfork handle and it struck Alice in the ribs and staggered her. She clung tightly to the pitchfork, knowing that if she let go Cole would spring upon her and even badly wounded could still kill her.

She dug her feet into the barn floor, gathered all her strength and gave the pitchfork a powerful thrust. The steel tines penetrated deeper, punching a path upward inside Cole's ribcage. Two of the slender tines punctured Cole's lungs. One tine pierced his throbbing heart. Its powerful beat weakened and fluttered erratically.

Cole sank to his knees. He turned his head and stared over his shoulders with an expression of terror. His eyes found Alice. "You've killed me, you little bitch," Cole muttered with bloody bubbles from his punctured lungs bursting on his lips. His heart stopped its beat and he fell and lay in the dirt of the barn floor.

Alice felt the vibration from Cole's quivering, dying body running along the pitchfork handle and she hurriedly released her hold upon it. She began to shiver as the enormity of what she had done overwhelmed her. She sank weakly down to sit upon the ground. She had killed a man. But she was still alive.

"Oh, my God," Matty called out from the doorway of the barn. She hastened to Alice. "I saw part of what happened. And I can imagine the rest of it." She knelt and put her arms around the trembling Alice.

Alice leaned into Matty's arms. "He said he was going to kill me."

"He meant it too and deserved to die," Matty said and hugged Alice tightly.

After a time, Alice controlled her trembling body and spoke in a whisper to Matty. "Shouldn't we tell somebody what happened? Tell exactly what Cole tried to do to me?"

Matty released her hug of Alice and drew back to look into her face. "Who would we tell that'd save you? Not Oscar. He'd finish what Cole started. You're in terrible danger and you've got to get away from here as fast as you can."

"Yes, Matty, I'd like to go a long, long way from here. I could go back to England except I don't have any money."

"I have some but not enough. And anyway Oscar could catch you before you got out of the country."

"How about going to another state?"

"That won't work. Oscar would just get the law in the other state to find you and bring you back here. That'd put you in Oscar's hands." Matty fell silent, the possibilities of Alice's escaping from Oscar running through her mind. Then she spoke, "You've got to go to Canada. Other orphans have done that and were never seen or heard of again."

"How far away is Canada?"

"About a hundred miles straight north. There's one road, State Route 72 that runs all the way. But you couldn't use it for that's the first place Oscar will look for you, if he couldn't find you around here. The distance would be much further than a hundred miles, what with most of the way through deep woods with thickets and fallen trees and lakes. It could be a hundred and twenty miles, or even more. The further north you go the fewer the farms and the more woods, and so there's less chance of finding shelter. You'll have to camp in the woods most every night"

Matty clasped Alice's hands that were folded in her lap. "I think Canada would be best for you. The Mounties don't like Oscar for the way he comes into their country and arrests men and drags them back across the border without getting their permission. So they wouldn't do much to help Oscar. You can hide there. Are you game to give it a try?"

"If you think that's best, then I'll go."

"It's damn cold and the snow is deep. You'll have to walk every step of the way."

"How long will it take?"

"It'll take several days of tough hiking. And that's if you don't get lost."

"I'll walk until I find a safe place, no matter how far and how tough. And I'll stay out of peoples' sight."

"You'll need blankets and food and other things. I can outfit you with things I have at the house."

Alice pointed at Cole's corpse, its eyes open and staring and seeing nothing. "What about him?"

"I'll take care of Cole."

Chapter Nine

The Forest Of Snow

Alice walked north through the snow covered forest of huge trees. The cold was intense with the wind in her face. Every step through the ankle deep snow was an effort, and she was weary to the core. She leaned heavily on the stout walking staff she had cut from the stem of an oak sapling with her knife. Her hand, though gloved, felt frozen around the staff. Every breath of the frigid air burned her throat.

The winter sun was low in the southwestern sky. In the deep forest with each tree crowding its neighbors for space, most of the feeble light of the dying day was blocked and shadows shortened vision to but a few yards. Alice admitted to herself that she was afraid in the dark forest and was even more afraid of the blackness of the night that was but a short time away.

She anguished over the killing that she had been forced to do to save her life. Yet glad that she had been strong enough to accomplish the deed. Would she escape from Sheriff Taggert? Matty had told her that he was a cruel and vindictive man and he must surely be racing after her. Just keep walking, she told herself.

Without the compass Matty had given her, she would have been lost in the cold, silent, vastness of the forest with no sense at all of where the north bearing lay that would take her to Canada. Matty had prepared Alice for the journey. Into an old backpack that Cole had brought home with him from the time when he was a soldier in the last war, she had loaded two blankets, several cans of food, the last batch of nearly a dozen biscuits she had baked, less one that Alice had taken and hungrily eaten, a hatchet, rope, twine, matches, a piece of canvas, and a small pan. She had hung the compass around Alice's neck.

"Do you know how to use a compass," Matty had asked.

Alice nodded yes. "My father showed me how to hold it level and use the needle to find different directions."

"Good, just followed the needle north. Hide your tracks when you can. Now you'll have to cross the Red Lakes Indian Reservation. Don't let them catch you on their land for I don't know how they would treat you. You'll know when you reach Canada for the border is the Rainy River. Find a bridge to cross and keep going north."

Lastly, Matty searched and found a burlap sack that had once held feed grain for the livestock. From one, she cut broad strips of the cloth and wrapped them around Alice's boots and lower legs and tied all firmly in place with cord. She told Alice that the coarse burlap fabric would help keep her feet dry and warm, and not slip on the snow. The remainder of the burlap sack went into the pack.

Matty had given Alice a tight hug, a few dollars, and then helped her hoist the heavy pack onto her shoulders. Alice had begun the long trek north, crossing farm fields for the first few miles and then entering the forest.

She had walked steadily through the day with only a few rest periods, and a biscuit for lunch. Now it was getting late and she had to find a spot to camp before dark.

She pulled the compass out of the front of her coat and sighted along the needle and checked the north bearing. She moved off along the compass course.

Minutes later, she broke from the woods and into an open area of four or five acres. A three strand barbed wire fence ran around the border of the land, with sections of the wire sagging from rotting posts. A small log cabin stood in the middle of the snow covered clearing.

Alice checked the cabin, looking for any smoke coming from the chimney. As cold as it was, there should be a fire if somebody lived there.

After a few minutes of observing the cabin, she decided it was empty and moved into the field. The cabin would be a good place to spend the night for it would offer shelter and make a great difference in keeping warm as opposed to sleeping in the open.

The closer Alice came to the cabin the more certain she was that it was abandoned. Her spirits lifted. She had learned months ago just how important a roof over her head really was to give a degree of safety

Alice hurried to the door that stood half open. She halted and stared down at tracks in the snow. Large tracks, resembling house cat tracks but many times larger, were visible showing the animal going into the cabin and coming out.

Alice stared at the tracks. Were they made by the big cats the Americans called panthers? Dare she invade the animal's lair? The freshest tracks appeared to be those coming out and that gave her courage and she pushed the door open and entered.

The cabin was small, a single room filled with the dark shadows of coming night. A loft was close overhead. About half of it had collapsed onto the cabin floor. A hand made table and two stools were in the center of the space. A fireplace made of stone occupied most of one end of the room. A tiny window with a single pane of unbroken glass was in the front wall. The bones of rabbits, squirrels and birds of several sizes littered the floor made of hand hewn lumber. The big cat had brought its kills back to the cabin to eat. She looked in more detail at the panther's tracks and saw them in the dust on top of the table. There they were close together where the animal had gathered itself and made a long jump up into the loft. It must sleep up there, thought Alice. Tonight, she would take possession of the panther's cabin.

Alice leaned her walking staff against the wall and dropped the pack from her tired sore shoulders. She shut the door and dropped the latch into its slot. Now to build a fire and get warm.

She took the hatchet and went to the boards and supporting beams of the loft that had fallen onto the floor. After several minutes, she had cut a large pile of firewood. Using splinters of wood as kindling, she struck a match and started a fire in the fireplace. From the pack, she removed a can of pork and beans. It was frozen solid. Using her knife, she opened the can and placed it on the hearth near the fire so that the food would thaw. Once she had warm food inside her, she would feel stronger.

She carried one of the stools up close to the fireplace and sat down, pulled off her gloves and held her hands out to the flames. Wonderful, so very wonderful, she thought and rubbing her hands together in the heat of the flames. How far had she come this day? Twelve miles, maybe fifteen. Not bad considering having to walk in deep snow. Tomorrow she would have a full day and could walk a greater distance. She was thankful that she had found the cabin and had a fire. Now she had the night to rest. Tomorrow she would push herself to the limit. The sheriff would be after her and must not overtake her before she crossed the border into Canada. She hoped it would snow and hide her tracks. And that she would find other places to find shelter and sleep under a roof.

She was very thirsty. She dug the small pan from her pack and went outside and packed it with snow. This she sat on the hearth beside the can of food where the paper label was curling and charring and the food inside was beginning to steam.

She dragged the table up close to the fireplace. From the pack she took a spoon. She lifted up the can of bubbling food and sat it on the table to cool. She couldn't carry everything needed for so many days of travel and so would eat short rations until reaching Canada. She ate the beans directly from the can.

Alice looked about at the small single room of the cabin. Somebody had made a home here. Two stools told that two people, probably a man and woman, had live here. But why did they leave without their furniture? What was the real story? For some unidentifiable reason, she thought it would be a sad one.

The fire burned down and Alice stoked it with fresh wood, large pieces that would burn for hours. Near the fire she spread the canvass and the blankets. She tipped the table to lie on its side and parallel to the fireplace so that its flat top would reflect the heat from the fire back upon the blankets. She would sleep with all her clothes on with half of the blankets and canvas under her and half over her, and she would keep the fire burning all night for the temperature would fall during the darkness.

She removed her boots and held her bare feet out to the fire. The warmth felt grand. She had almost walked through the burlap that had been wrapped around the boots and she cut new pieces from the burlap sack and added a new layer to what was there. In the flickering firelight, she drew on the boots and went to the door and checked the latch, judged it a flimsy piece of wood but hoped it would keep out any intruder. She lay down on the pallet and placed the walking staff close to her side for a weapon if one should be needed.

Alice pulled the blankets and canvas down tightly around her. She lay listening to the north wind striking the side of the cabin and the rattling the wooden roof shingles as it continued its journey south. She was exhausted but still she could not sleep. She thought of the panther that had used the cabin and the other wild animals of the forest, and of Oscar who would surely kill her.

She pulled a breath of the cold cabin air and turtled her head under the blankets. As she drifted off to sleep, a loud scratching sounded on the door and a weight was thrown against it. She snapped fully awake with her heart thudding. The big cat had returned.

She leapt from her pallet, grabbed up her club and sprang to the door. She pressed her back against the door, spread her feet on the floor and pushed with all her strength to hold it shut. She must prevent the animal from breaking into the cabin.

The scratching came again, up high as if the panther was standing on its hind legs. Alice felts it weight, the door pressing against the latch and her back. The beast gave a powerful shove and uttered a guttural growl. After a handful of seconds, the panther's weight against the door fell away. There was silence for a moment, and then the panther moved off, marking its withdrawal by growls of disappointment.

Alice's fear lessened and she breathed again. She had won the battle against the big animal. A sense of pride in not panicking, in her strength and will to fight came pleasantly over her.

She returned to her bed and lay ready to spring from the blankets and again defend herself against the panther. She did not know when she went to sleep. She awoke to the fire burned low. She reached out from under the blankets and fed fresh wood to the hot coals of the fire. For a moment she thought of the cat. Then sleep again took her weary body.

Chapter Ten

The Pursuit

Oscar's powerful right hand gripped Matty's neck and held her pressed against the horse stall in the barn. His angry face was within inches of hers. At their feet lay Cole's frozen corpse. The pitchfork was still embedded in Cole's side.

"Now tell me again everything you saw and did." Oscar's voice held a venomous softness. "Leave nothing out for if you lie to me, I'll know it."

Oscar felt the woman trembling with fear and that was good. Now he watched for the steadiness of the eye that told she spoke the truth, or the blink, or that tiny change of expression that exposed the lie, or the half lie.

"It's like I told you already." Matty's voice quivered. "Cole left this morning to buy some feed for the livestock. Afterwards, the girl we took in gets up and I send her to the barn to fetch eggs for breakfast. I turn on the Victrola and listen to the music while I'm cooking. You know that I often listen to the Victrola. Because of the music, I don't hear Cole drive past the house to the barn. When the girl doesn't come with the eggs, I go to the barn to see what's keeping her. She's not there. The truck is, but not Cole. The dogs have followed me and they start barking at the pile of hay and then start digging in it. I see Cole's foot and I uncover him the rest of the way to see if he's alive. He wasn't breathing."

Matty tried to look away from Oscar but couldn't break her eyes free of his. "I saw the pitchfork stuck in his side and the blood. I didn't think she could kill him by herself so I looked around the outside of the barn in the snow to see if somebody had helped her. But there was only her tracks going off to the north. I wanted to tell you quick as I could. So I drove the truck to Bemiji to get you and bring you out here to show you."

"And?" Oscar asked. He closed his hand tighter around Matty's throat and stopped the flow of her breath. After a few seconds, he released his grip sufficiently to allow her to breathe. "I know there's more. In fact I think you kill Cole. Or helped the girl do it. Out with it."

Matty sucked in a fast breath of air, and then another. She would speak the truth for she had not helped Alice. Oscar must believe her. "Cole broke into her bedroom last night, but I talked him out of hurting her. She was terribly afraid of him. I think she saw a chance to kill him went into the barn where she was gathering eggs and rammed the pitchfork into him. I swear that's all there is to tell, Oscar. I wouldn't hurt Cole. Please don't kill me."

Satisfied that he had the true story, Oscar removed his hand from Matty's throat. "Why, Matty, what ever made you think that I was going to kill you. Be a good girl and show me those tracks that you mentioned."

"Yes. Yes, Oscar. I'll show you." Matty led Oscar to the side door of the barn through which Alice had left. She had planned the location of the tracks to agree with her story. She pointed at the tracks in the snow.

Oscar readily interpreted the tracks. "It seems you told the truth. Come with me."

He caught Matty by the arm and propelled her to his sheriff's car parked near the barn. There he opened the trunk of the car and clothed himself in a heavy wool coat and a pair of fleece lined boots. He buckled on snow shoes and settled a pack onto his shoulders.

"You take my car and drive to Bemiji and tell Sam what you told me and that I'm going to catch the girl. She's got a short head start on me of about six hours, but I've got her tracks to follow and I'll catch her late today or early tomorrow. You and Sam take care of Cole's body. You got all that?"

"Yes, Oscar, I'll tell him exactly that."

Oscar strode away to fall upon Alice's tracks. He stretched his snow shoe stride until three of his engulfed four of Alice's steps.

***

Matty sat across the desk from her nephew Sam in the Sheriff's Office in Bemiji and in a tight voice relayed to him what she had told Oscar about Cole's murder. She suddenly leaned toward Sam and her voice became sharp with anger, "Sam, Oscar choked me." She lifted her chin to show the red bruises on her throat. "He shouldn't have done that. It wasn't right."

Sam rose abruptly from his chair and stood rigid with his fists clenched. Slowly he lowered himself back into his seat. "The sonofabitch."

"That he is Sam. Now he's going to kill that girl. I'm sure Cole tried to rape the girl and somehow Alice managed to kill him with the pitchfork. But she'll never have a chance to tell a judge her story for then it would come out that Oscar and Cole killed those other two girls."

"What!" Sam was on his feet again. "What did you say?"

"They killed those two girls we took off the Orphan Train that was supposed to have run away. The one this past April and the one last year. Hid their bodies somewhere. Now after what happened to Alice, I'm sure of it."

"What makes you think that?"

"Both girls seemed happy to be with us on the farm. They laughed at my old jokes. They just seemed really happy. Then each one just disappeared without a word. Something wasn't right. I asked Cole what he thought about them being gone and he cursed me for asking and walked away."

"Why didn't you tell somebody? Tell me?"

"I was afraid for you. Jan Johansson, that deputy before you, came around once when Cole wasn't home and asked me questions about the girl that had run off in April and where was Cole when she disappeared. I told him that Cole had gone off fishing. Johansson asked me if he caught any fish. I said no, that Cole told me that they weren't biting. Shortly after that, Johansson was found dead. Now I think he made a mistake by mentioning his suspicions of Cole to Oscar. And then either Cole or Oscar killed him."

"How do you tie Oscar into this?"

"The first night Alice was here, Cole went into her bedroom. She started yelling and I went in. She had this knife in her hand and was trying to keep him off her. When I told Cole that Oscar wouldn't like him bothering the girl, he said something strange. He said that he couldn't wait for Oscar. When he said that, those two girls that disappeared came to my mind. I think Cole and Oscar together killed those two girls and buried them someplace."

"Where were you the time this last girl vanished?"

"I was visiting your mom. We hadn't seen each other for a few weeks and I drove over there to have a talk with her."

"Is there anything else that I should know?"

Matty made a hard smile. "Oscar thinks Cole was killed this morning. It was yesterday morning that it happened."

"Yesterday?"

"Yes. I wanted to give the girl a head start toward Canada. So I waited to call Oscar. I just had to for I felt responsible for her being where Cole could get his hands on her. I should never have agreed to taking her

157

in, not with all that I suspected. Sam, you've got to find that girl and keep Oscar from killing her."

"If what you've said is true, he'll kill you for lying to him."

"I've thought of that too. It would be best if he never returned. Alive anyway."

Sam ignored his aunt's suggestion.

"You ride with me in my car. Then I'll spend the night there and leave at first light."

Sam stepped to the door that led down a long hallway to the jail. He called out in a loud voice to the junior deputy who had his small office close enough to the jail to watch the prisoners. "Charlie, Oscar is after a runaway and wants me to help him catch her. I don't know how long I'll be gone. You've got the office until Oscar or I get back. It may be a few days."

"Right, Sam. I'll take care of everything."

***

Sam parked his sheriff's car at Matty's house and climbed out. Matty hurried to stand near him.

"First off, I want to see Cole's body," Sam said.

"This way," said Matty.

She led Sam to the barn and to Cole's body lying in the hay. Sam studied it for a moment.

"God damn the Taggerts to hell," Sam exclaimed.

"Amen to that," Matty spoke in a hushed voice. Then her voice became savage, "Kill Oscar, Sam. I'm afraid that if you bring him back for trial that somehow he'll not be convicted. And he'll sure find a way to kill me for testifying against him for I damn sure intend to."

"If anybody asks what Oscar and I are doing, just say we're after a runaway," Sam said and giving no sign he had heard Matty.

"All right. But hear me, nephew, I'm begging you to just kill that raping, murdering bastard."

"I'm a lawman, Aunt Maddy."

"Then that is even more reason to do justice for these poor little girls. Now you do it. Hear me!"

Sam turned and stared north. He thought of the girl Alice running north through the woods with Oscar closing on her. Make the right choice when you overtake Oscar, he told himself.

***

Alice leaned against the broad trunk of the pine tree and rested. This was the evening of the second day and for the last several hours she had seen no sign that humans had ever been here. Nothing moved within her view, and the total stillness of the dense forest held an eeriness, a threatening presence. She knew nothing of forests for her life had been one of towns with houses and people always within a shout. She wished that she had somebody with her to lessen the aloneness she felt so sharply.

She looked about at the forest where the big trees were elbowing each other for space. A little poem came to her.

> Forest, oh forest,
> You know not what you do,
> Open up an avenue,
> And let me pass through.

She struck off through the trees. In the edge of night, and where the thick forest met the shore of a frozen lake, Alice made her camp near a large dead pine tree that had fallen to the ground. As the tree fell, it had struck a live pine and stripped the limbs from one side. Now the trunk of the dead tree and the green boughs of the live tree lay in a shattered mass. The great abundance of readily available firewood caused her to stop the laborious journey through the forest.

She built a fire of hot burning pine knots and warmed her cold body and thawed a can of food for the evening meal. She ate the simple fare standing close to the fire, and finished the meal with water from melted snow.

Alice gathered a large quantity of wood and placed it where it would be available to keep the fire burning during the night. Then exhausted, she sat down upon the pile of wood and removed her gloves and boots and held her hands and feet out to the fire. She examined a chafed area on her right heel. She examined her boot and, and finding the rough spot that had caused the rubbing, smoothed it with her knife.

Close by the fire, she leveled a place in the carpet of needles beneath the live pine and made her bed of canvas and blankets. Then using limbs from the pine, she constructed a crude lean-to, copying a picture of one she had once seen in a book, with its open front facing the fire and so would guide its heat upon her bed.

She took a seat on the wood pile and stared out across the snow covered the lake. Not far away on the lake surface, the wind picked up a skein of snow many yards long and spun it away in a miniature snow storm. Farther away, the dark line of the forest on the opposite shore of the lake was visible. She judged the distance two miles. In the north, storm clouds were moving upon her. She shivered; the night would be a cold one.

Alice sat wearily in the warmth of the fire as the black wave of the night crept closer and objects lost their form. Gradually the last fleeting memories of daylight fled from the forest. Out on the lake, the snow became but a lighter shade of darkness.

Alice did not like the darkness. She raised her eyes and looked to the eastern horizon where the edge of a full moon had appeared. She wished the moon was up high enough to give her light for the cold didn't seem to bite so harshly when she could see around her. It would take several hours for the moon to reach the middle of the sky where its light could reach her in the woods.

She turned back to the fire where the leaping flames chased her shadow back and forth over the trunks of the close by trees. In the openings between the trees, her shadow vanished, swallowed by the night's blackness. A puff of wind came down from the sky and made the flames dance wildly and tore sparks from the ashes and sent them streaking off like brilliantly colored butterflies among the boles of the trees. Alice inched closer to the fire.

***

Alice awoke with cold fingers seeming to stroke her cheeks. She thought she had heard somebody whispered her name. She opened her eyes and stared out into the small bubble of light created by the flames of her campfire. The forest was full of wind and falling snowflakes. The trees swayed to the push of the wind and a multitude of snowflakes swirled about. Snowflakes had been blown in beneath the lean-to and upon her cheeks. She brushed them away.

"Alice," a low, whispery voice spoke. Though Alice barely heard the word, the voice sounded like her mother's. It seemed to be coming from a far distance. She sat up and held her breath, listening.

"Alice," the voice spoke again and it held urgency.

Alice's heart surged for the voice was indeed that of her mother. More than that, she felt the presence of her mother. Could that really be?

"Mother, is that you?" Alice whispered and staring hard into the wind tormented fall of snow.

Alice sensed the presence of her mother growing stronger, a presence just there close by and hidden by the snow. "Mother, let me see you." Alice spoke more strongly and willed the loving presence into being. "Talk to me!"

The wind's eddies and currents and the snowflakes that rode upon them slowed and moved in a measured way. The snowflakes began to congregate and to form a pattern against the tall pine tree on the opposite side of the fire. The wind shook the top of the tree where the branches were most heavily laden with snow and they shed their burdens. The falling snow struck the branches below and triggered them to drop their snow. Down and down the snow fell, its quantity swelling and spreading. The wind took possession of part of the cascading snow and added it to the snow patterns that it was drawing. The remaining snowflakes formed a white curtain against the pine.

Alice gasped for the figure of a woman wearing a long, rippling dress that reached below her feet, had taken form suspended in the wind's snow filled currents in front of the pine tree. Her arms were ribbons of downward pouring snow. Her hands and fingers were splayed strips of falling snow. A wavering snow face took shape, a brow, nose and eyes, and all tinted by the light of the fire to give it substance. The face held a haunted and worried expression. Alice recognized her mother in the spectral being.

"Alice," the snow and wind figure whispered.

The figure was not Alice's imagination for she had seen the mouth move. She must go and talk with her mother. She cast off the blankets and canvas that covered her and crawled out from the lean-to and into the wind and snow and the awful cold. The air that had had all scent frozen out of it before was suddenly full of the fresh smell of pine. She circled the fire and wondering was this truly happening, or was she dreaming. Her footsteps slowed and she hesitantly drew close to the figure held by the wind against the pine tree.

"I'm here, mother," Alice said shakily, and looking up at the snow face that resembled her mother's, but blurred.

Alice listened to the voice that held the sigh of the wind and the soft whisper of falling snow. Some of the words were difficult to understand for they were distorted and rose and fell in volume. As she concentrated to hear, she feared that this was all imagination or a dream and not really happening. Still the voice was that of her mother and she could not close her eyes or refuse to hear. The voice ceased to speak and the arm that was made of a stream of snowflakes, swung out toward her.

Alice hesitated but a moment and then reached out to take hold of the extended hand. Even as she moved, the hand and wrist unraveled into hundreds of snowflakes and fell away. The stump of the arm withdrew.

Alice hastily pulled her hand back. Even as she did so, the hand of the figure began to reform with snow streaming down the arm from the shoulder. The hand did not offer itself again.

Alice looked up at the face of the figure and saw its mouth move.

"Danger," the voice whispered with its volume frail and fading.

Alice turned her head left and right, straining to hear the voice that was rapidly weakening, seemingly coming from an ever greater distance. Then all that Alice could hear was the sighing of the wind and the whisper of falling snow. The dress and arms of the snowflake figure elongated, stretching down to touch the ground. The face flattened and tore diagonally from the left forehead to the right edge of the mouth. The body became translucent, then transparent with the pine tree behind showing through. The ethereal figure blended into the falling snow and became but part of the multitude of snowflakes riding on the ever-changing currents of the wind.

Alice stood staring at the pine tree with its branches catching snow and bowing to the wind. Had the spirit of her dead mother crossed from the spirit world and created a body from the snow and wind so as to be able to warn her of danger? That seemed impossible, and yet Alice could not deny what she had seen and heard.

The glacial wind buffeted Alice and cut through her clothing, and her thoughts. She wrapped her arms about herself and hurried back to the lean-to, where she stooped and crawl under its roof of pine boughs.

Had she really seen the spirit of her mother, really heard her voice? Or had the killing and the hours of flight through the cold, snowy forest affected her reasoning?

It was not my imagination. Alice hardened that thought in her mind. It was her mother warning that a man who wanted to harm her was close. And she must leave and hurry on.

Alice had been going straight north. Come daylight, she would go left, to the west, for a ways, maybe two miles, and then turn back north toward the Canada. With the new snow hiding her footprints, Oscar wouldn't be able to follow her. Now she must rest and sleep. She slid underneath the covers. Her mother was watching over her. Alice smiled for the very first time in days.

***

Alice shouldered her pack, and propelling herself along with her walking staff, went out onto the snow and ice covered lake just as the first rays of the sun fell upon it. Nothing moved upon that broad expanse of frozen white for the wind had ceased to blow and the snow to fall. Behind her on the shore, the tops of the snow laden trees glowed carmine in the rising morning sun and lied about being warm. In the north sky, a huge mass of dark storm clouds was driving swiftly upon her. She must hurry and reach the far side of the lake before the storm fell upon her.

She moved off across the ice, her sore muscles aching. On the snow, the shadows of her legs mimicked her every step. Oh, if only her real legs could move so easily.

***

Alice had barely passed mid-point of the lake when the storm fall upon her like a white, billowing curtain traveling swiftly with its top farther advanced than the bottom and overhanging the lake. The far shore with its green pine forest vanished within the whiteness. Half a minute later, the lake in front of her disappeared and a powerful wind struck her in the face with a wall of snow and a cold so biting that she gasped and halted and turned her back to it.

She could freeze to death on the lake with no shelter. She had to get into the trees on the shore where the wind would not be so strong and she could build a fire. She could not see and must follow the compass. She pulled it from inside her coat, and with her face angled down to protect it from the lash of the glacial wind and the sting of the icy snow flakes, moved off at a right angle to the compass's north pointing needle and toward the nearest woods.

Alice plowed ahead with the deep snow trying to trip her and the wind slamming her about. Tears were torn tears from her eyes and froze upon her cheeks. She had been cold before, but never like this. She had to find shelter soon or she would surely die.

***

Alice raised her head from watching the compass and threw a look ahead into the wind and snow. She jerked, startled, for not but a score of steps away and inside the edge of the forest, a big fire blazed orange and yellow. She had stumbled upon somebody's camp.

A man stood on the far side of the leaping flames of the fire and watched her. He wore a long sheepskin coat with the fleece turned inside and a fleece lined cap pulled low on his head until only his eyes showed. Snow lay thick upon his shoulders and head. He stared directly at her.

For a frightening moment, Alice feared the man was the sheriff and he had somehow gotten ahead of them. Then through a break in the thick snow, she saw the face of a young man, not much older than Alice.

"Who in the hell are you?" the fellow shouted out in a challenging voice.

"Somebody who needs to share your fire," Alice called back. The fellow was a stranger, but stranger or not, she must have a fire.

"Well come on in. The fire don't care who it warms." The fellow motioned with his left hand. He held his right hand hidden behind his leg.

Alice moved ahead and halted near the fire. She leaned her staff against her shoulder and, using her teeth, pulled the gloves off her stiff, frozen hands and held them out to the wondrous heat of the flames. She scrutinized the young man. He was quite slender. The coat was too large for him and he had it cinched in around his lean body with a leather belt. Knee high boots protected his feet from the snow and cold. His head was somewhat narrow with a large, high nose and a large mouth. His eyes, large for his thin face, held a worried, alert expression.

The young man scowled at Alice. "Now who the hell are you?" he questioned in a rough tone.

"My name is Alice."

"What's your name?" Alice asked.

"Call me Will," the young man said and kept a sharp focus on Alice. "Where in hell you going in a storm like this'n?"

"I'm headed north to Canada."

Will gave Alice a knowing grin. "That's what I suspected. That's where most of the runaways go."

"Where're you heading in the same storm?" Alice asked.

"The same place." Will brought a revolver into view from behind his leg and held it up for Alice to see. "For a time there in the snow I thought you might be somebody chasing me. I don't intend to let anybody take me back south."

"You'd use a gun to stop somebody from doing that?"

"If I had to. And I'm a good shot." Will cocked the revolver and then lowered the hammer. "I'm betting you're a girl off the Orphan Train and now running off to Canada because people are mean to you and hit you."

"I'd say you're one of those too."

"People learn quick not ever to hit me." Will waved the pistol up at the wind tossed pine boughs above his head.

Alice watched Will's display with the gun. Had he committed a crime? Had he killed someone, as she had done? She must not think about what she had done.

"Is anybody chasing you for something you done back there?" Alice asked.

"Haven't seen anybody chasing me."

"That's not what I asked."

"That's my answer."

Will studied Alice. "You've got the smell of bad luck."

"You do too," Alice said, not to be outdone.

"I was good luck to you what with my fire when you needed one."

"True enough and I won't deny it."

Alice hoped Will wasn't as violent as he acted. She tightened her grip upon her walking staff. She would use it as a club if the need was forced upon her.

Will's scowl lessened at Alice's admittance of his help and he spoke more friendly. "You're going to need something to keep the wind and snow off you. If you got a hatchet or something to cut with, I'll help you built a lean-to there beside mine on the up-wind side of the fire." He shoved the revolver into a side pocket of his coat.

Alice dropped her pack and dug out the hatchet. With its sharp blade, the hatchet would make a deadly weapon. Keeping a wary eye on Will, she began to chop branches off the nearby pines. They gathered the branches up and carried them close to the fire. Then working together, they constructed a lean-to adjacent to Will's, and as near the fire as they dared and not be burned.

Alice placed the last of the pine boughs in a mat under the structure to sit on and keep her bottom off the snow. She took up her pack, stooped, ducked her head and entered the lean-too and seated herself. She extended her cold feet out to the fire.

Will took a seat in the entrance of his shelter, and there hunched his shoulders to shield a pouch of tobacco from the wind and rolled a cigarette. He popped a wooden match into flame with a thumbnail and lit the cigarette.

"You want a smoke?" Will asked and holding the pouch of tobacco out to Alice.

"No. I don't smoke."

"That's the best for a poke of tobacco cost ten cents. And girls shouldn't smoke anyway."

They sat without talking and the pine trees around them bucking and bowing and their limbs thrashing and the snow slanting down in a torrent of white on all sides. Snowflakes fell into the fire where they boiled and hissed for an instant and vanished.

A swift burst of wind reached down through the trees and rode up over the sloping back sides of the two shelters and struck the fire. The tall flames bent and flattened and stretched long downwind and spat a multitude of red sparks out over the ice imprisoned lake.

"The storm acts like it'll last a while," Will said.

"Looks that way," Alice replied.

"I'm going to sleep for a while and wait for the storm to stop," Will said. He crawled into his lean-to.

Alice remained silent. She was exhausted and cold, but dare she close her eyes and rest with not knowing the character of the fellow?

She spread the canvas and blankets upon the mat of pine boughs. Placing the hatchet ready to her hand, she pulled the covers over her and lay facing the fire. Her eyelids felt as if lead weights were pulling them down. She would close her eyes and rest just for a moment. She went instantly to sleep.

***

Alice awoke shivering with the cold. She twisted about and peered out from under the shelter. The snow had stopped falling. The wind had raced off to some distant place and the pine trees surrounding the camp stood rigid in the intense cold. Wood smoke lay in a thin, motionless gray fog between the lowest limbs of the pine trees and the snowy ground. The fire had burned itself away too only a pile of coals frosted with grayish ash.

She turned to Will's shelter. He appeared to be sleeping soundly and that was a good thing for he had worried her. However it seemed that he meant her no harm regardless of his tough talk.

She rolled out from under the lean-to and tossed fresh wood upon the bed of coals. Flames, waiting only to be awakened, sprang to life. She threw on more wood and the flames greedily ate and grew to stand tall in the windless day.

Alice spread her cold hands out to the flames and listened to their crackling talk as she looked at the lake wearing a wave tossed covering of snow drifts. The stiff polar wind had performed a Herculean task of creating snow drifts tall as Alice's chest and many yards long. Every drift was aligned north to south. In the alleyways between the drifts, the snow lay but thinly, and in many places the ice had been swept clean. She noted a frequent linking of one snow free area with another. Her eyes turned upward to the sky that held a hard blue color, and then to the south where the sun was small and pale and gave no warmth to the frozen forest and lake.

She called out to Will. "The storm is over."

Will sat up and tossed off his blankets. He sat for a time and silently looked at Alice. "We're going in the same direction. You want to go with me. I'm strong and can help you. And I'd like somebody to talk with."

Alice silently considered the proposition. He seemed friendly enough and he had made no trouble for her as she had slept. She admitted to herself, that she wanted somebody to travel with, to share the dangers that must lie ahead. Also, she judged him strong even with his slenderness.

"I can help you fight off the wolves." Will said, as if reading her thoughts.

"Are you trying to scare me?"

"No. Just telling you the truth."

"I'll go with you until we cross the border."

"You're a stout girl," Will said and for the first time he smiled at Alice.

"Not so stout." Then to herself, just scared of who might be close behind me.

Alice pointed at the lake. "Why don't we travel on the lake for the wind has blown snow off in places. That'll make for easier walking than through the woods."

Will scrutinized the lake with its snow drifts. "That'll work just fine for Canada is straight north up the lake."

They gathered their possessions quickly. Walking abreast in the snow free pathways, they struck out over the ice.

***

Alice was exhausted, her legs rubbery and breath coming hard. She was terribly cold. Using the channels between the snow dunes, they had walked for miles across the frozen lake. At times they were forced to laboriously break through a tall drift to get to another snow-free pathway leading north.

"I've got to rest for a minute," she called to Will. "Just for a minute," she added for she did not like to complain.

Will looked at Alice's taut, strained face and halted. Not once had she complained at the fast pace he had set. She was a good companion and he should have been watching her more closely. "All right. We've come a fair distance."

***

The two journeyers were still far out upon the frozen lake and searching for paths through the snow drifts when the sun rolled down its ancient sky path and hid below the rim of the world. The ice covered lake filled with dusk. The cold deepened.

Will called to Alice. "It's getting dark. But we'll have the North Star to guide us when it shows."

Alice looked at the north sky where night was birthing. She murmured to herself.

> Oh, North Star,
> Hear our plight.
> Surrender the day
> Come early tonight
> To Guide our way,
> Oh, North Star.

She would write the poem down in her book so as to remember it. One day in the future, she would read the little poems to her children and tell them about her adventures, should she have a future and children.

Alice struggled on while the sky darkened and the first big evening star came out. Her spirits rose as a few minutes later Will pointed at the sky.

"There's the North Star. Can you see it Alice?"

Alice looked up into the sky, and as her father had taught her, found the Big Dipper and the two stars of the dipper's cup that pointed at the North Star. "Yes, I see it. I'm always surprised at how small it is."

"It's not much of a star, that's the truth."

They set their course to bear on the star. A weary distance later, Alice could see the shore of the lake. They trudged on and reached the land. A treeless area lay before them, its size hidden by darkness. A line of wooden post supporting a three strand barbed wire fence blocked their entry upon the land.

"We should be close to the Red Lake Indian Reservation," Will said. "Maybe on the other side of that fence. I don't know what the Indians would do to us if they caught on their land."

"We won't let them catch us," Alice said.

"That'd sure be best."

"I smell smoke," Alice said and smelling the air. "There has to be a fire someplace close." A fire meant warmth, if they were allowed to come close. She looked through the darkness lying upon the snow covered land. A tiny yellow pinpoint of light showed far away.

"There's a house out there for I see a light," she called out and pointed. "Let's go and see if we can find a place to sleep tonight before I freeze to death."

"I see it too."

Will pressed down the top wire of the fence and stepped over. The fence was too tall for Alice to step over. She lay down and scooted under the bottom strand. Will helped her to her feet and brushed the snow off her. As they went into the field, the full moon lifted its round head above the forest in the east and its light fell upon the field of snow and turned it into a shimmering plain of silver. They waded onto the silver plain.

***

Alice and Will slowed as the point of light they had seen from the lake, grew into an orange square of lamplight in a window of a small frame house. A small stream of smoke rose from the stone chimney. A barn, silhouetted against the snow covered land, was close by the house. The lowing of a cow came from the barn.

"The people will have finished all their chores by now and be in the house," Will said in a low voice. "Since they have livestock, there'll be hay for us to use as a bed. I hope they don't have an ornery dog."

"Me too," Alice said. "We should wait until they've gone to sleep and maybe they won't see or hear us go into the barn."

They waited with the cold deepening. On the snow, the barn shadow and the house shadow and their own thin shadows shortened as the moon climbed higher. An orange shooting star passed overhead and vanished silently in the void of the north. Alice hardly noticed the streak of fire for her legs were growing ever weaker and she was wobbly on her feet and she stood erect only by propping herself up with the staff.

"I wish they'd go to bed," Alice whispered. Even as the last word left her lips, the lamplight in the window went black.

"I'll be damned, Alice, you're a witch. Now let's have a look in the barn."

They crept over the snow to the barn. The door made a low grinding sound on its hinges as Will pushed it open and closed it behind them. He struck a match and held it up to see the barn interior. A tan cow was in a small section of the barn and a team of black horses in a second, larger section. In the open part of the barn was a horse drawn hay mower, a hay rake, a wagon and a sled. Various farm tools lay on a work bench, or hung on wooden pegs on the walls. Hay lay in a mound in the loft.

"There's plenty of hay to make us a good bed."

"That'll be better than the pine limbs we've been sleeping on," Alice replied.

Will doused the match that had burned down to his fingers and the barn went dark. He struck another.

"I want to check something."

Will walked slowly toward the cow that watched him with large, liquid brown eyes reflecting the match. "Easy, Old Jerse," he called to her as he stepped over the railing of the partition and into her portion of the barn. As he drew even closer, he blew the match out so as not to frighten the cow with its flame.

He touched the cow's side with his bare hand and ran it down her ribs and flank and then lower and felt her bag-like udder. He squeezed the closer of the four teats. He licked his fingers and began to chuckle softly.

"Alice, how would you like to have fresh milk for supper?" he called out through the darkness of the barn.

"How could we have that?" Alice had a sudden yearning for a glass of milk.

"The cow is giving milk. I'm sure she was milked earlier this evening but she has made more by now. She's a jersey and they have the richest milk."

"I wonder where the calf is," Alice said. "Do you think they ate it?"

"Probably sold it for cash. These small farmers always need cash."

"What can we use to catch the milk?"

"I have a tin cup we can use." Will dug into his pack and drew out the cup.

Will knelt and began to milk the cow. Alice heard the streams of milk rattle on the cup.

Will halted his effort and turned to Alice. "Here, you drink first."

"Thanks." Alice took the offered cup and lifted it to her mouth. She drank hastily, shivering with delight, her taste buds strumming with the taste of the sweet, warm milk heavy with fat that her starving body craved. A cow hair came into her mouth and she isolated it with her tongue and spit it out. The cow hair had no importance when compared to her hunger. She drank the last of the milk.

She handed the cup to Will. "Your turn."

"Right."

Will began to milk, the squirts of milk rattling against the tin of the cup.

Alice rose to her feet and stepped away. Will was turning out to be a good traveling companion. A poem came to her.

> A shared hate made friends of strangers
> A shared fear made friends of strangers
> She thought of Cole Taggert and added
> Hate gave you strength
> Hate gave you courage
> Hate made you cherish love

She would remember the poem, and when and where it had come to her.

Alice moved close to the cow's shoulder and dug her fingers deeply into the thick winter hair and down to the skin and pressed them tightly there to absorb the warmth of the living heat. She stood thus, hearing the squirt of milk and then Will swallowing the richness and knowing his great pleasure at the food. She could still taste her own feast of the liquid goodness of the cow. She leaned her weary head upon the Jersey's hairy shoulder and rested.

***

Alice and Will slept in the hay mow of the old barn. Throughout the night the walls and roof creaked with the cold and the cow and horses stomped and moved about. In the morning twilight, hungry and stiff with cold, they stole from the barn and closed the door.

Alice was surprised to see the moon still in the sky. It had driven its course across the night sky and now rested as a large, glistening silver-gold sphere on the western horizon. She lowered her eyes to look at the house, about the size of her home in England. Along the front of the house was a large flower bed with the dead heads of several types of flowers sticking above the snow. A fair size garden surrounded by a woven wire fence was to the left of the house. An orchard of at least a dozen leafless fruit trees stood evenly spaced one from another in a neat square just beyond the garden. Now in the dead of winter, the farm appeared bleak and cold and lonely.

"Best we hurry on before the farmer wakes up and sees us," Will said.

They struck off over the snow covered field north of the house. As they entered the forest on the far side, Alice looked to the rear. A person trailed by a dog was walking from the house to the barn. They had barely escaped being caught trespassing.

They forged a trail in the deep snow through the long forenoon of the day. In the afternoon, they came upon a lake. They left the dark tunnels of the forest and went out upon the flat, frozen surface with its wind hammered snowdrifts. They took a course near the right hand shore. As evening dusk built in the east, dense snow began to fall, large snowflakes fluttering down like small, white birds that had frozen to death while flying in the cold air. A north wind came alive and pushed the snowflakes into their cold faces.

Alice raised a hand to brush away snowflakes that had attached themselves to her eyelashes. As she lowered the hand, she caught movement on her right and turned hastily. The grayish brown forms of several deer were in a brush thicket not far off. Every animal was watching the two journeyers.

They moved on for a ways when Will halted and stared ahead through the falling snow. "Alice, I think I see buildings off there on the shore of the lake."

Alice looked where Will indicated. "Yes, yes. I see them too," she exclaimed.

"It's a logging camp for I see big piles of logs. And men are there for I can see smoke. We'll try to buy some food from them."

"It's nearly dark and the wind is growing stronger. Maybe they'll let us sleep inside where it's warm."

"I sure hope so. Let's go and ask them."

Will strode off with long strides. Alice hurried to keep up.

The daylight faded swiftly and the logging camp began to lose its form and to blend into the great piles of logs that lay about it. The logs in turn were fading into the dark forest where night had arrived early.

"It's going to be dark before we can get there," Will called out.

Alice did not respond. She needed all of her breath for the arduous task of keeping up with the long steeping Will.

In the black forest not a quarter mile off in the forest, a cacophony of barks, yaps, and howls rose shrill and penetrating on the cold, dense air. She halted abruptly, startled by the explosion of sound.

"What's that," she cried out.

Will stopped and faced about. "That's wolves rounding up their pack for a hunt. They're the first we've heard. Sounds like there are about five or six of them. I've been told that the farther north we go the more wolves we'll hear."

Alice stood transfixed by the wild, strident cries rushing unbound from among the giant pines and out onto the lake. As she listened to the voices, the volume rapidly increased and she feared the wolves themselves were racing from the darkening forest and upon her. Then she realized that was not so, that the greater loudness was caused by additional wolves joining the outcry.

As Alice listened to the wolves' voices, their barks and yaps and howls combined into a harmonious melding of pitch and tone and volume that resembled a human yodeling, a surprisingly pure sound that was truly pleasant. She cupped her ears in her hands and leaned in the direction of the source of the song. As she eavesdropped upon the wolves, her fear of them lessened and she sensed the kinship each of them must have for all the others, and their readiness for the hunt.

The joining of animal voices into the enjoyable vocal sound held for a slow count of six. Then the synchronization of the many voices broke apart and once again they were but a clamoring of barks and yaps and howls of the wolf pack. The volume lessened and then the last yap sounded and silence fell upon the forest. Alice pictured the wolves, ready for the chase and the kill, loping off over the snow led by their leader, a large, strong animal.

Alice silently composed a poem to remember this strange event.

> I hear the wolf's wild lament.
> The savage bite is his passion.
> I hear him howl his wild intent.
> The starry sky echoes his obsession.

Before she slept tonight, she would write the poem in her little book.

"Alice, we must hurry while we can still see."

They pushed into the wind with snow falling more heavily. As they drew closer to the camp, men were seen coming from the forest and entering the larger of the buildings.

Chapter Eleven

The Logging Camp

Will rapped on the stout wooden door of the building at the logging camp and waited for a response from those inside with their fire. Nobody came to open the door. He knocked more loudly and waited and still no one responded.

"Hit it hard and make them hear," Alice called out as she leaned her shoulder against the log wall of the building to keep from being blown down by the powerful wind. She was freezing and hungry and exhausted.

As Will raised his fist to hammer the door, it swung away and a tall, rawboned man with a reddish beard stood in the opening. He peered through the snowflakes streaming past and swept Will and Alice with a quick appraisal.

"What the hell!" he exclaimed. "Come in. Come in." Immediately he reached out his big hands and caught Will by the arm and Alice by the front of her coat and dragged them inside the building. He kicked the door shut.

"It's not fit for man nor beast to be outside on a day like this." The man said in a hearty voice. "Hustle yourselves over to the stove and get thawed out." He motioned at the huge iron heating stove in the middle of the spacious room.

Alice was astonished, but pleased by the man's vigorous welcoming. She leaned her staff against the wall and trailed closely behind Will toward the stove, feeling its increasing warmth, a physical force touching her cold body. She wanted to smile, however her face was too cold and stiff for that, and so the smile got no further than her thankful heart.

She and Will took a vacant space among the three men sitting around the stove with their feet propped up on a metal ring surrounding its bottom and a foot off the floor. The men appeared to have been awakened from snoozes. Alice stripped off her gloves and unbuttoned her coat and held it open so that the heat could get to her shivering body.

She sensed the presence of other people in the room and looked about its spacious interior that was both a barracks and a work room. She saw a score or so of bearded men, dressed in heavy woolen shirts and trousers, scattered about in various situations. Every man in the room had halted what he had been doing and now Alice and Will were the focus of their attention. Their eyes held curiosity, a wondering as to how these two young people had suddenly entered their province.

Alice smelled the odors of the room, pine wood smoke, tobacco smoke and unwashed bodies, and the oil used to waterproof leather boots, and other scents faint and stale that she could not identify. She caught a whiff of food being cooked and her mouth moistened.

"I'm Jack Dawson and the camp boss. What might you two be named?"

"I'm Alice." She was going to speak for herself from now on.

"My name is Will."

"You're not lost, are you?"

"No, we're not lost."

"And where might you be leading you?"

"North to Canada," Alice replied.

"Well, you're almost there. About ten more will get you to the Rainy River that marks the border. But don't try to cross the river on the ice. The river flows fast and the ice is thin in places. You'll have to find the bridge on State Route 72 to cross, and it's off to the west of us about four miles."

"My-o-my, what do we have here?" Two Doves asked from the doorway of the kitchen. She was wiping her hands on a white apron tied about her waist.

"Two Doves, meet Alice and Will. They're going to stay for supper and spend the night with us." He looked at the two. "Isn't that right?"

Both nodded quick agreement.

"That's just fine for I've cooked plenty of food," Two Doves said in a hearty voice. "Alice, why don't you come into the kitchen? Its warm and you can wash up there."

"Thank you," Alice said. "I would like to clean up a bit."

"Then come along. Jack, have your dirty loggers wash up for supper." Two Doves led Alice into the kitchen.

Alice followed the short, broad woman with a large bosom and well rounded hips, and clothed in a brightly flowered springtime dress. The woman was half a hand shorter than Alice.

In the kitchen Two Doves dipped warm water from a reservoir attached to the end of the cooking stove and filled a washbasin nearly full. This she placed on a wash stand where there was a bar of soap in a small dish, a towel and a mirror on the wall.

"Help yourself," Two Doves said and gesturing at the washbasin.

Alice removed her coat and cap and hung them on the hook fastened to the wall near the wash stand. She examined her face in the mirror and saw that the wind and cold and her weariness made her appear older than she was. She scrubbed her hands and face with warm, soapy water, and dried them on the towel. She combed her tangled yellow hair as best she could with her fingers.

***

At Two Dove's call, the loggers filed into the kitchen and took seats around the long rectangular table. Two Doves guided Alice to a seat between Will and Jack at the end of the table, and then hurried off to her kitchen. Will gave Alice a quick, short smile showing his pleasure at being warm and about to feast.

Alice gazed upon the table where three coal oil lamps, one of outsize dimensions, sat in a row along the center and illuminated the large bowls of steaming venison stew, sliced ham upon a platter, large loaves of hot bread on cutting boards, dried apple pies in their metal pans, black coffee and cans of rich condensed milk to enrich it and sugar in bowls to sweeten it. The rich aroma of the food overwhelmed Alice in her hunger and she felt faint. She fought the weakness and filled her plate as the food was passed around the table and came to her. As was her habit, she ate slowly, chewing the food thoroughly and savoring the flavor to the utmost.

The men ate with gusto, their forks and spoons rattling against the crockery as they dipped and ladled food. She glanced up once from her plate and noted that Will was eating as sturdily as the loggers, and that brought a smile to her face.

Alice finished her food and looked about at the men. All had finished eating and had lit their pipes or cigarettes and were puffing away and creating a cloud of smoke. Their brushy beards and the squint marks around their eyes from staring into wind and sun, and the obvious strength in their muscular bodies, confirmed their occupation as woodsmen.

Her attention was drawn to the extra-large oil lamp that was directly in front of her in the center of the table. In the globe made of thin, clear glass, a golden flame rose in a broad, shallow U from the end of the wick. The warm air surrounding the hot globe was rising and spinning in a counter-clockwise vortex some one foot in diameter. The column of air was drawing in the gray smoke of the men's tobacco and every strand and thread of it was distinct. Upon striking the ceiling, the rotating column fragmented into a formless mixture of smoky air.

Jack noticed Alice fascination with the lamp. "The lamp makes that whirling smoke when a pretty girl eats at the table."

Alice blushed. "I don't believe that at all," she murmured.

"It's the total truth. Ask any man here."

Every man's heads, save Will's, nodded sagely in affirmation of Jack's statement.

Two Doves had come from the stove with a steaming coffee pot. "It's the truth," she said with a laugh. "When I first came here, I was much younger and just a slender slip of a girl, it swirled like that for me."

A great roar of laughter erupted around the table. "True, true, for I was here when it happened," one of the loggers shouted out.

"Now let the girl drink her coffee in peace" Two Doves directed and tipped her pot and poured Alice a cup full of the black brew.

"And, Jack," Two Doves continued, "when you're done eating, move one of the empty bunks into the kitchen near my bed. Alice can sleep there."

"Right, good idea" Jack said.

"I thought so," said Two Doves. She turned away to her work at the stove.

The men took up their coffee mugs and streamed off into the barracks. Alice remained at the table and sipping her coffee. She was reluctant to leave Two Doves and go into the barracks with the men. But why should she be? She rose and walked into the barracks and to the heating stove.

The woodsmen sat about the room drinking their coffee, smoking and talking in deep, rumbling voices that filled the space. At Alice's entrance, they ceased talking and focused on her. In the weaker lamp-light of the big room the loggers watched her with eyes hidden in dark caves beneath their brows. Thought she could not read what was in their minds, their expressions, those of the younger men especially, caused her cheeks to warm and she knew she was blushing. She felt not ready for what they were thinking. Still, she had read that in some countries girls became married as young as eleven and twelve.

Alice was tired of running from men. Whatever these woodsmen were thinking wasn't going to drive her away from the heating stove. She seated herself on a chair beside Will who sat with his weary head lowered and half asleep. She watched the leaping flames of the fire through the little clear mica windows in the door of the stove.

Jack and another man passed by carrying a bunk bed. "The kitchen is Two Dove's country," Jack said to Alice. "And no one goes in there without her permission." With those words, Alice knew Jack understood her plight and was telling her that she would be safe there.

***

Alice, with weariness pressing her eyelids closed, had nodded off in the grand warmth of the big cast iron stove when a loud crash filled the room as the outside door was flung inward and slammed against the wall. The frigid wind rushed into the room and swarmed over the occupants and fueled the flames in the stove and they roared out with a thunderous WHUMP that set the stovepipe vibrating and rattling and ready to tear itself to pieces.

She jerked awake at the cascade of noise and whirled to look at the source of the wind. A billowing cloud of snowflakes had blown into the room and blocked her view of the doorway. A shadowy figure moved within the cloud and the door closed. The fog of snowflakes, now cut off from its supply, settled speedily and a man in a long wolf skin coat with a hood hiding his face became visible. A bulky pack was strapped to his back, a roll of furs was clamped under his left arm, and a rifle hung over his right shoulder. A large gray dog was close on his left.

The last snowflakes fell and lay upon the barracks floor. Paul Bouc-card, his shoulders, hood and backpack thickly covered with snow, stood upon the white layer of snow. More snow fell in a shower as he dropped the furs from under his arm and flung back the hood of the coat. He smiled with a broad show of teeth and surveyed the room.

Alice was astounded by the obvious goodwill that showed so bright-ly in the young man as he bestowed his magnificent smile upon the room's occupants one after the other. He seemed to be sharing with them his own peace of mind, his delight in the world and where he was at the moment. She caught herself up, wasn't she reading too much into him?

"Paul, come in out of the cold," Jack called and moved across the room to greet Paul.

"I already have, thank you, Jack," Paul replied in a joking tone.

"Night almost caught you out in the storm," Jack said.

"It did catch me and with all the snow blowing about it's pitch black out there. But I had Brutus to guide me and he never gets lost."

He signaled Brutus into a stay position. Brutus sank down to sit on his haunches, and began to observe the humans with their sharp body scents.

Paul moved half a dozen steps into the room, and then his sight came upon Alice and his smile widened in utmost wonderment at the vision of a golden haired girl in the logging camp. He snatched off the billed cap that he wore under the hood of his coat. Without consciously deciding to do so, he bowed to the beauty of the girl.

As he straightened, a man's voice burst forth loud with fury. "There's that goddamn dog that bit me. I'm going to chop him into mincemeat."

Oroville leapt from his chair and snatched up an ax from the work bench near him. With his face contorted with rage, he spun toward Paul and advanced upon him and Brutus.

"Hold there, Oroville," Paul called out warningly. "Nobody hurts Brutus."

"I'm going to kill that crazy dog and that's for damn certain," Oroville snarled. He raised the ax above his head, and ready to strike, continued to move forward.

Paul shook the strap of the rifle off his shoulder, seized hold of the gun as it fell and rotated the black iron barrel to point at Oroville.

"Oroville, I'm telling you to stop. I don't want to have to shoot you."

Brutus recognized his old enemy and remembered the taste of his blood and flesh. He also knew the danger from the upraised ax. His master was angry at the man and was pointing his gun at him. Brutus's duty was to help in the coming battle. His hackles rose, and he crouched and spread his toes with their arched toenails to best grip the floor, and waited with every muscle tensed. When his master gave the hand signal, Brutus would launch himself upon their enemy.

"You'd not shoot a man over a damn dog that deserves killing for its meanness."

"Don't gamble your life on that for then you'd be dead wrong." Paul cocked the rifle, the click of the hammer loud in the stillness of the room.

"Damn you, Oroville," Jack shouted as he hurried to intercept the man. "There'll be no killing in my camp."

He came up on Oroville from the side and grabbed hold of the ax handle, and wrenching powerfully, tore it from his hands. "You stupid bastard, he'll shoot you for sure."

"If he's going to use a gun on me then I'll get mine." Oroville stepped to his bunk, but a few feet away, and reaching beneath the mattress, pulled out a revolver.

"Now we're even," Oroville shouted and cocked the pistol and pointed it at Paul.

Jack took one long step toward Oroville and swung the handle of the ax into him. The hard hickory wood struck Oroville in the chest and knocked him backward against his bunk. The blow caused him to squeeze the trigger and the pistol fired and spewed a bullet chased by a lance of incandescence and smoke. The bullet zipped past Paul with the buzz of an angry bee and thudded into the door.

Jack checked Paul and saw he was lowering his rifle. He then leaned over Oroville sitting crumpled on the floor and holding his chest and trying to breathe. He took the pistol from the man's slack hand. "I just saved your life, Oroville." He prodded the man in the ribs with the toe of his boot. "Do you hear me, Oroville? I just saved your life."

The battered man gulped air into his lungs and looked up with a murderous expression at Jack. "Dawson, that's the one and only time you'll ever hit me."

"If you behave yourself until tomorrow morning, then I won't have to hit you again. You're fired. In the morning, pack your things and get the hell out of my camp."

"Nothing would suit me better."

"Then there's nothing more to say."

Jack moved to stand near Paul. "Maybe it'd be better if you left. There's just too much bad blood between you two."

"I think so too," Paul replied and lowered the hammer on his rifle. "Will you be all right with him?" He nodded at Oroville.

"I have his pistol so he'll behave himself. And he's made enemies here and we'll all keep an eye on him until tomorrow. The next time you come, you stay the night with us."

"I will. Thanks."

Paul slung the rifle over his shoulder, took up the pack of furs, and pulled the hood over his head. He motioned to Brutus who promptly took station on his left.

"Another cold night for us, Brutus," Paul said.

He stepped to the door and tripped the latch and a blizzard of snow stormed into the room. He lowered his head and plunged into the white swirling mass. He reached back and pulled the door shut.

Alice stared at the door where Paul had gone. She remembered his appraisal of her. What had been his thoughts? Why should she care? Yet she did.

Jack spoke from beside her. "Something bothering you little miss?"

"Will he be all right out there in the storm?'

"Don't worry too much about Paul for he's half wolf and will be all right."

"It's an awful storm."

"That it is, worst one I've ever seen."

"Where will he go?"

"He'll find a place to hole up for the night."

"I hope he doesn't freeze to death. I wouldn't want to be out there in all that wind." Alice shivered with the thought.

"Your right, it's the wind that makes it so damn cold."

"I hate it. I'm glad we found your camp." She gave Jack a smile.

"So am I. You'll sleep all snug there in the kitchen with Two Doves."

"I like her," Alice said.

"She's a rare one and that's for sure," said Jack.

***

Paul was blind in the night, the blizzard blocking off all light from the heavens and the darkness absolute. He braced himself against the wall of the barracks to keep from being blown down. The glacial wind was ripping away his body heat and driving ice flakes to lash his face. He must find shelter to survive. He had two possibilities, the barn with the oxen and horses, or the cold room. The cold room was the better for it was more wind proof.

He pictured its location in relation to his position and moved off along the wall, and sliding his shoulders upon the logs to keep his footing. At the corner of the building, he turned to the right and again followed the wall. When he judged he had progressed half the way to the next corner, he pivoted a quarter turn to the left and struck out with a gloved hand extended in front of him.

The wind struck and swirled and struck again, each time from a different direction as it tried to confuse him of his course. He dared not miss the cold room and wander lost in the blizzard.

His hand encountered the wall of the cold room before he could see it. He felt along the logs of the structure until he felt the door. He pulled the bolt to free the door and stumbled into the room. He quickly shoved the door closed against the deadly wind.

In the Stygian darkness of the windowless cold room, he found the lamp that always sat on the table in the center of the space. He lit it with a match from the box beside the lamp and the room filled with a yellow light that flickered in sync with the wavering flame.

His furs from previous trips hung in a corner. He placed his newest catch beside those earlier ones. He dropped his pack and leaned his rifle upon it.

Paul sliced off two large pieces of meat from one of the hams that hung on a cord from the rafters. He tossed one piece to Brutus, who snatched it out of the air.

He was weary from the storm and the miles of travel running his trap line, and from the trouble with Oroville. He ate his ham quickly and spread his sleeping robe on the floor. He placed his rifle within reach and set the lamp and the matches close by. He lay down on the robe, reached out with a cupped hand just above the top of the chimney, and blew out the flame. He pulled the robe tightly around him. Brutus came and laid down on the edge of the robe.

Oroville could rightly reason that Paul would choose the cold room for the night and come wanting revenge. However neither man nor beast could steal upon Brutus without him hearing or smelling him. His thoughts turned to the girl with the loggers, and the boy who most likely was with her. How did they come to be here? He would ask Jack the next time he spoke with him. That could be days away for he planned to leave at first light so as not to encounter Oroville. But the girl now? With that question on his mind, Paul breathed twice and was asleep.

***

Alice slept snug and warm on the logger's bunk in the kitchen. She awoke once during the night and stared into the darkness trying to determine what had awakened her. A few feet away, Two Doves breathed with a soft sighing sound as she slept. From the barracks came the sound of men snoring. Outside the storm was gathering ever more madness and violence as it walked the dark world. She heard the wind pounding the walls and whistling as it was cut by the eaves and roaring as it raced over the roof top.

She thought of Paul outside in the terrible storm. Jack had said Paul would find a place to endure the night. Alice fervently hoped that was so.

Chapter Twelve

Black Face

Alice and Will left the logging camp barracks just as the sun brought daylight upon the lake and forest. A new layer of snow some three inches thick blanketed the old. The wind was but a frail ghost of its nighttime power and barely strong enough to tumble a snowflake. The cold was intense, seeming to have a density that required an effort for her to move through. Each breath of air stung her nostrils.

"This is the coldest it's ever been," Alice said and shivering as the cold cut through her clothing.

"It's a bad one and that's for sure. I'd like to reach the river before dark and cross into Canada where we'll be safe."

"Yes, let's try." Alice said. With her breath pluming out white and frosty, she walked into the waiting day. It would be another long one of slogging through the snow that now reached half way to her knees.

They had progressed about a mile when Will called out excitedly and pointed ahead to where the lake narrowed just before it ended. "Alice, there go two wolves."

Alice saw two grayish black animals racing over the snow not far ahead. They had obviously come out of the forest on the left shore of the lake and were heading for the forest on the opposite shore. The larger and darker colored wolf led, with the smaller wolf following its path. The lead wolf gave Alice and Will a short glance over its shoulder, and then looked back to the front.

Alice marveled at the effortless way the wolves moved, leaping with great bounds, seeming almost to float as if they weighed nothing at all. Only the geysers of snow that erupted and glistened in the sunlight as they leapt told that their feet did truly touch the ground. The two wolves vanished into the forest like phantoms.

"They act as if they're afraid of us."

"Wolves usually stay away from people."

"I hope these two stay away from us."

***

Black Face lay in the snow under the low hanging limbs of a giant pine and watched the two humans make their way over the last half mile of the frozen lake and enter the forest. Beside him and was the young female with the black and gray fur and white throat patch that he had stolen from the Rainy River pack.

Black Face had laid claim to the land around Head Lake as his domain and the need to know the identity of the two humans was strong within him. He had spied upon the humans that cut down the big trees and knew each by sight and by his scent. Were these two from that group? He would find out. He rose and trotted off among the trees bordering the lake.

As Black Face moved away from his mate, she barked once to question his intention. He ignored her query and continued on. She hesitated but a moment and then sprang forward and followed close behind.

Black Face found the two sets of human footprints in the snow and lowered his nose to catch the scents that were on them and rising into the air from them. The moist, olfactory nerve endings within his nose could detect and identify one tiny bit of a particular scent from a myriad of other smells that floated upon the air.

He possessed an uncountable number of odors stored in his memory; from the simple pine needle to the white butterfly of summer, from the lowly earthworm to the eagle that soared in the high sky. He knew the loggers scent, and those of the hunters who prowled the woods with their guns, and the fishermen who walked the shores of the lake.

Black Face compared the odors of these two humans with all the scores of other human smells that he knew and found they were strange to him. More than that, the scent of one of the humans possessed a unique quality, one he could not match with a known one. Yet at the same time there was something about it that seemed somehow familiar.

Close beside him his mate was also sniffing at the tracks and that drew Black Face's attention to her. As her smell registered anew, the riddle of the unique human scent was answered. This particular human carried the scent of a female, the first Black Face had ever come upon.

He breathed in a lung full of the air and allowed it to stream out slowly through his nose. He sorted out the female smell from that of the usual human smell, and it was tantalizing in its strange newness. The smell was irresistible to Black Face, and though there would be danger, he must go close to this female human.

He struck off at a trot along the pair of tracks. His mate followed, whining worriedly. Black Face gave her a look over his shoulder and she fell silent.

***

When the sun passed over its zenith and began its short wintertime fall to the horizon, Alice and Will halted in the forest near a fallen pine tree with many limbs. They scraped the snow away from the ground as best they could with their burlap wrapped feet, and built a fire with the dead wood of the pine. They sat upon the trunk of the tree near the fire and ate ham sandwiches from the supply of food Two Doves and Jack had insisted they take.

The worry came again to Alice, as it had so many times during the days of travel, what would she find in Canada, what kind of life could she make for herself there? She wanted to believe that she would find work to earn money for food and a place to sleep. She wanted to meet kind people like Sister Marie, or Eduardo Sandoval the old shoe cobbler.

She peered at Will and saw he must be having thoughts similar to Alice's for his face held a worried, haggard expression. What had he left behind? He had volunteered nothing about his past life. Alice had asked no questions.

Alice finished her sandwich and spoke to Will. "I have to go off a little ways by myself. "

"I wouldn't go far."

"I won't. Just beyond those trees." She pointed.

***

From a patch of bushes among the trees and down wind, Black Face stealthily observed the two humans at the fire and eating. His mate lay beside him and also viewing the two. He had quickly identified the odors coming from the humans. The female human scent, strong now that he was close, came from the smaller of the two. As he observed her, she made the sounds one human made to another and left the fire and walked off among the trees.

Black Face signaled his mate to remain hidden. Then he rose and stole among the trees and ever closer to the human female. He stopped instantly when she halted and looked back in the direction of the fire, now hidden from her view by the trunks of several trees. She began to unbuckle the belt to her pants.

Without a sound, Black Face crept closer to Alice.

Alice looked about one last time before dropping her pants. She flinched sharply for a huge male wolf was but a dozen steps away and creeping through the snow toward her. Her pulse was suddenly pounding. She hastily buckled the belt.

The moment her eyes had fallen upon the wolf, he stopped and stood with his muzzle pointed directly at her. He was motionless except for the movement of his chest as he breathed in her scent. His face and back were black, his sides gray, and that graded to reddish tan below. His brush of a tail was curved slightly upward. His eyes were yellow with brown centers, and those eyes were fixed unblinkingly upon her.

Alice started to whirl around and run. She caught herself up short, if she turned her back and ran, might that provoke the wolf to spring upon her. She must remain very, very still and look the wolf in the eyes. If she showed no fear, might that keep it from attacking her? She was awfully scared and wished for her walking staff, that she had left behind at the fire, to use as a club.

As Alice faced the wolf, a strange thought came to her. She sensed no menace from the wolf. Or was it that she did not recognize it? The wolf's eyes opened wide to a full circle of concentration upon her. Was the animal trying to read her intentions as she was trying to read its? Wolves did not think that way. Or did they?

The wolf lifted its nose and drew in a deep breath of her scent. At that he wagged his brush of a tail twice. Alice knew what that meant, if he had been a dog. Wasn't a wolf the cousin of a dog? Was this wolf telling her that he intended no harm to her? Could it be that her special way with dogs could protect her from this wolf? She held her green eyes locked upon the yellow eyes of the wolf and willed the animal to understand that she was friendly and for it not to hurt her. To show her desire to be a friend, she slowly offered her hand to the wolf. The wolf broke eye contact and looked at the offered hand.

At that instant, thunder exploded among the trees not far off on Alice's right. A powerful blow struck the wolf on the left side and knocked him rolling, his tumbling body flinging snow into the air. He came to rest on his side and lay motionless. Then after a short moment, he turned weakly to his stomach and slowly raised the front half of himself up on two trembling legs. Blood streamed from his side and made crimson splashes upon the pristine snow. His eyes, questioning what had happened to him, looked searchingly to Alice for the answer. Then the pain came and he knew that he had been injured and his eyes filled with accusation. That gave way to hate and he growled raw and savagely at Alice. His growl dwindled to silence, and with the accusatory expression rapidly fading, he sank into the snow. His legs worked and churned the snow a bit as if he was trying to run and escape from this hazardous place. He let out his breath, and shuddered, and died.

From her hiding place in the bushes, the young female Black Face had chosen for his mate, had observed the killing. She barked out in fear and bolted away through the forest, running with all her strength and swiftness.

Alice was stunned at the crash of the rifle shot and the violent death of the wolf. The expression with which the wolf had stared at her, blaming her for his wound as he died, was hurtful and her heart cramped.

There was movement among the trees to her right and Alice saw Paul Bouccard and his dog run into sight. Paul carried a rifle and Alice knew he was responsible for shooting the wolf.

"Are you all right?" Paul shouted out.

"Yes. Yes. I'm all right." Alice replied. He had killed the wolf to protect her. "Did you have to shoot the wolf?"

"I was afraid he was going to jump on you." Paul answered and much surprised at Alice's reply.

"I don't believe he was going to hurt me at all. I think he was just curious about me."

"And how do you know that?"

"I know because it was in his eyes. And his tail wagged."

"His tail wagged? Well you could be right for wolves have a great amount of curiosity. I surely didn't want to shoot him for I saw he had a mate. But when I saw him trailing you, I figured I'd better follow and make sure you weren't attacked." Paul continued on in a sad tone that told his regret at having killed the wolf. "It's done now and nothing can change that."

"You did what you thought was needed."

"If I was wrong about him, then it was a bad thing."

"We can never know the answer to that."

"No, we can't."

Paul, with Brutus beside him, went to Black Face and knelt in the snow. "I'm truly sorry, Black Face," Paul whispered. "I wish this hadn't happened." Days earlier, he had ceased hunting the wolf when he saw him with the female and knew he had broken away from the pack and would start his own in the spring breeding season soon to come. A pack of Black Face's offspring would now never come to be and the loss to the forest was large and Paul was the cause of that. For the first and last time, he ran his hand over the wolf's black face, over his pointed ears and along his back. He avoided touching the gaping bullet wound and the blood that had ceased to flow. Black Face looked smaller in death than he had running wild and free through the woods. "I'm sorry," Paul whispered again.

Will ran from the trees and stopped near Alice. "What happened? Are you hurt?"

"I'm all right. He shot a wolf that was close to me," Alice said and nodding toward Paul.

"He's the trapper fellow we saw at the logging camp," Will said and looking at Paul who was rising from beside the wolf. "Are you going to skin the wolf?"

"No. I couldn't bring myself to skin Black Face. This is his land and I'll let him lie here and become part of it."

"You had a name for him?" Alice asked.

"Yes, I've seen him in the woods these last three years. He had this distinctive coloring about his head and so I gave him the name. He came to seem like an old friend."

"I can see why you wouldn't want to skin him," Alice said.

Paul came a few steps closer to Alice and Will. "We didn't have time to get introduced at the lumber camp," Paul said. "My name is Paul."

"Mine is Alice."

"I'm Will. Do you know how far it is to the border with Canada?"

"Sure. About four miles. You'll want to find the bridge. It's in that direction." Paul pointed off through the pine trees. "If you come to the river first, then turn left toward the bridge. If you see the road first, then turn right and follow it to the bridge." That they were runaways showed plainly. But why did they choose January, the worst possible time to do it?

"Thanks," Will said.

"Do you know anybody in Canada?" Paul wondered what relationship existed between the two.

"No," Alice replied.

"You'll find it hard to find work this time of year."

"We'll make out," Alice said.

Will nodded his head in agreement with Alice.

Paul considered the brave answers. The two would find it very difficult in Canada.

"Where were you going before all of this happened?" Alice asked.

"I had finished running my trap line and was heading home. My mother and I have a farm there along the Rainy River." Paul pointed as if he could see through forest to the farm. "And I'd best get moving for I got chores to do before it gets dark."

"We had better go too," Alice said. She turned to Will. "Are you ready?"

"Yes."

"Good luck to both of you," Paul said and looking directly at Alice.

"The same to you," Alice said. "I'm sorry about your wolf."

"I wish he was still alive," Paul replied. "And, of course, you not hurt." Paul turned about, and with Brutus at his side, walked away among the big pines and was lost from view.

"Let's hurry," Will said.

"Yes," said Alice.

Alice followed Will back to the fire where they gathered up their belongings and hastened away through the snowy forest.

Chapter Thirteen

"I see the bridge, Will, I see the bridge!" Alice cried out joyfully and pointing along the road. "We've made it to Canada where we'll be safe."

"Not until we cross the river to the far side," Will replied.

Alice and Will had come out from among the big trees of the woods and onto the road but a moment before. The bridge, a few score steps ahead, was an ancient iron structure with much rust showing through its peeling brown paint. Its builders had selected a site for the bridge where the Rainy River was pinched down to but a couple hundred feet wide between two bluffs. The bridge was narrow and provided space for only one vehicle at a time to cross. A low metal railing ran along each side of the bridge. The ends of the bridge rested on stone abutments. Its center section was supported by two equally spaced stone pillars rearing up through the ice from the river bottom.

Alice shivered from the severe cold. She had no feeling in her feet and feared they were frozen. She had 'walked through the burlap that had provided insulation from the snow. The burlap now hung in tatters from the cords that had bound it to her legs. Strips of the burlap flopped about on the snow with each of her steps.

"Will, I'm so cold I can hardly walk. I've got to have a fire to keep from freezing to death."

"I'm darn cold myself. The snow is too deep to get a fire burning in the woods. Let's build one on the bridge where the snow has been mostly blown away."

"Build it on the Canada end of the bridge," Alice said. "Then if we see somebody coming we can run into the woods and hide."

Will led the way onward along the road toward the bridge. He halted where a narrow road came in from the right and joined the main road. He pointed and spoke to Alice. "A horse pulling a sleigh went down the lane and then came back out and went north over the bridge."

"Let's hurry on and get the fire started," Alice said shaking with the cold.

With both of them walking in the same sleigh track, Will led to the bridge. As they stepped upon its end, he gestured ahead with his gloved hand. "There's the sign we've been looking for, Alice, Canadian Border."

"A very fine sight," Alice said. Her heart lifted as she read the much weathered and faded lettering on the metal sign fastened to the bridge railing at the river's mid-point.

Beyond the sign, Will dropped his pack on the bridge and spoke to Alice. "You sit down and rest while I go get wood for the fire."

"Thanks, Will." Alice was glad to rest for she was so terribly cold and weary.

As Will hastened off into the thick woods on the Canadian shore, Alice sat down on the pack and shoved her hands deeply into the pockets of her coat. She leaned against the bridge railing and looked down at the river that marked the place upon the earth that Will and she had journeyed so desperately to reach. One of the bridge's pillars was directly below her and the swift current of water swirled and gurgled as it argued with the stone that interfered with its passage. She noted that due to the turbulence of the water near the pillar, the frigid temperature had been unable to freeze it into a sheet of ice, and instead had created an area of slush ice several inches thick, some three feet wide and extending several feet downstream from the bridge. The thousands of ice crystal of the slush ice whispered with a low rasping sound as they were constantly being churned by the movement of the river current.

She looked downstream along the ice imprisoned river to where it curved away to her right and out of sight between heavily forested banks. She looked more broadly about and saw no animal of the earth, nor bird of the sky, only snow and ice, and the dark trees of the forest and they were frozen to their heartwood. She had enough of gloomy forests and snow. She tried to picture how the land might look in springtime with new greenness and flowers and song birds, and the river free of its ice mask and its waters running free and sparkling in warm sunlight. She failed to create the picture because the desolate view lying before her dominated her mind and she shivered ever more.

She must do something to generate some warmth in her body. She stood and hugged herself and began to stomp around on one foot and then the other, with the torn strips of burlap swinging about her feet. Then as she made to lift a foot, she could not for a length of the burlap attached to it was caught beneath the other foot. The inability to lift the foot threw her off balance and she tripped and stumbled into the pack and that knocked her feet from under her and she fell backwards upon the iron railing of the bridge. She tumbled over the railing and into space.

Alice rotated half a turn as she fell and struck the slush ice of the river head first and vanished beneath the water. The momentum of her fall drove her down deeply and the swift current seized her in its frigid embrace and swept her downstream. Don't breathe! Don't breathe! Alice warned herself for then you will die.

She strained to see through the water that was made murky by being shut off from the daylight by the thick ice. She could only make out the gray up toward the ice and the black of the bottom. She did not know how to swim, but her natural instinct started her to pawing at the water with her gloved hands. She moved slowly for every muscle was stiff from the cold and the heavy boots and clothing were hampering her effort. Gradually she climbed upward toward the pale light above.

A swirl of the current caught her and carried her down deeper and her feet touched the gravely river bottom. Panicked with fear of drowning, she kicked off stoutly and shot upward. Unable to judge the distance to the surface of the shadow filled water, she came up too swiftly and her head crashed into the ice with a brutal blow. She knew she had a nasty cut. The injury had no importance when death threatened.

She hammered the underside of the ice with both fists. She must reach the life giving air only inches away. Her blows drove her down in the water and away from the ice. She paddled back up to the ice and beat upon it again. Again she was driven away from the ice, and again she paddled up and hit at it with her fists. Nothing gave to her blows for the ice was stone to her flesh and bone knuckles.

The shock of the frigid water upon her body slowed her heart beat. Controlled by an ancient instinct, the reduced flow of blood was shunted to her brain and lungs.

Her body cried out for her to breathe. She fought the desperate urge for her fear of drowning overrode the agony of having no air.

The current hurried Alice downstream, sliding her along the smooth underside of the ice. Enfeebled by cold and the lack of oxygen, she paddled feebly to keep near the ice and hoping desperately to find a hole through which she could climb from the water and into the air.

An image of Alice's mother appeared and she cried out silently, "Oh, Mother, how strange it is that we both die by drowning. I should have died in your arms in the deep ocean instead of here in a river of a strange land. She waited for an answer. Her mother smiled benignly at her and said not a word. Her mother's silence angered Alice. Why don't you talk to me? Her mother only smiled with that gentle smile.

Alice's felt a powerful urge to breathe. She fought the urge for she must use only logic and it told her not to breathe until she found an opening in the ice. Could a person hold their breath long enough to kill herself?

Alice's heart labored and beat ever more slowly. The fires of her mind were surrendering to the lack of oxygen. Her thoughts were fragile and difficult to hold onto. Blackness was closing upon her from all sides. That blackness must be death. The terror of dying left her. Even so she must not surrender while there was still an ounce of strength in her body. Her mother's figure was fading. Mother, please don't leave me to die alone. She concentrated intently so as to hold onto the image and reached out toward it. As Alice's mind went dark, she felt her mother clasped the hand firmly and pull. Yes, dear mother, we shall die together as it should be. Alice breathed where there was not one particle of air.

***

In the long shadows of late evening, Will sat on his pack and leaned on the bridge railing and looked down at the slush ice where Alice had vanished into the river. He had cried bitter tears for in the short time he had known Alice, he had become very fond of her, and he had cried at his inability to protect her as he wanted. He hated the river that had killed her. It should be permanently marked, scarred in some manner for it murderous deed.

Will had been returning to the bridge with an armload of firewood when he had seen Alice fall over the railing and into the river. He had rushed to the spot and stripped off his coat in preparation to jumping in after her. He leaned over the railing and saw where she had vanished beneath the slush ice. He noted the swiftness of the current and knew she was being carried speedily downstream. How far away was she? How could he find her under the thick ice that sheathed the river? Another thought came, the ice would imprison him and only death awaited him beneath it. His death would not bring Alice back to life.

He had pulled his coat back on and sat down on his pack and cried as he listened to the rasping of the slush ice and the creak and groan of the solid ice. Oh, God, how he missed the strong girl with her rare beauty. He had known her for just these few days during the journey north and that time was much too short. Her death left a great pain and he mourned for her.

Will heard the crunch of snow close by and hastily started to rise. A hand fell upon his shoulder and bore down with a heavy pressure and held him but half erect. Will hastily looked up. Oscar Taggert stood glaring down at him. He held a pistol pointed into Will's face.

"Just stay right there," Oscar said in a harsh voice. "And don't do anything that'll make me shoot you."

Will sat down on the pack. The open barrel of the pistol but inches from his face.

"I'm Oscar Taggert."

"I know who you are. You can't arrest me for I'm on the Canadian end of the bridge." Will again made to get to his feet.

"Stay down there damn you," Oscar growled. He leaned more heavily on Will and dug his bony fingers into the flesh of his shoulder. "I've been following you and saw your tracks with the girl's. Where is she? Where's Alice Childs?"

"I don't have to tell you anything for you don't have any authority here," Will said and grimacing with the pain of Oscar's iron fingers. He slid his hand closer to his pocket with the pistol.

Oscar studied the young face intently watching him. "You're right", he said in an agreeing tone. "This is out of Beltrami County and out of my jurisdiction."

Oscar removed his hand from Will's shoulder and moved back a step. He holstered his pistol.

"But tell me where the girl is."

Will had heard about the sheriff and all of them told him not to trust the man. Still he could see no harm in telling him about Alice. "She's down there." Will nodded down at the river.

Oscar surveyed the frozen river to where it curved out of view and into the forest. He faced back to Will.

"Why didn't you go with her?"

Will realized the lawman had misunderstood and believed Alice had gone off downstream. Well, just let him think that for it would be a worthy trick to play on him.

"She got mad at me and struck off on her own."

"Then why were you sitting here?"

"Trying to decide whether to go after her," Will lied.

"I don't believe you'd let her go off by herself. There's more to this than what you've said,"

"Well, that's what happened. I don't care if you believe me or not. She's not here, is she?" Will was glad that his and Taggert's foot prints had erased Alice's tracks.

Oscar again looked down the river channel that was being filled with evening dusk, and then turned his eyes to the dense woods where the dusk was almost darkness.

"I'm going north now," Will said, and anxious to go quickly into the sanctuary of Canada. He made to rise and expecting the sheriff to take some action to stop him.

"Better take your pack," said the sheriff.

"Yeah. Sure." Will, surprised at the ease of escaping from the sheriff, took up the pack and settled it onto his back.

The sheriff fell in beside Will. "I'll walk along with you for a short ways. I want to be sure you leave Beltrami County."

Will did not want the sheriff to accompany him, but said nothing. He left the bridge and went into the big woods of Canada. The sheriff matched his stride.

A short time later, a pistol shot shattered the stillness of the Canadian woods. An equal time later, the sheriff returned to the bridge and crossed over it into Beltrami County. He made his night camp there.

***

Paul cut ice at his usual place on Rainy River just upstream from his home. Each of his strokes with the sharp ice saw cut half an inch gash in the ice that was some eight inches thick. In the past hour of work, he had removed ice from an area of river some thirty feet long and half that distance in width.

Heather was on the ice near Paul. When he finished cutting one of the blocks of ice and dragged it upon the ice shelf, she snagged it with her ice hook and skidded it to the bank. From time to time, Paul would stop sawing and with his superior strength, lift the blocks and load them onto the farm sled that was close by on the river bank.

The brown horse, harnessed and hitched to the sled, stood patiently in its long haired winter coat and dozed. Brutus was on his pallet of straw on the front of the sled. He lay on his stomach with head resting on his outstretched front paws. He watched Paul and Heather harvest the blocks of ice from the river and pile them onto the sled. He was alert for his master might call to him at any moment, or signal a command. Brutus must always be ready to obey.

Paul pulled the saw and severed the last thin neck of ice holding a block fastened to the ice sheet. The block began to float away on the lazy current. He dropped the saw on the ice shelf and took up the ice hook with its long wooden handle. He leaned over the water and reached out to catch the drifting block and draw it to him. The iron hook glanced off the hard, slick surface of the ice and plunged into the water.

He started to withdraw the ice hook when it caught onto something heavy that was submerged in the water. He pulled stoutly to free the hook and brought a gloved hand to the surface, followed by an arm in a heavy coat, and then by the face of a girl with startlingly white skin and green eyes open wide and staring. Long blond hair trailed out behind. He recognized Alice.

"Mom, come quick," Paul shouted out. "There's a girl in the river." He braced his feet as best he could on the slippery ice and hauled the ice hook toward him.

The girl's body came up against the cut edge of the ice shelf. Paul dropped to his knees and quickly caught hold of the front of the girl's coat and held the body from sinking back into the depths of the river. Water had splashed upon the ice and increased its slipperiness and he fought to keep from sliding into the river.

"My God!" Heather cried out as she came up beside Paul. She knelt beside him and took hold of the girl's hand. "Lift, Paul, lift. Quick get her out of the water."

Paul heaved mightily on the body made heavy by the thick, wet clothing. Heather took hold of Alice's and pulled. The body, dripping water, came up over the ledge of ice and onto its flat surface.

"It's the girl Alice that I saw at the logging camp and later in the woods." An ache came alive in Paul's chest as he stared down at the body. It wasn't right for someone so young to die.

"Hurry, open her clothing and let me see if she's still alive," Heather directed.

"Is that possible?" Paul asked as he sprang to the task of prying open the buttons of the coat rapidly stiffening with the cold.

"Stop fooling with the buttons, Paul, rip them off. Hurry, every second is vital. I've heard of people living after being under water for several minutes when water is this cold."

Paul grabbed the coat in both hands and yanked and the buttons tore loose and bounced away over the ice. Heather lowered her head and pressed her ear to Alice's cold chest and listened.

"Yes! Yes! I hear a beat. It's weak, but her heart beats. Lift her up with her head down and let's get the water out of her lungs."

Paul encircled Alice's waist with his arms and raise her midsection with her head down. Heather seized Alice's chest and back between her hands and squeezed strongly. Water poured from Alice's mouth. Heather squeezed again with less water came, then none at the third attempt. Alice's lungs began to expand and contract, but feebly

"She's breathing on her own." Heather said. "Hurry now, pick her up and carry her to the house. Run, Paul! Run! We must get her warm as fast as possible. She can still die."

Paul scooped Alice's wet body up in his arms and ran. The water droplets clinging to her hair froze swiftly into crystals in the frigid temperature. Paul heard the ice crystals striking against one another and tinkling and chiming like little bells telling him to hurry! Hurry! She must not die!

Heather raced ahead of Paul to the house and opened the door for him. He hastened inside and close to the heating stove and there placed Alice on the warm boards of the floor.

"Build up the fire real hot and then hold blankets close to the stove until they're real hot to wrap her in," Heather directed. "We've got to get her warm quick."

Paul rushed to obey.

Heather hurriedly began to strip Alice of her clothing. With his eyes turned away from Alice's nude body, Paul brought the first warm blanket.

"Don't be bashful," Heather said. "Help me get her clothes off and wrapped in the blanket. Then heat another one really warm."

Paul untied Alice's boots and removed them and then helped strip the boys' pants off her. In but seconds, Alice lay nude before him, skin a pearly white, a blond puff of youthful hair at the V of her legs, shoulders bony, ribs showing painfully, girlish breast taut from the cold. She's so fragile and so awfully vulnerable, Paul thought as he stared down at Alice. She must not die.

They wrapped Alice in hot blankets. When one cooled a little they wrapped her in one freshly heated, and then another, and another. Finally Alice's flesh felt warm to the touch and her breathing came evenly and her heart beat strongly. They prepared a bed for her on a cot they brought close to the stove and covered her snugly.

Paul loaded wood in the stove and came and sat down on a chair near Heather. For a time they sat silently together each with their own private thoughts and watching the rise and fall of the blankets as Alice breathed.

"She hasn't spoken a word," Paul said worriedly. "I hope she lives."

"I think she'll be all right since her heart never stopped," Heather replied. "She'll regain conscious just as soon as her body can heal itself from the cold and the damage the water did to her lungs."

"I sure hope so. I wonder what happened to Will, that boy she was with."

"Do you think they were brother and sister?"

"I don't know. They didn't look much alike. I think they might be two of the orphans they've been bringing from the big cities in the east."

"It's dark now. Tomorrow you should go looking for him."

"That's what I was thinking. I'll look for tracks. Maybe they tried crossing the river on the ice and it broke through with them."

"If you can't find him, and she is an orphan, we could ask her to stay with us. Instead of going to Canada like they obviously planned."

"That's what I was thinking," Paul replied with a thoughtful expression.

"Better bring in more wood for we want to keep the fire going all night."

Paul rose and put on his coat. "I'll keep it burning."

Chapter Fourteen

The Trap

Alice came awake floating up from the dark pit of unconsciousness where she had lain close to death. She opened her eyes to a brightly sunlit window but a few feet away. A wide, snow covered field was framed by the window, and beyond the field in the far distance, lay a woods.

She lay quietly observing the view beyond the glass. Then the incongruity of the scene jerked her completely awake and she hastily reached out to gather her thoughts. The last thing she remembered was being beneath the ice of the river and her mother taking her by the hand. Now this. Was she alive? Where was she? What had happened between being in the river and now? She opened her mouth and breathed deeply. She drew in sweet air and not water. She was warm, blessedly warm under several blankets.

Her spirit soared. I'm alive! By some miracle I'm out of the river and alive! But how could that be?

She turned her head to look about and her eyes fell at once upon Paul sitting on a chair beside the bed. He appeared very real and he was gazing steadily at her. The big, gray dog lay on the floor by his side. It too watched Alice.

"You?" Alice said, her voice coming weak and scratchy from a raw throat.

"Yes, me."

"And you're real?" Alice asked wanting assurance that she wasn't imagining being alive.

"Sure enough real."

"Then I'm really alive?"

"You're surely not dead," Paul replied with a magnificent smile and glorying in the girl's happiness. Her face was drawn with weakness from her ordeal and still a beauty showed like none Paul had ever seen before. Her nearness caused his heart to throb with pleasure.

Alice in turn was evaluating Paul. His light brown eyes showed relief and pleasure as he looked at her.

"But I thought you were when I pulled you from the river," Paul said.

"You pulled me from the river?"

"With help from my mother."

"I was one lucky girl for you to be there for I was drowning under the ice."

"You almost did."

"Where are we?"

"At our farm. My mom's and my farm," Paul replied.

"I remember you mentioning that you had a farm."

"How did you get in the river?"

"I tripped and fell off the bridge while Will was gathering wood. Have you seen him?"

"No."

"I want to know if he's all right."

"Then soon as you're taken care of, I'll go looking for him." Paul raised his voice and shouted out. "Mom, she's awake."

Alice heard quick footsteps approaching and Heather entered the door at the end of the room. She hastened to the bed and clasped Alice's hands. "I'm Heather, and I'm so glad to see you're all right. We were terribly worried about you."

Heather examined Alice and was pleased with what she saw. During the long hours of the night, the girl's body had recovered from the near drowning in the frigid water and her unconsciousness had become sleep. The girl's gaunt body showed her frailty. She needed days of wholesome food and rest. Heather believed Alice needed something more, the absence of fear.

"Please tell me more of how I came to be here," Alice said. "Tell me all if it. How long have I been here?"

Paul spoke. "Since yesterday evening just before dark. I was cutting ice on the river when I caught your glove with the ice hook. We pulled you out of the river and carried you to the house and thawed you out. Mother knew what to do. She's the one who really saved you."

Alice squeezed Heather's hands that still held hers. She liked the woman from the first sight of her, the gentle eyes and caring expression. The proud way Heather looked at her son almost made Alice smile. Still holding Heather's hand, Alice held her other hand out to Paul who seized it gladly.

"I owe both of you my life. I don't know how I can ever repay."

"You can tell us your story," Heather said. "How you came to be on the river, all of it. But that can wait until later. For now, are you hungry?

"I'm starved. Almost drowning turns out to be good for the appetite."

"Do you feel well enough to get up and eat or should I fix you a plate of food and bring it in here?"

"I'm ready to get up to eat

"Good. Your clothes are ready for you." Heather nodded at the garments freshly laundered and neatly folded on the foot of the cot. She gestured at the small bedside table holding Alice's poem book and her father's watch. "We dried your little book with its rhymes and the picture. Paul took the back off the watch and dried it. It seems to be running just fine."

"Thank you very much for all of them means a lot to me."

"You're very welcome," Heather said with a smile. She turned to Paul. "Tend to the food on the stove while I help Alice dress."

"Yes, mom." Paul gave Alice a quick look and strode off toward the kitchen. Brutus trailed behind with his hard claws tapping upon the wooden floor

Alice swung her legs out from under the blankets and sat on the edge of the bed. She began to shake from weakness and she felt lightheaded. "I guess I'm not as strong as I thought."

"You have good reason to be." Heather sat down beside Alice and put an arm around her and held her. "Just take it slow and easy. I can still bring you a plate."

"No. I want to get up to prove to myself that I'm really alive. Just help me a little."

Alice felt her strength returning as she donned the garments, aided by Heather. She walked slowly, but unaided to the kitchen. Heather guided Alice to the table and she seated herself.

"It's wonderful to have you here, and I hope you will stay a long time with us. Now you just rest while I finish breakfast for all of us."

"Thank you." Alice felt at ease, even secure in the friendly company of Heather and the stalwart Paul.

Heather brought a jar from a pantry and placed it on the table and then hot food from the stove. "Let's all eat," she said in a cheery voice.

Alice helped herself to a large portion of fried steak, boiled potatoes and cabbage and freshly baked biscuits. She poured a tall glass full of milk.

Heather handed her a pitcher of amber fluid. "Pour some sun nectar over your biscuits," she said.

"Sun nectar?" Alice said.

"Yes, nectar made by the sun and flowers and wild bees."

"Oh, that'd be honey."

"That's right. A liquid suited for the gods."

"I think so too," Alice replied.

She split a biscuit and poured a liberal measure of honey upon it and began to eat. From time to time, she looked at Paul and Heather and found they were observing her as she was them. Their presence and gentle expressions made the world feel safe, for the moment.

Heather noted the obvious pleasure the girl had from the food and was pleased. She would try to persuade Alice to remain with them instead of going north into Canada. She pictured the three of them on a sleigh ride behind the horse, or fishing on the ice, or having a picnic in the springtime warmth, and all laughing and talking together. And then there was the matter of finding Paul a suitable wife when the time was right. She smiled at the possibilities the girl had brought.

Heather's contemplation of the future was banished by a series of loud, imperative knocks sounding on the kitchen door leading to the front yard.

"Now who could that be so early in the morning?" Heather said as she glanced at Alice and then at Paul. She rose to her feet and went to the door and opened it.

Alice, looking past Heather, gasped and shrank back for she saw Oscar Taggert standing on the stoop. She recognized him from Bemiji when Cole chose her from among the other girls. Her worst fears had come to be. She felt the thudding of her frightened heart to the tips of her fingers.

"How can I help you?" Heather asked and closely observing the big man dressed in heavy winter clothing and with a pack on his back and a holster with a pistol strapped to his side.

"I'm Oscar Taggert the county sheriff. You probably heard my name during the last election."

"I've heard your name. What can I do for you?"

"I'm searching for a blond haired girl of thirteen or so with the name of Alice Childs. I was told that she came down river from the bridge. Have you seen her?"

Oscar looked past Heather and into the kitchen. "Well, hell now. I see that very person." He shoved past Heather and came into the room and up to the table close to Alice.

"The chase is over, girl," Oscar said with hard satisfaction. "You gave me a good run, but it's over."

Alice broke from the shock at seeing the sheriff and jumped to her feet, ready to flee. She swept a look around. She was trapped within the house. Only Heather and Paul could save her now. But how could they? Would they try?

Oscar saw the panic in Alice. "The running is over. You're going back to Bemiji with me."

Heather stepped between Oscar and Alice. "What has she done that you'd chase her from Bemiji?"

"Just murder, that's all," Oscar replied in a harsh voice. "She killed a man."

"Murder?" Heather turned and fastened disbelieving, questioning eyes on Alice.

"I fought to save my life," Alice said strongly. "It was his brother Cole. I was one of the girls that got off the train in Bemiji. Cole and his wife Matty took me in. He caught me in the barn and tried to rape me. I knew he would kill me."

"That's self defense," Paul said and fear for Alice building.

"She can tell all of that to the judge when I get her back to Bemiji. Get you coat on, girl, and let's go. We've got a long trip ahead of us."

"She's too weak to walk to Bemiji," Heather objected. "And I didn't see that you had a car."

"She won't have to. I'll stop at the first farm house with a car and have somebody drive us to Bemiji."

"Heather, he's going to kill me." Alice cried out in a stricken voice and fastened pleading eyes on the woman. "Please don't let him take me. I fought to save my life, Heather, and that's the truth."

"She has nothing to say about you coming with me," Oscar said roughly. He raised a hand as if to strike Alice. "Move, damn you."

"You can't take her," Paul said and moved to stand beside Alice. "Mother and I'll bring her to Bemiji ourselves."

Oscar eyes narrowed and he put a hand on the butt of his pistol. "What's that? I can't take her?"

Heather saw the flat, deadly expression in the sheriff's eyes and the movement of his hand to the pistol. She feared for Paul and hastily moved to his side and caught him by the arm. "Paul, he's the sheriff and has the authority to arrest Alice and take her back for trial."

"Alice is afraid of him. Maybe she's right, that he plans to kill her. We would keep our word and bring her to Bemiji."

"Yes we would," Heather agreed and speaking to Oscar. "Let us do that."

"That's not the way it's going to be. Are you two trying to stop me from making an arrest?"

Heather felt Paul's muscles grow taut and she gripped his arm tightly. "Certainly not," she said to Oscar. "You're the sheriff and we trust you to do what's right."

"You're a wise woman," Oscar said.

Heather spoke to Alice. "Put on all your clothes for it's terribly cold outside."

"No! No! Please don't make me go with him!" Alice cried out. Why didn't they believe that she was telling the truth?

"Just do it," Heather said in a flat, emotionless voice.

Paul stared disbelievingly at his mother. "But, we would…"

"The sheriff is only doing his sworn duty," Heather interrupted in a tone that told Paul to be silent. She motioned impatiently to Alice. "Go get your clothes and put them on here in the kitchen."

Alice stifled a sob and straightened to full height. She had expected help from Heather and Paul. That help had been withheld. She was once again all alone, as she had been for many long months. She went to her bed and brought her outerwear into the kitchen and dressed. She felt the weight of the knife in the coat pocket. That sharp blade was the only thing that might yet save her life. She would wait for the sheriff to be off guard and she would stab him. The odds were long against her succeeding in killing the big man before he killed her. She knew that was what he intended.

She lifted her eyes to Paul, pleading silently for his help. He stared back, his eyes half closed and hiding what he was thinking

"Go on," Oscar told Alice and gestured for her to walk ahead of him. He gave Paul a hard look, and then spoke to Heather. "She'll be all right. The judge will give her a fair hearing."

Oscar shoved Alice to the kitchen door and into the yard. Paul followed. Heather reached the doorway first and there spread her arms and caught hold of the facing of the door on both sides.

"No, Paul" she said fiercely. "No!"

Paul, with his superior strength, could have broken his mother's hold on the door frame and lifted her aside. However he obeyed her and silently watched the sheriff take Alice by the shoulder and draw her along with him. Man and girl left the yard and entered the lane and shortly entered the woods and out of sight.

"They're gone," Heather said and turned to Paul.

"Now I must catch them and take her away from him," he said as he swiftly drew on his coat. He grabbed up his cap.

"He'll kill you. Didn't you see his pistol? He could shoot you and never be punished."

"I saw the pistol and that's why I didn't do anything to stop him from taking Alice. I don't trust him. I believe what she said, that she'll never reach Bemiji alive."

"Paul, you're all that I've got. If something happens to you, I'd die."

"Mom, I've got to bring her back to us," Paul said. He felt that Alice belonged to him after he had saved her from drowning and watching her through the night? Any man who would not fight for his woman was no man at all.

"Yes, you must go after them and bring her back," Heather said, relenting for she saw the man in her son. He would from now on do as he thought best.

"You knew this all the time?"

"I was afraid it was so. Hurry and get ready."

Paul went to the gun rack where he kept his rifle and the cartridge belt with its loops full and took them down. He loaded the magazine of the weapon and levered a cartridge into the firing chamber.

Brutus had seen the rifle and knew a hunt was coming. Wagging his tail with anticipation, he came and stood beside Paul.

"I'll cut through the woods and get ahead of them, and then wait for them to come along the road."

"Don't give him a chance to fight you for he's trained to use guns and will kill you."

Paul nodded. He would kill the sheriff as if he was one of the devil wolverines that robbed his traps and destroyed his prize of furs for no reason except pure evil. This time the prize was Alice.

Paul, with Brutus at his side, left the house and sprinted away across the yard and into the forest.

***

"That'll do" Oscar said and surveying the treeless area of some half acre lying adjacent to the road. They had traveled a mile or so and it was now time for the next step. "Come along, girl, for we haven't much time." Pulling Alice along with him by the arm, he led her to the center of the cleared area.

"Sit down," he ordered.

"In the snow? It's too cold." Alice was shivering and felt faint from weakness.

"Sit I say" Oscar growled and put his hands on Alice's shoulders and shoved her down roughly onto the snow.

From a coat pocket, he extracted a strong cord. Working swiftly, he tied Alice's ankles together and then her hands, wrist over wrist.

"Now you wait for me here until I get back," Oscar said with a laugh. "I've got something to do."

He strode away across the clearing and into the woods.

Hope surged in Alice as Oscar disappeared among the trees. This was her chance to escape. She brought her tied hands around to reach the knife buried in her right coat pocket. She sat on the long tail of the coat and the pocket was under her hip. She hoisted herself up on an elbow and slid her rump to the side and reached for the pocket. Her fingers pushed the flap of the pocket aside and slid inside and found the knife. Hurriedly she pulled the knife from it sheath and brought it out and twisted to the front and began to saw frantically on the cord binding her feet. Hurry, cut your feet free and run.

***

Big flakes of snow were falling as Paul cautiously approached the road visible but a short distance ahead through the trees. At the edge of the woods, he looked both ways along the road. Nobody was in sight. Holding his rifle ready, he went out onto the road and checked for tracks. No tracks showed of Alice and the sheriff heading south. The two must be back along the road between him and the lane to the farm. Paul reentered the woods, and with Brutus close by his side, stole along the road.

He caught sight of movement through the trees. A few steps more and he recognized Alice sitting in the snow in a clearing. She was leaning forward over her feet and her arms were moving.

Paul scanned the woods for sight of the sheriff. He saw no sign of the man. Somehow Alice had escaped her captor. Why was she sitting in the snow? Was she injured and could not walk?

Paul dashed from the trees and dropped to his knees beside Alice. "I've come to get you," he said. Then he saw Alice's knife and the cords binding her hands and legs. His blood chilled. Oh, damn fool! The sheriff had set a trap for him using Alice for bait. He leapt to his feet and whirled to look for Taggert.

"Don't move!" the sheriff's voice came hard and pleased.

Paul pivoted to look over his shoulder. The sheriff had come out of the woods and into the clearing. He held his pistol aimed at Paul.

"I knew you'd be coming for I saw it in your eyes." The sheriff laughed heartily. "You were easy to catch."

"I was stupid," Paul said. Because of that stupidity, Alice was going to die. And so would Paul. He moved a finger closer to the trigger of his rifle. If the sheriff as much as blinked, Paul would use that time to try to shoot him.

"Hold it, damn you!" Oscar laughter had ceased abruptly. "Now get your hand away from that trigger."

Paul lowered his hand to hang beside his leg and near Brutus's head, and the dog's watchful eyes. Brutus sensed Paul's hate of the man with the gun and accepted it as his own hate. Paul flattened his hand and bit by bit pointed it at the sheriff. Brutus saw the signal and every muscle and tendon of his body tightened. He drew himself together, coiling for the attack. He but waited for Paul's signal to release him.

Paul thrust his hand at the sheriff. "HUNT!" he commanded Brutus.

Brutus hurled his lean, muscular body toward the sheriff, devouring the distance between them with huge bounds.

Paul hurled himself to the side and down. As he rolled in the snow, he aimed his rifle and fired at the sheriff.

For a tiny fraction of time, the sheriff was surprised by the young man launching an attack directly into the open bore of his pistol. Then swiftly he fired. The bullet struck Paul on the side and tore flesh as it skittered over his ribs. The punch of the bullet knocked his breath from him with an explosion of air.

Oscar heard Paul's rifle bullet pass by his ear with a hiss and suck of air as he swung his pistol to aim at the wolfhound charging upon him. The beast was a fearsome creature with its rippling muscles, its jaws opened wide and the lips pulled back to expose its sharp white fangs.

The Brutus made a great leap at the man. Oscar fired into the dog's chest as it crashed into him. Oscar was knocked backward and off his feet by Brutus hurtling body and upon the snow covered ground. The dog landed on top of him.

Brutus shuddered at the shock and the pain from his bullet shattered chest and burst lungs. Still he was driven by the will to obey Paul's command to kill the enemy. He struck at the man's soft, vital throat. He closed his mighty jaws and ripped away a mouthful of flesh and gullet and throbbing jugular. Brutus collapsed upon his enemy.

Oscar raised a hand to the gaping wound beneath his chin and felt the rhythmic pulse of warm blood spurting from his severed jugular. The dog had killed him. Never had he foreseen that he would be the one to die and not the girl. He tried to shove the dog off him but could not for his strength was fading swiftly. He stared upward into the falling snow flakes. His mind repeated the awful reality; the Goddamned dog had killed him. The quivering flesh of the dying man and dying dog joined in a last spasm of fleeing life.

"Paul, are you hurt bad?" Alice cried out.

"My ribs sure ache." Paul replied as he rose from the snow. He gave Brutus and Oscar a quick look. "But I'm still alive. Let's get you cut loose." He took Alice's knife from her and finished cutting the cords that bound her.

He opened his coat and shirt and examined his wound. Blood flowed from the raw edges of torn flesh. Not too bad. His mother could sew the wound closed and apply a poultice. He buttoned his clothing and rose and went to Brutus lying on top of the sheriff. Both lay motionless. He checked the bodies for life and found none existed. Grieving, he ran his hand gently over Brutus's head. The dog had been a constant part of his life for many years.

"Hello there," a man called from the road. Without further words, he left the road and came into the clearing. He looked at Alice, who had come to stand near Paul. "Are both of you all right?" the man asked.

"We're okay," Paul replied and wondering who the fellow was. He put his arm protectively around Alice's shoulders

"I saw what happened and you're lucky to be alive for the sheriff is a crack pistol shot. Oh, by the way, I'm Sam Horton, Deputy Sheriff." He paused as a thought came to him. "Actually, now that Taggert is dead, I'm the Sheriff of Beltrami County.

At Sam's pronouncement, Paul glanced at his rifle lying in the snow.

"You won't need that for I'm on your side. I followed Taggert to stop him from killing Alice."

"What did you say?" Alice asked quickly and not believing what she had heard.

"Matty told me about Oscar and I came to stop him from killing you. Further I know that you killed Cole in self defense." He gave Alice a sad look. "I'm sorry about that fellow you were traveling with these last miles."

"What about Will?" Alice asked hastily.

"I've been following Oscar's tracks and they led me straight to Will's body. Oscar killed him over there in Canada just beyond the bridge."

"He was good to me," Alice said and her eyes misting. She wanted to cry for Will. She would do that when she was alone.

"What about him?" Paul asked and gestured at Oscar's body.

"My lawman's deduction from the visible evidence is that a wild dog killed the sheriff. In fact I see the dog lying on top of his victim. I'll take its body back with Oscar's as proof."

Paul did not like the thought of Brutus being taken to Bemiji for display and declared to be a wild killer. Brutus deserved a proper burial at the farm. Still brave and faithful Brutus would want his body used to protect Paul as it had before in other dangerous situations. Paul locked eyes with the lawman and nodded. Sam nodded back and there was complete understanding and agreement between the two.

"Then we're both really free to go?" Alice said.

Sam turned to Alice. "Like I said, I believe you killed Cole in self defense. If there are any questions about Cole's or Oscar's death, then I'll drive up here and get a statement from you two. But I don't think there will be any for Oscar wasn't much liked. My job now is to report several deaths and arrange funerals for the dead."

Paul picked his rifle up from the snow. "Alice, let's go home so my mom can doctor my wound."

"Home?"

"Yes. Mom said to bring you home to live with us." Paul put his arm around Alice's shoulders and pulled her against him.

Alice in turn put her arm around Paul. She had a home and a family. A warm, secure feeling evicted the cold loneliness that had dwelled in her heart for such a very long time.

"You two take good care of each other," Sam called and gave them a smile.

"We'll do that very thing." Paul replied. "And thanks."

Alice and Paul, side by side, walked away through the falling snow.

About the Author

F.M. Parker has worked as a sheepherder, lumberman, sailor, geologist, and as a manager of wild horses, wild, free roaming buffalo and live-stock grazing. For several years he was the manager of five million acres of Public Domain Land in eastern Oregon. His highly acclaimed novels include the *Coldiron* Series, *The Searcher*, *The Assassins*, *Predators and Prey*, and *The Shadow Man*.

Coming Soon!

THE HIGHBINDERS
BY
F.M. PARKER

THEY LEFT HIM FOR DEAD . . .
AND NOW IT WAS HIS TURN TO KILL.

The time is 1869. On the Black Rock Badlands, Tom Galaway is mistaken for another man, a thief, and shot. Delirious and near death, he wanders into the mountains of the Snake River Country. Sigh Ho and his 30 comrade gold miners find Tom unconscious on the river bank and nurse him back to health. The lonely Chinamen have pooled their money and sent to China to buy a woman and have her brought to California to provide love for them in the foreign land of America . . .

For more information
visit: www.SpeakingVolumes.us

On Sale Now!

BESTSELLING AUTHOR
F.M. PARKER

COLDIRON SERIES

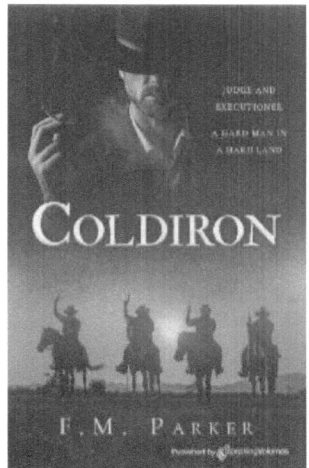

**For more information
visit:** www.SpeakingVolumes.us

On Sale Now!

GREG HUNT
THE BORDERLAND TRILOGY

For more information
visit: www.SpeakingVolumes.us